THE
ONLY
GOOD
INDIANS

THE
ONLY
GOOD
INDIANS

a novel

STEPHEN GRAHAM JONES

SAGA PRESS

LONDON SYDNEY **NEW YORK** TORONTO NEW DELHI

AN IMPRINT OF SIMON & SCHUSTER, INC.

1230 AVENUE OF THE AMERICAS, NEW YORK, NEW YORK 10020

First Saga Press hardcover edition July 2020

SAGA PRESS and colophon are trademarks of Simon & Schuster, Inc.

For information about special discounts for bulk purchases, please contact Simon & Schuster Special Sales at 1-866-506-1949 or business@simonandschuster.com.

The Simon & Schuster Speakers Bureau can bring authors to your live event. For more information or to book an event, contact the Simon & Schuster Speakers Bureau at 1-866-248-3049 or visit our website at www.simonspeakers.com.

Interior design by Michelle Marchese

Manufactured in the United States of America

7 9 10 8 6

Library of Congress Cataloging-in-Publication Data

Names: Jones, Stephen Graham, 1972– author.
Title: The only good Indians : a novel / Stephen Graham Jones.
Description: First edition. | New York : Saga Press, [2020]
Identifiers: LCCN 2019032510 (print) | LCCN 2019032511 (ebook) |
ISBN 9781982136451 (hardcover) | ISBN 9781982136475 (ebook)
Subjects: GSAFD: Horror fiction.
Classification: LCC PS3560.O5395 O55 2020 (print) |
LCC PS3560.O5395 (ebook) | DDC 813/.54--dc23
LC record available at https://lccn.loc.gov/2019032510
LC ebook record available at https://lccn.loc.gov/2019032511

ISBN 978-1-9821-3645-1
ISBN 978-1-9821-3647-5 (ebook)

For Jim Kuhn.
He was a real horror fan.

This scene of terror is repeated all too often in elk country every season. Over the years, the hunters' screams of anguish have rocked the timber.

—Don Laubach and Mark Henkel, Elk Talk

WILLISTON, NORTH DAKOTA

The headline for Richard Boss Ribs would be INDIAN MAN KILLED IN DISPUTE OUTSIDE BAR.

That's one way to say it.

Ricky had hired on with a drilling crew over in North Dakota. Because he was the only Indian, he was Chief. Because he was new and probably temporary, he was always the one getting sent down to guide the chain. Each time he came back with all his fingers he would flash thumbs-up all around the platform to show how he was lucky, how none of this was ever going to touch him.

Ricky Boss Ribs.

He'd split from the reservation all at once, when his little brother Cheeto had overdosed in someone's living room, the television, Ricky was told, tuned to that camera that just looks down on the IGA parking lot all the time. That was the part Ricky couldn't stop cycling through his head: that's the channel only the serious-*old* of the elders watched. It was just a running reminder how shit the reservation was, how boring, how nothing. And his little brother didn't even watch normal television much, couldn't sit still for it, would have been reading comic books if anything.

Instead of shuffling around the wake and standing out at the family plot up behind East Glacier, everybody parked on the logging road behind it so they'd have to come right up to the graves to turn their cars around, Ricky ran away to North Dakota. His plan was Minneapolis—he knew some cats there—but then halfway there the oil crew had been hiring, and said they liked Indians because of their built-in cold resistance. It meant they might not slip off in winter.

Ricky, sitting in the orange doghouse trailer for that interview, had nodded yeah, Blackfeet didn't care about the cold, and no, he wouldn't leave them shorthanded in the middle of a week. What he didn't say was that you don't get cold-resistant because your jackets suck, you just stop complaining about it after a while, because complaining doesn't make you any warmer. He also didn't say that, first paycheck, he was gone to Minneapolis, bye.

The foreman interviewing him had been thick and windburned and sort of blond, with a beard like a Brillo pad. When he'd reached across the table to shake Ricky's hand and look him in the eye while he did it, the modern world had fallen away for a long blink and the two of them were standing in a canvas tent, the foreman in a cavalry jacket, and Ricky already had designs on that jacket's brass buttons, wasn't thinking at all of the paper on the table between them that he'd just made his mark on.

This had been happening more and more to him the last few months. Ever since hunting went bad last winter and right up through the interview to now, not even stopping for Cheeto dying on that couch.

Cheeto hadn't been his born name, but he had freckles and orange hair, so it wasn't a name he could shake, either.

Ricky wondered how the funeral had gone. He wondered if right now there was a big mulie nosing up to the chicken-wire fence around all these dead Indians. He wondered what that big mulie saw, really. If it was just waiting all of these two-leggers out.

Cheeto would have thought it was a pretty deer, Ricky figured. He had never been a kid to get up early with Ricky to be out in the trees when light broke. He hadn't liked killing anything except beers, probably would have been vegetarian if that was an option on the rez. His orange hair put enough of a bull's-eye on his back, though. Eating rabbit food would have just got more dumb Indians lining up to put him down.

But then he'd died on that couch anyway, not even from anybody else, just from himself, at which point Ricky figured he'd get out as well, screw it. Sure, he could be this crew's chain monkey for a week or two. Yeah, he could sleep four to a doghouse with all these white boys, the wind rocking the trailer. No, he didn't mind being Chief, though he knew that, had he been around back in the days of raiding and running down buffalo, he'd have been a grunt then as well. Whatever the bow-and-arrow version of a chain monkey was, that'd be Ricky Boss Ribs's station.

When he was a kid there'd been a picture book in the library, about Heads-Smashed-In or whatever it was called—the buffalo jump, where the old-time Blackfeet ran herd after herd off the cliff. Ricky remembered that the boy selected to drape a calf robe over his shoulders and run out in front of all those buffalo, he'd been the one to win all the races the elders had put him and all the other kids in, and he'd been the one to climb all the trees the best, because you needed to be fast to run ahead of all those tons of meat, and you needed good hands to, at the last moment after sailing off the cliff, grab on to the rope the men had already left there, that would tuck you up under, safe.

What had it been like, sitting there while the buffalo flowed down through the air within arm's reach, bellowing, their legs probably stiff because they didn't know for sure when the ground was coming?

What had it felt like, bringing meat to the whole tribe?

They'd almost done it last Thanksgiving, him and Gabe and Lewis and Cass, they'd *meant* to, they were going to be those kinds of Indians for once, they had been going to show everybody in Browning that this is the way it's done, but then the big wet snow had come in and everything had gone pretty much straight to hell, leaving Ricky out here in North Dakota like he didn't know any better than to come in out of the cold.

Fuck it.

All he was going to hunt in Minneapolis was tacos, and a bed.

But, until then, this beer would work.

The bar was all roughnecks, wall-to-wall. No fights yet, but give it time. There was another Indian, Dakota probably, nursing a bottle in a corner by the pool tables. He'd acknowledged Ricky and Ricky had nodded back, but there was as much distance between the two of them as there was between Ricky and his crew.

More important, there was a blond waitress balancing a tray of empties between and among. Fifty sets of eyes were tracking her, easy. To Ricky she looked like the tall girl Lewis had run off to Great Falls with in July, but she'd probably already left his ass, meaning now Lewis was sitting in a bar down there just like this one, peeling the label off his beer just the same.

Ricky lifted his bottle in greeting, across all the miles.

Four beers and nine country songs later, he was standing in line for the urinal. Except the line was snaking all back down the hall already, and the last time he'd been in there there'd already been guys pissing in the trash can and the sink both. The air in there was gritty and yellow, almost crunched between Ricky's teeth when he'd accidentally opened his mouth. It wasn't any worse than the honeypots out at the rig, but out at the rig you could just unzip wherever, let fly.

Ricky backed out, drained his beer because cops love an Indian with a beer bottle in the great outdoors, and made to push his way out for a breath of fresh air, maybe a fence post in desperate need of watering.

At the exit the bouncer opened his meaty hand against Ricky's chest, warned him about leaving. Something about the head count and the fire marshal.

Ricky looked past the open door to the clump of roughnecks and cowboys waiting to come in, their eyes flashing up to him but not asking for anything. It was the queue Ricky would have to mill around in to wait his turn to get back in. But it was starting to not really be his decision anymore, right? Inside of maybe ninety seconds, here, he was going to be peeing, so any way he could up the chances of being someplace where he could do that without making a mess of himself, well.

He could stand in a thirty-minute line to eyeball that blond waitress some more, sure. Ricky turned sideways to slip past the bouncer, nodding that he knew what he was doing, and already a roughneck was stepping forward to take his place.

There wasn't even any time to stiff-leg it over beside the bar, by the steaming pile of bags the dumpsters were. Ricky just walked straight ahead, out into the sea of crew cab trucks parked more or less in rows, and on the way he unleashed almost before he could come to a stop, had to lean back from it because this was a serious fire-hose situation.

He closed his eyes from the purest pleasure he'd felt in weeks, and when he opened them, he had the feeling he wasn't alone anymore.

He steeled himself.

Only stupid Indians brush past a bunch of hard-handed white dudes, each of them sure that seat you had in the bar, it should have, by right, been theirs. They're cool with the Chief among them being the chain monkey, but when it comes down to who has an eyeline on the white woman, well, that's another thing altogether, isn't it?

Stupid, Ricky told himself. *Stupid stupid stupid.*

He looked ahead, to the hood he was going to hip-slide over, the bed of the truck he hoped wasn't piled with ankle-breaking equipment, because that was his next step. A clump of white men can beat an Indian into the ground, yeah, no doubt about it, happens every weekend up here on the Hi-Line. But they have to catch his ass first.

And now that he was, by his figuring, about three fluid pounds lighter, and sobering up fast, no way was even the ex–running back of them going to hook a finger into Ricky's shirt.

Ricky grinned a tight-lipped grin to himself and nodded for courage, dislodging all the rifles he couldn't keep stacked up in his head, rifles that were *actually* behind the seat of his truck back at the site. When he'd left Browning he'd taken them all, even his uncles' and granddad's—they were all in the same closet by the front door—and then grabbed the gallon baggie of random shells, figuring some of them had to go to these guns.

The idea had been that he was going to need stake-money when he hit Minneapolis, and rifles turn into cash faster than just about anything. Except then he'd found work along the way. And he'd got to thinking about his uncles needing to fill their freezer for the winter.

Standing in the sprawling parking lot of the roughneck bar in North Dakota, Ricky promised to mail every one of those back. Would he have to pull the bolts, though, mail them in separate packages from the rifles, so the rifles wouldn't really be rifles anymore?

Ricky didn't know, but he did know that right now he wanted that pump .30-06 in his hands. To shoot if it came to that, but mostly just to swing around, the open end of the barrel leaving half-moons in cheeks and eyebrows and rib cages, the butt perfect for jaws.

He might be going down in this parking lot in a puddle of his own piss, but these grimy white boys were going to remember this Blackfeet, and think twice the next time they saw one of him walking into their bar.

If only Gabe were here. Gabe liked this kind of shit—playing cowboys and Indians in all the parking lots of the world. He'd do his stupid war whoop and just rush the hell in. It might as well have been a hundred and fifty years ago for him, every single day of his ridiculous life.

When you're with him, though, with Gabe . . . Ricky narrowed his eyes, nodded to himself again for strength. To fake it anyway—to try to be like Gabe, here. When Ricky was with Gabe, he'd always want to give a whoop like that too, the kind that made it where, when he turned around to face these white boys, it'd feel like he was holding a tomahawk in his hand. It'd feel like his face was painted in harsh crumbly blacks and whites, maybe a single finger-wide line of red on the right side.

The years can just fall away, man.

"So," Ricky said, his hands balled into fists, chest already heaving, and turned around to get this over with, his teeth clenched tight so that if he was turning around into a fist it wouldn't rattle him too much.

But . . . no one?

"What the—?" Ricky said, cutting himself off because there *was* something, yeah.

A huge dark form, clambering over a pearly white, out-of-place 280Z.

Not a horse, either, like he'd knee-jerked into his head. Ricky had to smile. This was an elk, wasn't it? A big meaty spike, too dumb to know this was where the people went, not the animals.

It blew once through its nostrils and launched into the truck to its right, leaving the pretty sloped-down hood of that little Nissan taco'd up at the edges, stomped all down in the middle. But at least the car had been quiet about it. The truck the elk had slammed into was much more insulted, screaming its shrill alarm loud enough that the spike grabbed onto the ground with all four hooves. Instead of the twenty logical paths it could have taken away from this sound, it scrabbled up across the loud truck's hood, fell off into the between space on the other side.

And now that drunk little elk was banging into another truck, and another.

All the alarms were going off, *all* the lights going back and forth.

"What is into you, man?" Ricky said to the spike, impressed.

The feeling didn't last long. Now the spike was turned around, was barreling down an aisle between the cars, Ricky right in its path, its head down like a mature bull—

Ricky threw himself to the side, into *another* truck, setting off *another* alarm.

"You want some of me?" Ricky yelled to the elk, reaching over into the bed of a random truck. He came up with a jawless oversized crescent wrench that would be a good enough deterrent, he figured. He hoped.

Never mind he was outweighed by a cool five hundred pounds.

Never mind that elk don't *do* this.

When he heard the spike blow behind him he turned already swinging, crashing the crescent wrench's round head into the side mirror of a tall Ford. The big Ford's alarm screamed, flashed every light it had, and when Ricky turned around to shuffling hooves behind him, it wasn't hooves this time, but boots.

All the roughnecks and cowboys waiting to get into the bar.

"He . . . he—" Ricky said, holding the wrench like a tire beater, every second truck in his immediate area flashing in pain, and showing the pounding they'd just taken. He saw it too, saw *them* seeing it: this Indian had got hisself mistreated in the bar, didn't know who drove what, so he was taking it out on every truck in the parking lot.

Typical. Momentarily one of these white boys was going to say something about Ricky being off the reservation, and then what was supposed to happen could get proper-started.

Unless Ricky, say, wanted to maybe *live*.

He dropped the wrench into the slush, held his hand out, said, "No, no, you don't understand—"

But they did.

When they stepped forward to put him down in time-honored fashion, Ricky turned, flopped half over the 280Z he *hadn't* trashed, endured a bad moment when somebody's reaching fingers were hooked into a belt loop, but he spun his hips hard, tore through, fell down and ahead, his hands to the ground for a few overbalanced steps. A beer bottle whipped by his head, shattered on a grille guard right in front of him, and he threw his hands up to keep his eyes safe, veered what he thought was around that truck but not enough—his hip caught the last upright of the guard, spun him around, into *another* truck, with *another* stupid alarm.

"*Fuck you!*" he yelled to the truck, to all the trucks, all the cowboys, just North Dakota and oil fields and America in general, and then, running hard down a lane between trucks, hitching himself ahead with more mirrors, two of them coming off in his hands, he felt a smile well up on his face, Gabe's smile.

This is what it feels like, then.

"Yes!" Ricky screamed, the rush of adrenaline and fear sloshing up behind his eyes, crashing over his every thought. He turned around and ran backward so he could point with both hands at the roughnecks. Four steps into this big important gesture he fell out into open space, kind of like a turnrow in a plowed field, caught his left boot heel on a rock or frozen clump of bullshit grass, went sprawling.

Behind him he could see dark shapes vaulting over whole truck beds, their cowboy hats lifting with them, not coming down, just becoming part of the night.

"White boys can move . . ." he said to himself, less certain of all this, and pivoted, rose, was moving again, too.

When the footfalls and boot slaps were too close, close enough he couldn't handle it, knew this was it, Ricky grabbed a fiberglass dually fender, used it to swing himself a sharp and sudden ninety degrees, into what would have been the truck's long side, what should have been its side, but he was sliding now, he was going under, leading with the slick heels of his work boots.

This was the kind of getting away he'd learned at twelve years old, when he could slither and snake.

The truck was just tall enough for him to slide under, through the muck, his momentum carrying him halfway across. To get across the rest of the truck's width, he reached up for a handhold, the skin of his palm and the underside of his fingers immediately smoking from the three-inch exhaust pipe.

Ricky yelped but kept moving, came up on the other side of the truck fast enough that he slammed into a beater that didn't have an alarm. Two truck lengths ahead, the dark shapes were pulling their best one-eighty, casting left and right for the Indian.

Duck, Ricky told himself, and disappeared, ran at a crouch that felt military, like he was in a trench, like shells were flying. And they might as well be.

"There he is!" a roughneck bellowed, and his voice was far enough off that Ricky knew he was wrong, that they were about to pile onto somebody else for ten or twenty seconds, until they realized this was no Indian.

Ten trucks between him and them finally, Ricky stood to his full height to make sure it wasn't that Dakota dude catching the heat.

"I'm right here," Ricky said to the roughnecks, not really loud enough, then turned, stepped through the last line of trucks, out into the ditch of the narrow ribbon of blacktop that had brought him here, that ran between the bar's parking lot and miles and miles of frozen grasslands.

So it was going to be a walking night, then. A hiding from every pair of headlights night. A cold night. Good thing I'm Indian, he told himself, sucking in to get the zipper on his jacket started. Cold doesn't matter to Indians, does it?

He snorted a laugh, flipped the whole bar off without turning around, just an over-the-shoulder thing with his smoldering hand, then stepped up onto the faded asphalt right as a bottle burst beside his boot.

He flinched, drew in, looked behind him to the mass of shadows that were just arms and legs and crew cuts now, moving over the trucks.

They'd seen him, made his Indian silhouette out against all this pale frozen grass.

He hissed a pissed-off blast of air through his teeth, shook his head once side to side, and straight-legged it across the asphalt to see how committed they might be. They want an Indian bad enough tonight to run out into the open prairie in November, or would it be enough just to run him off?

Instead of trusting the gravel and ice of the opposite shoulder, Ricky took it at a slide, let his momentum stand him up once his boot heels caught grass, then transferred all that into a leaning-forward run that was going to have been a fall even if he hadn't caught the top strand of fence in the gut. He flipped over easy as anything, the strand giving up its staples halfway through, just to be sure his face planted *all* the way into the crunchy grass on the other side.

Ricky rolled over, his face to the wash of stars spread against all the blackness, and considered that he maybe should have just stayed home, gone to Cheeto's funeral, he maybe shouldn't have stolen his family's guns. He maybe should have never even left the rez at all.

He was right.

When he stood, there was a sea of green eyes staring back at him from *right there*, where there was just supposed to be frozen grass and distance.

It was a great herd of elk, waiting, blocking him in, and there was a great herd pressing in behind him, too, a herd of men already on the blacktop themselves, their voices rising, hands balled into fists, eyes flashing white.

INDIAN MAN KILLED IN DISPUTE OUTSIDE BAR.

That's one way to say it.

THE HOUSE THAT RAN RED

FRIDAY

Lewis is standing in the vaulted living room of his and Peta's new rent house, staring straight up at the spotlight over the mantel, daring it to flicker on now that he's looking at it.

So far it only comes on with its thready glow at completely random times. Maybe in relation to some arcane and unlikely combination of light switches in the house, or maybe from the iron being plugged into a kitchen socket while the clock upstairs *isn't*—or is?—plugged in. And don't even get him started on all the possibilities between the garage door and the freezer and the floodlights aimed down at the driveway.

It's a mystery, is what it is. But—more important—it's a mystery he's going to solve as a surprise for Peta, and in the time it takes her to drive down to the grocery store and back for dinner. Outside, Harley, Lewis's malamutant, is barking steady and pitiful from being tied to the laundry line, but the barks are already getting hoarse. He'll give it up soon enough, Lewis knows. Unhooking his collar now would be the dog training him, instead of the other way around. Not that Harley's young enough *to* be trained anymore, but not like Lewis is, either. Really, Lewis imagines, he deserves some big Indian award for having made it to thirty-six without pulling into the drive-through for a burger and fries, easing away with diabetes and high blood pressure and leukemia. And he gets the rest of the trophies for having avoided all the car crashes and jail time and alcoholism on his cultural dance card. Or maybe the reward for lucking through all that—meth too, he guesses—is having been married ten years now to Peta, who doesn't *have* to put up with motorcycle parts soaking in the sink, with the drips of Wolf-brand chili he always leaves between the coffee table and the couch, with the tribal junk he always tries to sneak up onto the walls of their next house.

Like he's been doing for years, he imagines the headline on the *Glacier Reporter* back home: FORMER BASKETBALL STAR CAN'T EVEN HANG GRADUATION BLANKET IN OWN HOME. Never mind that it's not because Peta draws the line at full-sized blankets, but more because he used it for padding around a free dishwasher he was bringing home a couple of years ago, and the dishwasher tumped over in the bed of the truck on the very last turn, spilled clotty rancid gunk directly into Hudson's Bay.

Also never mind that he wasn't exactly a basketball star, half a lifetime ago.

It's not like anybody but him reads this mental newspaper.

And tomorrow's headline?

THE INDIAN WHO CLIMBED TOO HIGH. Full story on 12b.

Which is to say: that spotlight in the ceiling's not coming down to him, so he's going to have to go up to it.

Lewis finds the fourteen-foot aluminum ladder under boxes in the garage, Three Stooges it into the backyard, scrapes it through the sliding glass door he's promised to figure out a way to lock, and sets it up under this stupid little spotlight, the one that all it'll do if it ever works is shine straight down on the apron of bricks in front of the fireplace that Peta says is a "hearth."

White girls know the names of everything.

It's kind of a joke between them, since it's how they started out. Twenty-four-year-old Peta had been sitting at a picnic table over beside the big lodge in East Glacier, and twenty-six-year-old Lewis had finally got caught mowing the same strip of grass over and over, trying to see what she was sketching.

"So you're, what, scalping it?" she'd called out to him, full-on loud enough.

"Um," Lewis had said back, letting the push mower die down.

She explained it wasn't some big insult, it was just the term for cutting a lawn down low like he was doing. Lewis sat down opposite her, asked was she a backpacker or a summer girl or what, and she'd liked his hair (it was long then), he'd wanted to see all her tattoos (she was already maxed out), and within a couple weeks they were an every night kind of thing in her tent, and on the bench seat of Lewis's truck, and pretty much all over his cousin's living room, at least until Lewis told her he was busting out, leaving the reservation, screw this place.

How he knew Peta was a real girl was that she didn't look around and say, *But it's so pretty* or *How can you* or—worst—*But this is your* land. She took it more like a dare, Lewis thought at the time, and inside of three weeks they were a nighttime *and* a daytime kind of thing, living in her aunt's basement down here in Great Falls, making a go of it. One that's still not over somehow, maybe because of good surprises like fixing the unfixable light.

Lewis spiders up the shaky ladder and immediately has to jump it over about ten inches, to keep from getting whapped in the face by the fan hanging down on its four-foot brass pole. If he'd checked *The Book of Common Sense* for stunts like this—if he even knew what shelf that particular volume might be on—he imagines page one would say that before going up the ladder, consider turning off all spinny things that can break your fool nose.

Still, once he's up higher than the fan, when he can feel the tips of the blades trying to kiss his hipbone through his jeans, his fingertips to the slanted ceiling to keep steady, he does what anybody would: looks down through this midair whirlpool, each blade slicing through the same part of the room for so long now that . . . that . . .

That they've carved *into* something?

Not just the past, but a past Lewis recognizes.

Lying on her side through the blurry clock hands of the fan is a young cow elk. Lewis can tell she's young just from her body size—lack of filled-outness, really, and kind of just a general lankiness, a gangliness. Were he to climb down and still be able to see her with his feet on the floor, he knows that if he dug around in her mouth with a knife, there wouldn't be any ivory. That's how young she still is.

Because she's dead, too, she wouldn't care about the knife in her gums.

And Lewis knows for sure she's dead. He knows because, ten years ago, he was the one who made her that way. Her hide is even still in the freezer in the garage, to make gloves from if Peta ever gets her tanning operation going again. The only real difference between the living room and the last time he saw this elk is that, ten years ago, she was on blood-misted snow. Now she's on a beige, kind of dingy carpet.

Lewis leans over to get a different angle down through the fan, see her hindquarters, if that first gunshot is still there, but then he stops, makes himself come back to where he was.

Her yellow right eye . . . was it open before?

When it blinks Lewis lets out a little yip, completely involuntary, and flinches back, lets go of the ladder to wheel his arms for balance, and knows in that instant of weightlessness that this is it, that he's already used all his get-out-of-the-graveyard-free coupons, that this time he's going down, that the cornermost brick of the "hearth" is already pointing up more than usual, to crack into the back of his head.

The ladder tilts the opposite way, like it doesn't want to be involved in anything this ugly, and all of this is in the slowest possible motion for Lewis, his head snapping as many pictures as it can on the way down, like they can stack up under him, break his fall.

One of those snapshots is Peta, standing at the light switch, a bag of groceries in her left arm.

Because she's Peta, too, onetime college pole vaulter, high school triple-jump state champion, compulsive sprinter even now when she can make time, because she's *Peta*, who's never known a single moment of indecision in her whole life, in the next snapshot she's already dropping that bag of groceries that was going to be dinner, and she's somehow shriking across the living room not really to catch Lewis, that wouldn't do any good, but to slam him hard with her shoulder on his way down, direct him away from this certain death he's falling onto.

Her running tackle crashes him into the wall with enough force to shake the window in its frame, enough force to send the ceiling fan wobbling on its long pole, and an instant later she's on her knees, her fingertips tracing Lewis's face, his collarbones, and then she's screaming that he's stupid, he's so, so *stupid*, she can't lose him, he's got to be more careful, he's got to start caring about himself, he's got to start making better decisions, please please *please*.

At the end she's hitting him in the chest with the sides of her fists, real hits that really hurt. Lewis pulls her to him and she's crying now, her heart beating hard enough for her and Lewis both.

Raining down over the two of them now—Lewis almost smiles, seeing it—is the finest washed-out brown-grey dust from the fan, which Lewis must have hit with his hand on the way down.

The dust is like ash, is like confectioner's sugar if confectioner's sugar were made from rubbed-off human skin. It dissolves against Lewis's lips, disappears against the wet of his open eyes.

And there are no elk in the living room with them, though he cranes his head up over Peta to be sure.

There are no elk because that elk *couldn't* have been here, he tells himself. Not this far from the reservation.

It was just his guilty mind, slipping back when he wasn't paying enough attention.

"Hey, look," he says to the top of Peta's blond head.

She rouses slowly, turns to the side to follow where he's meaning.

The ceiling of the living room. That spotlight.

It's flickering yellow.

SATURDAY

On break at work—he's supposed to be training the new girl, Shaney—Lewis calls Cass.

"Long time, no hear," Cass says, his reservation accent a singsong kind of pure Lewis hasn't heard for he doesn't know how long. In response, Lewis's voice, smoothed down flat from only ever talking to white people, rises like it never even left. It feels unfamiliar in his mouth, in his ears, and he wonders if he's faking it somehow.

"Had to call your dad to get your number," he says to Cass.

"What happens when you move away for ten years, yeah?"

Lewis shifts the phone to his other ear.

"So what's going?" Cass asks. "Not calling from jail, are you? Post office finally figure out you're Indian, what?"

"Pretty sure they know," Lewis says. "It's the first checkbox."

"Then it's her," Cass says with what sounds like a grin. "*She* finally figured out you're Indian, enit?"

What Cass and Gabe and Ricky had told him when he was running off with Peta was that he should get his return address tattooed on his forearm, so he could get his ass shipped back home when she got tired of playing Dr. Quinn and the Red Man.

"You wish she'd figure it out," Lewis tells Cass on the phone, turning to be sure Shaney, his shadow for the day, isn't standing in the break room doorway soaking all this in. "She even lets me hang my Indian junk on all the walls."

"Like *Indian*-Indian," Cass says, "or Indian just because an Indian owns it?"

"I called to ask a question," Lewis says, quieter, closer.

Of Gabe and Ricky and Cass, Cass was always the one he could dial down to "serious" easiest. Like the real him, the real and actual person, wasn't buried as deep under attitude and jokes and bluster as it was with Ricky and Gabe.

Not that Ricky, being dead, really has a telephone number anymore.

Shit, Lewis says inside.

He hasn't thought about Ricky for nearly ten years now. Not since he heard.

The headline flashes in his head: INDIAN MAN HAS NO ROOTS, THINKS HE'S STILL INDIAN IF HE TALKS LIKE AN INDIAN.

Lewis breathes in, covers the handset to breathe out, so Cass won't hear it across all these miles.

"Those elk," he says.

After a long enough time that he can be sure Cass knows exactly the elk he's talking about, Cass says, "Yeah?"

"Do you ever . . ." Lewis says, still unsure how to say it, even though he ran it through his head all last night and all the way in to work. "Do you ever, you know, *think* about them?"

"Am I still pissed off about them?" Cass fires right back. "I see Denny on fire on the side of the road, you think I stop to piss on him?"

Denny Pease, the game warden.

"He's still on the job?" Lewis asks.

"Running the office now," Cass says.

"Still a hard-ass?"

"He fights for Bambi," Cass says, like that's still in circulation all this time later. It was what they all used to say about the game crew: anytime Man was in the forest, all the wardens' ears perked up, and their citation books flapped open.

"Why you asking about him?" Cass says.

"Not him," Lewis says. "Just thinking, I guess. Ten-year anniversary, I don't know."

"Ten years in, what, a week?" Cass says.

"Two," Lewis says, shrugging like he doesn't mean to have it all figured down this precise. "It was the last Saturday before Thanksgiving, wasn't it?"

"Yeah, yeah," Cass says. "Last day of the season . . ."

Lewis winces without any sound, closes his eyes tight. The way Cass dragged that last part out all suggestive, it's the same as reminding Lewis it *wasn't* the last day of the season. Just, the last day they'd been able to all get together to hunt.

But it was also, as it turned out, the last day of their season in a different way, he guesses.

He shakes his head three times like trying to clear it, and tells himself again that no way did he see that young elk on the floor of his living room.

She's dead, she's gone.

To pay for her, even, the day before he left with Peta, he'd taken all the packaged-up meat of her and gone door-to-door down Death Row, giving it to the elders. Because she'd come from the elders' section—the good country saved back for them up by Duck Lake, so they could fill their freezers from the field instead of the IGA—because she'd *come* from there, it was all full circle and Indian, hand-delivering the meat to their doors. Never mind that Lewis couldn't find any of his meat stamps, had to use Ricky's little sister's stamps. So, instead of STEAK or GROUND or ROAST, all the butcher paper the young elk was wrapped in had a black raccoon handprint on it, because that was the only one she had that wasn't a flower or a rainbow or a heart.

But no way could that elk be coming up from thirty stew pots all this time later, walking a hundred and twenty miles south to haunt Lewis. First because elk don't do that, but second because, in the end, her meat had got where it was meant to get, he hadn't even done anything wrong. Not really.

"Gotta go, man," he tells Cass. "My boss."

"It's Saturday," Cass says back.

"Rain nor sleet nor weekends," Lewis says back, and hangs up more abruptly than he means, holds the phone on its cradle for a full half minute before lifting it back.

He dials in the number Cass's dad gave him for Gabe. It's Gabe's dad's number, actually, but Cass's dad had looked out the window, said he could see Gabe's truck over there right now.

"Tippy's Tacos," Gabe says after the second ring. It's how he always answers, wherever he is, whoever's phone. There was never a place called that on the reservation, as far as Lewis knows.

"Two with venison," Lewis answers back.

"Ah, *Indian* tacos . . ." Gabe says, playing along.

"And two beers," Lewis adds.

"You must be Navajo," Gabe says right back, "maybe a fish tribe. If you were Blackfeet, you'd want a six with that."

"I've known some Navajo can flat put it away," Lewis says, a deviation from the usual routine, like bringing it down, breaking it. For maybe five seconds Gabe doesn't say anything, then, "*Lewdog?*"

"First try," Lewis says, his face warming just to be known.

"You in jail?" Gabe asks.

"Still a comedian," Lewis tells him.

"Among other things," Gabe says back, then, probably to his dad, "It's Lewis, remember him, old man?"

Lewis doesn't hear the reply, but does hear a basketball game cranked up high enough to be blasting through the whole house.

"So what's up?" Gabe asks when he's back. "Need bus fare home, what? If so, I can hook you up with somebody. Little light at the moment myself."

"Still hunting?"

"That'd be under the 'Among Other Things' category, wouldn't it?" Gabe says.

Of course he's still hunting. Denny'd have to work 24/7 to write up even half of what Gabriel Cross Guns poaches on a weekly basis, and the rangers over in Glacier would have to work even harder to find his tracks, going back and forth across the Park line, the return prints a couple hundred pounds deeper than the ones sneaking in.

"How's Denorah?" Lewis says, because that's where you start after this long.

Denorah's Gabe's daughter by Trina, Trina Trigo, has to be twelve or thirteen by now—she was walking around already when Lewis left, anyway, he's pretty sure of that.

"My finals girl, you mean?" Gabe says, finally all the way into this call, it feels like.

"Your what?" Lewis asks all the same.

"You remember Whiteboy Curtis from Havre?" Gabe asks.

Lewis can't dredge up Whiteboy's actual last name—something German?—but yeah, he remembers: Curtis, the baller, this naturally gifted farm kid who was born for the court. He didn't see it all with his eyes, he *felt* the game through his feet like radar, and didn't even have to think to know which way to cut. And he had that basketball on a string, one hundred percent. Only thing kept him from going college was his height, and that he insisted he was a power forward, not a stop-and-pop sharpshooter. At high school height, sure, someone just six-two could crash in, dominate as a power forward. And he had some jumps, too, could rise up and flush it—only in pregame, with a lot of setup, but still. In the end, though, he wasn't built like Karl Malone, but like John Stockton. Just, he couldn't accept that, had the idea he could go inside at the next level, bang his way through the bigs, not be a pinball bouncing off them. Insisting he was that power forward, he'd lost so many teeth he looked like a hockey player, last Lewis had heard. And the concussions weren't exactly doing anything good for his short-term memory. It would have been better for the rest of his life if he'd never figured he could play.

Still?

"He had that jump shot," Lewis says, seeing it again, the way Whiteboy Curtis would just hang and hang, wait for everyone else to sink back down before releasing the ball so perfect, his eyes laser-guiding it up and up, and, finally, in.

"Denorah's like that," Gabe whispers, like the best secret ever. "Just, *better*, man. Serious. Browning's never seen nothing like her."

"I should come watch her play," Lewis says.

"You should," Gabe says. "Just, don't tell Trina I told you to come. Maybe don't even talk to her. If she looks at you? She does, maybe cut your hair, change your name, jump on a ship."

"She still out for blood?"

"Woman can hold a grudge," Gabe says. "Got to give her that."

"For no reason, of course," Lewis says, leaning back on the usual lines again.

"So to what do I owe this call, Mr. Postman?" Gabe says then, being all fake formal. "I forget to put a stamp on something, what?"

"Just been a while," Lewis says.

"It was a while eight, nine years ago," Gabe says. "You're talking to me, man."

A lump forms in Lewis's throat. He tilts his face back, closes his eyes.

"I was just remembering when Denny—"

"Fucked us permanent?" Gabe cuts in. "Yeah, something about that maybe rings a bell or two . . ."

"You ever been back there by Duck Lake again?" Lewis asks.

"You have to have an old-timer with you," Gabe says. "You know that, man. How long you been gone again?"

"I mean where it happened," Lewis says. "That drop-off place."

"That place, that place, yeah," Gabe says, driving a nail into Lewis's heart. "It's haunted, man, didn't you know? Elk don't go there anymore, even. I bet they even tell stories around the elk campfires, right? About what went down that day? Shit, we're legends to them, man. The four boogeymen—the four *butchers* of Duck Lake."

"Three," Lewis says. "The three boogeymen."

"They don't know that," Gabe says.

"But you really think they might remember?" Lewis asks, just hanging it all out there at last.

"*Remember?*" Gabe says, the smile one hundred percent there in his voice. "They're fucking elk, man. They don't really have campfires."

"And we killed them all anyway, yeah?" Lewis says, blinking the heat from his eyes. looking around again for Shaney.

"What's this about?" Gabe says then. "You still missing that crappy knife, what?"

Lewis has to strain to dial back to what Gabe's saying: that trading-post knife he'd bought, with the three or four interchangeable blades, one of them a weak little saw, for the breastbone and pelvis.

"That knife was a piece of shit," Lewis says. "If you find it, lose it again fast, yeah?"

"Will do," Gabe says, his voice far from the phone for a moment, basketball pouring into his end of the line. "Hey, we're watching a—"

"I got to get gone, too," Lewis says. "Nice hearing your dumb-ass voice again, though."

"Shit, I should charge by the minute," Gabe says, and ten, twenty seconds later the line's dead again, and Lewis is standing there with his shoulder against the wall, tapping the handset into his forehead like a drumstick.

"Should I be taking notes, Blackfeet?" Shaney asks from the doorway.

Lewis hangs the phone up.

Shaney's Crow, so calling him "Blackfeet" is this running joke, their tribes being longtime enemies.

"Something Peta said last night," Lewis lies, always trying to be sure to remind Shaney about his wife, and then say something about her again, just to be sure. Not because he's the ladies' man of the USPS—there isn't one—but because him and Shaney are the only two Indians at this station, and for the last week, ever since Shaney passed the background check and hired on, everybody's been doing that thing they do with armchairs or end tables when they match: trying to push him and her together over in the corner, leave them there to be this perfect set.

"Something your *wife* said?" Shaney asks, Lewis sliding past her, leading them back to the big sorting machine. He flicks it on to continue this lesson.

"We've got this crap light in the living room," he tells her. "Won't come on when it's supposed to. She thinks it might be a short in the wall. Was calling a guy I know who does electrician stuff on the side."

"On the side . . ." Shaney repeats, and nudges an envelope this way into the sorting machine instead of that way.

Lewis tracks that fast piece of mail up into the belly of the beast and shakes his head with wonder when nothing catches, nothing crumples.

Shaney grins a mischievous grin, bites her lower lip in at the end of it.

"Next time," she says, and hip-checks Lewis.

He rolls with it, doesn't push back, is miles and years away.

MONDAY

Duckwalking backward on his stripped-down, double-throaty Road King that's about to find its lope, Lewis clocks Jerry already at the edge of the post office's parking lot, hanging his loose right hand down by the rear wheel of his custom Springer, his index and middle fingers waggling in an upside-down peace sign before they curl up into his fast fist. Lewis has no idea what it means, never rode with a real and actual gang like Jerry did in his Easy Rider youth, but it must mean something like *This way* or *All clear* or *Smoke 'em if you got 'em*, because Eldon and Silas throttle in right behind him, leaving Lewis to watch the back door like always, even though where they're headed is *to* Lewis's new place way the hell over on 13th.

Pecking order's pecking order, though, and Lewis, even though this is his fifth year slinging mail, is still the new guy. Being last, though, that means that when Shaney comes running out the side door, Lewis's bitch seat is what she jumps onto, barely making it.

Her hands fall perfect to his hips, her front to his back, and very much right there.

"Hello?" he says, throttled down and wobbling.

"I want to see too," she says, shaking her head and loosening her hair.

Yeah, this is exactly what Peta needs to clock pulling into the driveway.

Still, Lewis grabs the next gear, falls in line, having to goose it to stay with.

Why they're all going to his place is because Harley, at nearly ten years old, has taken to jumping the six-foot fence like a young dog, a fact Eldon says he'll only believe when he sees it. So, he's going to see it. They all are, including, now, Shaney.

Third in line is Silas, on his rattletrap scrambler that's not good past fifty, but gets kind of fun at seventy-five, if near-death experiences are your thing. Eldon, snapping at Jerry's heels, is on his slammed bobber, which he can only swing because he lives close to the post office, can walk in if the weather's bad, so doesn't need to keep and insure a truck or a car. Of the four of them he's the only one not married, too, which frees up some funds, for sure. Jerry tells him to just wait, though, it'll happen—"They'll drop sooner or later," haw haw haw. At fifty-three, Jerry's the oldest of them, and comes complete with the silver handlebar stache, freckled-bald head, ratty ponytail, and icy blue eyes.

Silas is pretty much mute, and might even have some Indian in him somewhere, Lewis thinks. Not enough to have been Chief before Lewis earned that title, but . . . maybe as much Indian blood as Elvis had, however much that is? Like, enough to fill up a pair of blue suede shoes? Eldon claims to be Greek and Italian both, which is maybe a joke Lewis doesn't quite get. Jerry doesn't claim to be anything other than in constant need of another beer.

It's good to have found them, after losing Gabe and Cass and Ricky.

Well, after having left them.

No headlines about this. It's just the same old news as ever.

The five o'clock traffic they slip past on River all cranes a bit to keep Shaney in view ten or twenty feet longer. Meaning her button-up flannel's probably untucked and flapping, threatening to come off altogether.

Great.

Wonderful.

Lewis shouldn't have said anything about Harley, he knows. It would be better just to be headed home alone, to maybe sink a few free throws in the driveway before Peta's back. But—Harley, right? He's not just not-young, he's actually pretty damn old for a dog his size, has been hit twice on the road, one of those by a dump truck, and he's been shot once, in the hip. And that's just what Lewis knows about. There've been snakebites and porcupines and kids with pellet guns and all the usual dog fighting that any dog's going to get up to.

No way should Harley be able to clear that fence. No way should he even have a reason to try. Still, four times now Lewis has found him out in the road, and Peta's found him twice.

He *must* be jumping, maybe scrabbling a bit to get all the way over.

And Lewis should have kept it to himself.

Except?

Thinking and thinking about the young elk who couldn't have been on his living room floor, Harley barking it up outside, Lewis had finally made what felt like a connection between the two. Could Harley have been barking at her, at the elk? Can he see her *without* a spinning fan? Has she been there all along, these past ten years?

Worse, if Harley can sense her, then is that what's been driving him over the fence? Maybe it's not about getting *to* all the dogs in heat out there or whatever. Maybe it's about getting *away* from the house.

Never mind that the lease is for twelve months and they lose the deposit if they pack up, disappear.

"Hold on," Lewis says back to Shaney, and rolls the throttle back to shoot across the river, go weightless a bit over the train tracks on the other side, avoid the way they always rattle his teeth not once but twice—one for each rail.

Shaney does a whoop from the thrill of it and Lewis gears down for the slow turn onto 6th, gets all the way into fourth for the straight shot down American Ave, taking the lead because none of these jokers have been to his new place. Three fast turns later, maybe taking them a bit fast like to test Shaney, it's his driveway.

"This is it," Lewis says into the sudden silence of no panheads, no V-twins.

Jerry and Eldon and Lewis all cock their bikes over, but Lewis waits for Shaney.

"Oh yeah," she says, placing her hands on his back and pushing off the seat all at once, a dismount Lewis is glad he won't have cycling through his head for the rest of the week.

"So where's this great flying dog already?" Jerry croaks.

"Close to your bedtime, Granddad?" Eldon says, just out of arm's reach but going boxer-light on his feet anyway.

Silas grins up at the front of the house, settles on a high window, Lewis thinks. He studies it, too. It's just his and Peta's bedroom window, no curtains yet.

"Well, mailboy?" Jerry says again.

It's what he calls everybody, Lewis is pretty sure. Probably because names have started slipping out of his head.

Lewis does the code for the garage, makes a show of tapping his shoes at the door, then ushers them all into the World Famous Jumping Dog Show.

"He just started doing it," he says on the way through the kitchen, walking backward like a proper tour guide. "I always thought he had some wolf in him maybe, along with sled dog or pit fighter. Now I'm thinking kangaroo."

"Snow kangaroo," Jerry says, the leathery skin around his eyes crinkling.

Silas snickers, running the tips of his fingers along the top of the table and then looking at them like for grime.

"Dog needs what's on the other side of the fence, that's a dog'll learn to jump," Shaney informs them all.

Jerry says something about this through his stache but it's lost, and anytime Lewis asks him for a repeat Jerry just waves it off.

"Where's the little lady?" Eldon asks, clapping his big hand onto the back of the couch.

"Making the big bucks," Lewis says, miming the bright orange wands Peta parks planes with, using them both to direct this little tour group to his right, his right.

"Aren't any big bucks in Great Fa—" Eldon starts to say, doesn't get to finish, some of Peta's more lacy underthings suddenly drying on the back of a chair.

"Divert, divert," Lewis tells him, waving him back with his make-believe wands but smiling.

Still, "*Nice*," Shaney says to Lewis and only to Lewis about the showy bra when she passes.

Past her, thankfully, Silas has liberated the housing for the Road King's headlight assembly from the kitchen table, is holding it up to peer through it.

"Still looking for hard bags?" he asks.

"Got some?" Lewis says back, and flips the latch up on the sliding door. "What color?"

"Because everything else matches so well?" Eldon cuts in.

"Foul, foul," Lewis calls, shining his wands on him because evidently he's a ref now.

No, his bike doesn't all match yet. But it will. He's going to Pinocchio it up from the rolling skeleton it is now into the real bike it wants to be. The hard bags are what Peta's insisting on, since, in a skid, they take the heat from the asphalt, keep the flesh and muscle on your leg and hip. Lewis tried telling her that only matters for riders who lay it over, but that pretty much just warranted a glare, not even a halfway grin.

"Anything about Silas's scoot there suggest he's got extra parts of any color laying around?" Jerry says over his shoulder. "Any extra pieces, he just tacks them on, don't he?"

Silas's bike right now is mid-transformation, somewhere between a cafe racer and a twelve-year-old's drawing of his dream bike, but he has to grin and shrug about this, because it's true.

Lewis twirls the sawed-off broomstick up from the sliding door's track, swishes the glass back dramatically, and presents the backyard to these unbelievers, letting them go first so they can see there's no trickery involved.

How he knows Harley will be there instead of running wild from yard to yard, it's that he hooked Harley's chain to the rusted baling wire of the laundry line before work, like every morning. Last he saw, Harley was running back and forth, he had a water pan, some shade, some grass, a clueless look on his face—everything a dog could need. The laundry line isn't a permanent solution, but it's solution enough until Lewis finds some hog-wire panels for the top of the fence.

"Maybe he's a pole vaulter like his momma," Eldon calls back from the uneven deck.

Lewis has bragged to them all about Peta, and Jerry and Silas have even met her a couple of times when it was raining and she had to pick him up in the truck.

"Or an escape artist," Silas adds.

Lewis steps out after them, parts them to see from pole to rusted pole of the laundry line, and he's right: no Harley. Also, no baling wire running between the poles anymore, to clip wet clothes to.

"I'm going to kill that dog," he says, stepping out farther to make sure Harley's not just standing there watching the house, which is when Shaney, over at the next corner of the back of the house, finishes that thought: "Think you're a little late for that, Blackfeet."

With her lips she shows Lewis where to look, and from the way she's not joking, he gets a flash of warning, can feel regret washing up into his throat.

It's Harley. He's hanging by his chain from the top of the fence, eyes open but not seeing anything, gouges and furrows clawed into the fence because it took a while for him to strangle out, evidently.

"Well, shit," Jerry says.

Harley was the first gift Peta ever got Lewis, nine years ago. One of her other aunts' dogs had thrown a litter, and the dad was supposed to have been a real scrapper, and Lewis had already been talking about how the last good rez dog he'd had, he'd been a kid, and a horse in the parade had kicked it in the head while Lewis was grubbing for candy with the rest of the kids. So Harley, he'd been perfect, almost made Great Falls feel like home that first year—they grew into it together. And now he's dead on the chain Lewis tied him up with.

"Sorry, man," Eldon says, studying the high-dollar boots he always changes into for riding.

"Looks like he almost made it," Shaney says for all of them, meaning they believe Lewis about Harley having found springs in his legs late in life.

"Stupid dog," Lewis says, keeping it short because he doesn't trust his voice not to break into pieces, choke him up.

And then one of Harley's hind legs twitches once, exactly in rhythm somehow with the way that elk on the living room floor blinked her eyes. The elk that wasn't dead on the floor of Lewis's living room, that wasn't *alive* on the floor—that wasn't there at all.

Lewis's response to Harley being sort of alive isn't the right response, isn't the response he's proud of: he sucks air in and steps back, almost falls on his ass.

Of the five of them it's Silas who dives forward to hug on to Harley, lift him up, get the pressure off his throat. Jerry reaches up with a meaty paw, unhooks the chain from the top of the fence, and Shaney's already guiding Harley's bloody collar up over his head, being careful of his ears.

Silas turns around, Harley cradled in his arms, and Lewis pulls his eyes away for just a moment, finds himself watching Shaney, who's maybe going to step forward, hug Harley to her, but then she's jerking back all at once, startled from the wall of sound suddenly rushing at them all.

Eldon grabs Lewis's shoulder like to pull him out of the way, or use him to push off of, and even Jerry looks up faster than his walrus-looking self usually does.

The whole backyard is shaking and loud and fast and dangerous, the kind of sensory trauma where Lewis is pretty sure that, if there were a sprinkler rainbowing a wall of water back and forth, that iridescent sheet of color would collapse, turn to mist.

It's the train that runs behind this neighborhood twice a day, what Peta calls the Thunderball Express. It's why her and Lewis can swing rent on a place with a ceiling this high. It's also why Harley can't be getting out of the backyard anymore.

Lewis looks up at the coal and graffiti smearing past, sees tomorrow's headline in his head: ONCE-LOCAL MAN CAN'T EVEN TOUCH HIS OWN DYING DOG.

Sometimes the headlines get it right. And the story on 12b this time, it's accompanied by a small out-of-focus black-and-white photograph Lewis's mind takes on reflex, because he can't really deal with it in the moment, what with the train screaming past, tearing its necessary hole in the world: Harley's mouth yawning open, flashing teeth, snapping back at the source of what he thinks is the cause of all this pain.

Silas jerks his face away right as the bite's happening, right when Harley's teeth have hooked into the skin of his cheek, but that just makes it worse, really.

TUESDAY

Lewis is using little short tear-offs of masking tape to outline a certain dead animal on the carpet of the living room floor. It's to prove that it couldn't have happened, that she wouldn't have even fit right there. That's what he's telling himself anyway.

He's got the couch shoved back, Peta's grandmother's antique coffee table pushed the other way. Peta's family isn't old-money Great Falls—is there any such thing?—but they've been here in one way or another since about when the original reservation was staked out.

She's in the garage with Harley, on the nest of sleeping bags and blankets she pulled together for him when she walked home from the make-do park-n-ride two streets over, found Lewis and Shaney and Eldon on the back porch dribbling water into Harley's mouth. Jerry was gone in the truck, delivering Silas to the hospital, his face packed in towels.

After they'd pulled away, Jerry driving easy, one hand on the wheel, the other keeping Silas upright, Eldon said it figured that a mailman would get it from a dog, right?

Right.

According to Peta, who spent most of her childhood nursing dogs and cats and baby birds, Harley could still go either way. Silas was never in that kind of danger—though, before he left, Lewis could see yellowy teeth through the flapped-open cheek skin.

Jerry says Lewis shouldn't hold it against Harley. He didn't know what he was doing. When the whole world hurts, you bite it, don't you?

Harley's nest of sleeping bags and blankets were meant to be the insulation around the sweat lodge Lewis had planned for the backyard, but screw it. Maybe they still will be. Maybe, next year, wrapped in heat and darkness and steam, Lewis will dip some water out of the bucket and tip a little out for Harley. In memory of, all that.

You can do it for dogs the same as people, he's pretty sure. And, if not, some old chief gonna step down out of the sky, slap his wrist?

Lewis tears off another longish rectangle of masking tape, sticks it to the carpet in front of the couch, then peels it up and sticks it again, trying to get the slow turn down from the belly to the front of the back leg just right. Thing is, these re-stuck sections of tape all curl up after a few minutes, like retracting from the shape Lewis is forcing them to be part of.

The rear hoof is just starting to come together when Peta steps back in with the dishrag over her shoulder, the bottle of goat milk in her hand, and for a slice of an instant she's a mom, tired from one in diapers, one just balancing around on wobbly legs. But that's another life than this one, Lewis reminds himself. She doesn't want kids, was up-front about that even those first couple of weeks in East Glacier. Not because Lewis is Indian, but because she thinks her pre-Lewis self made enough bad decisions of the chemical variety that any kids she had would have to pay that tab, so they'd be starting out with the world stacked against them already.

The headline kicks up in Lewis's head on automatic, straight out of the reservation: not the FULLBLOOD TO DILUTE BLOODLINE he'd always expected if he married white, that he'd been prepping himself to deal with, because who knows, but FULLBOOD BETRAYS EVERY DEAD INDIAN BEFORE HIM. It's the guilt of having some pristine Native swimmers—they probably look like microscopic salmon, even though the Blackfeet are a horse tribe—it's the guilt of having those swimmers cocked and loaded but never pushing them downstream, meaning the few of his ancestors who made it through raids and plagues, massacres and genocide, diabetes and all the wobbly-tired cars the rest of America was done with, those Indians may as well have just stood up into that big Gatling gun of history, yeah?

"How's he?" Lewis says, tipping his head to the garage.

"I think it's helping," Peta says, holding the goat milk up.

According to one of the luggage guys at the airport, you can bring a parvo puppy back with goat milk. Harley's not that kind of sick, but if goat milk can keep a puppy alive when its insides are turning to slurry, then surely it can do something for a dog that spent most of yesterday dying and then coming back, right?

It makes as much sense as anything.

At some point, though, and Lewis hates hates hates this, at some point, and soon, it's going to come down to a rifle, and Harley's last walk, or carry, whatever.

It won't be because Harley was a bad dog. It'll be because he was the best dog.

It'll have to be the same rifle from ten years ago, too. He'll drive up to the reservation to bum it off Cass, even—it's the one he used for that young cow elk. The cow elk he's tracing out on the carpet with a hundred torn-off pieces of masking tape.

"Need some help?" Peta says about this little project.

Any other person, any other woman, any other wife of a stupid husband who's trying to hide from his dying dog by outlining an elk on the living room floor in masking tape, she'd tell him to quit messing her house up, to quit wasting tape, to be sure and clean up every bit of that when he's done.

Peta works her way down beside Lewis, takes the roll of tape, tears off squares, and holds them up on her fingertips for when he's ready.

Her theory about what he saw is that, the same way you can put lights on the spokes of a bike and they'll gel into a picture at speed and hold that blurry glowing image, there must have been some random pattern of light and dark dust on the back of the fan blades. They produced a kind of blob in all that spinning, and Lewis just took it to his guilty place: that young elk.

About which, he hasn't told her the whole story.

She's vegetarian, and not for health reasons, but ethical ones. More nights than not, he's eating potatoes or tofu or beans. And that's fine. Every middle-aged Indian needs a diet exactly like this. So, Peta *would* listen to the whole story, sure, and make the right noises, hold her eyes in a way that meant she was getting it, but it would hurt her to hear it, and she'd have to go down to the high school, run around and around the track to try to stay ahead of that story. It's better not to tell her all of it, then, not to burden her with it, scar her memory up. Who knows, even? She might just stand up after hearing it, walk away, not come back.

Twenty minutes later, maybe an hour, Lewis has the shape of the cow elk more or less roughed out, emphasis on the "rough."

He stands to see it from higher up, and has no clue how the bow-and-arrow Blackfeet did it back in the day. The horses they drew into ledgers or onto the sides of lodges weren't anatomically accurate—neither's this—but they did suggest a sort of intimacy with the shape, with the form, that this masking-tape elk doesn't even come close to. It's more like somebody told Lewis about an elk than that he ever saw one in real actual life.

Peta covers her mouth with her hand to keep from laughing, and Lewis has to smile as well.

"Looks like a five-year-old tried to trace a giant sheep, doesn't it?" he says. "While he was working on his third beer of the morning."

Peta collapses onto the pushed-back couch, pulls her legs up under her, adds, "But the sheep kept kicking, trying to get away."

"Sheep don't know anything about art," Lewis says, and falls into the couch beside her.

From this position, he of course ends up looking through the fan from the underside, and then at the little spotlight that's dead again up there. It's a mystery he's resigned to never solving. Some lights you never figure out, and shouldn't even try to.

"What next, then?" Peta asks.

For maybe thirty seconds Lewis doesn't answer, then, "It's stupid," he finally says.

"What?" Peta says. "You mean like climbing up a shaky ladder alone in the middle of the day and almost cracking your head open?"

Point.

After stopping to say hey to Harley, tell him that Eldon's covering the morning shift, Lewis walks the tall aluminum ladder around the side of the house again.

"It was here," Peta says, positioning the ladder just shy of directly under the fan.

"How can you tell?" Lewis asks.

To show, she pivots around to the other side, braces her feet wide to lower the ladder down until the red plastic cap at the top fits perfectly into the wedge slammed into the wall on the other side of the living room.

"Oh," Lewis says. "Think we're getting the deposit back?"

"Security deposits are overrated," Peta says back, and maybe she really is Indian, right?

"Wait," Lewis tells her, and retreats to the garage, comes back from the chest freezer with the trash bag that's gone-with through six rental houses and one never-finished basement.

It's maybe going to smell. But maybe not.

"We still have that?" Peta says.

Lewis tries to open the bag but it's more like peeling a plastic tamale, the bag's so old. Inside, kind of making his heart swell, is the hide he promised that young elk to use someday, to make everything she went through worth it.

The story he told Peta was that it was snowing thick, and she'd looked like a full-grown cow, not a teenager. That he never would have pulled the trigger if he'd seen her right.

It's not a complete lie. Just, it's not the complete truth, either.

Lewis swallows the memory down, gets back to whatever this is he's doing: re-creating the scene of the crime? No. More like staging the accident all over again. With, this time, props.

"Is it still . . . ?" Peta asks about the tight bundle of rolled elk hide, hair still on.

Lewis shrugs, doesn't know about the hide, if it's still all one piece, or crumbly. It has a lot of nicks and holes, he knows, because, first, he's a crap skinner, but second, that trading-post knife he was using only held its edge for like three minutes.

Should he thaw it before unrolling it? Would the microwave work? Would he ever be able to eat anything warmed in there again?

"I'll just—" he says, and ceremonially sets the hide down in the middle of the masking tape. It looks like a fat, hairy burrito, and Lewis has to focus to keep from coughing, because that'll turn into a gag, and he doesn't want to be rude to her memory.

"That's probably good enough," Peta says, sitting back and eye-balling the hide, the tape, the whole setup.

"Well, then," Lewis says, one foot already on the lowest rung, one hand up higher.

"The fan's at the same speed?" she asks.

"I haven't messed with it," he says. "You?"

She shakes her head no, nods for him to go, that she's watching.

"I was on this rung," he narrates, using his hand to touch where his foot was, and then he's going up, up.

He waits until the spinning blades of the fan are at his chest again to look down through them. At Peta, on the couch. At a dead elk made of masking tape, with a hairy burrito for a gut sack.

"Maybe it's the light," Peta says, and unfolds from the couch, backs into the edge of the living room, where she was standing when Lewis started his big slow-motion fall. "Am I making a shadow?" she calls up to him. She turns the hall light on and off behind her, keeping her feet in the same place.

"You had a bag," Lewis tells her, still holding on to the chance that this might work, that there might be an explanation.

"O-kay . . ." she says, not as confident in this bag-possibility as he is, but all the same, she bounds into the kitchen to dig one up.

While she's gone Lewis looks over the top of the fan, at the gouge the ladder left in the wall of the living room. The new wound in the house.

Moving there like an afterimage, like it was left behind, is just trying to creep past without being seen, he's ninety percent sure there's the shadow of a person up against that wall. A thin shadow, just for a flicker of a moment.

A woman with a head that's not human.

It's too heavy, too long.

When it turns as if to fix him in its wide-set eyes, he raises his hand to block her vision, to hide, but it's too late. It's been too late for ten years already. Ever since he pulled that trigger.

WEDNESDAY

What wakes him the next morning is . . . a basketball? Dribbling?

Lewis rolls out of bed and into the closest sweats, has to hold them up with his left hand all the way down the stairs—the dryer ate their drawstring back when they were brand-new.

There's definitely someone dribbling a basketball in the driveway.

Lewis steps down from the kitchen into the garage, says to Harley, "Who is it, bub?"

Harley thumps his heavy tail once against a Star Wars sleeping bag but that's all he can manage.

A neighbor kid, maybe? Did the former tenants tell all the kids on this street that they can come over anytime, shoot hoops?

If so, cool. Lewis needs someone to play with who's at his skill level. Playing against Peta—doing anything athletic with her—is a study in shame, pretty much. Even grabbing her waistband when she slides past, pushing her in the back when she's laying it up, he never can hit twenty-one before she does. He can never even get to *ten* before she wins.

Lewis bumps the garage door button with the side of his fist, his face pre-hard because that's what you do in what could be a trespassing situation, what could be the former tenant, drunk, weaving back to the home he sort of remembers.

Slowly—it's an old, heavy door—the sneakers out there become legs, then shape into a woman, then become . . . *Shaney*?

She spins around, making room against an imaginary defender, and comes back, rises into a fallaway that scissors her legs in the air, the back one touching down just as the ball banks in, smooth as butter. She shags the rebound, claps the ball between her hands like heads-up, and passes it across, a clean bounce right on target.

Lewis catches it because the other option is getting popped in the gut with it.

"I wake you, early bird?" she says like a challenge.

"Day off," Lewis says.

"To spend with him," Shaney says back, going to Harley now that the door's open.

She cups his wide head in her hand, draws her nose to his, and squeezes her eyes shut, keeps them like that.

"You smell it, don't you?" Lewis says.

"He's dying," she says, massaging his notched ears.

She rolls into a sitting position on the unassembled sweat, says about Harley and all his scars, "He's an old warrior, isn't he?"

"You come just to see him?" Lewis asks, trying not to make it sound confrontational. She hears it anyway.

"Your wife wouldn't want me here, right? White girls of red men are always the most jealous of my kind."

"Your kind?" Lewis says, though he kind of already knows.

"Indian, unattached, an ass like this," Shaney goes on. "I know Jerry says I'm bad news."

The headline back on the reservation: BASEBALL BASEBALL BASEBALL.

"What's her name about anyway?" Shaney asks. "She a white-girl tortilla, or all against wearing animal skins, what?"

"Peta with an *e*, not an *i*," Lewis recites, falling through Peta's own explanation. "She was supposed to have been a boy, her dad's name is Pete, so he put an *a* on his own name, handed it down."

Shaney nods like she can track that, sure, and when she threads her bangs away Lewis clocks that her left eye's all bloodshot, and that—has he ever even seen her forehead?—the skin above her eyebrow on that side's drawn tight and bumply, like from sudden contact with a dashboard, or an aerosol can exploding in a burning pile of trash.

The eye, though. Bad date last night, Lewis has to think. Either that or the wrong boyfriend. He doesn't ask, tries not to be too obvious about looking. Which pretty much means he telegraphs his thoughts word for word across to her, he knows.

"Anyway, I came over for a book, Mr. Library," she says, shaking her hair back over her forehead and eye. "Not to jump your bones. Call her up, tell her that, I'll wait. My day off, too, yeah?"

Lewis looks at her about this, about the book thing, because usually this kind of lead-in is the setup for some joke. Reading about wizards and druids at the mall, or werewolves and vampires being detectives, it doesn't exactly bump a thirty-six-year-old's cool meter up. And if anybody knew centaurs and mermaids are sometimes part of it? Or demons and angels? *Dragons?*

Keep those book covers folded all the way back, Lewis knows.

Except here's a girl actually asking to see them.

Even Peta doesn't really understand the fascination, the compulsion, the draw. How, camping, he always tucks a paperback or two in his pack, each inside its own separate ziplock bag. She's a super-athlete, though. She was always running too fast or jumping too high to pick up reading. It's nothing bad about her.

Keep saying that, Lewis tells himself.

Keep saying that and dribble out from under the garage, into the bright open sky. It's that kind of November day.

"Anything particular?" Lewis says back to Shaney without looking, all his fascination on the rim so he can come up onto his toes to shoot. What he has planned is a trip to the bank, to show off, to match the shot she just made look so easy, but then he has to collapse that idea at the last instant to keep his sweats on his body. Nothing underneath.

"Nothing I haven't seen before," Shaney says. "Tall Indian choking on the court, I mean."

The ball's bouncing through the junk lumber behind the goal. Lewis picks through barefoot to retrieve it, finds an even worse way back to the concrete pad.

"Court intrigue or heroic quests to save the realm?" Lewis asks. "Ships or horses, elves or—"

"I don't know, something *exciting*," Shaney says. "First in a series, maybe? Nice long series. Something to keep me busy all night."

Can she ever just talk about one thing?

"You being serious?" Lewis asks, chest-passing the ball across to her slow enough that she rips it from the air, like disgusted with the weakness of that lackluster pass. Her billowy T-shirt snags the grabby ball when she whips it across her midsection, though, so, pissed off about that, she bounces the ball high and wrenches her arms around behind her to tie her shirt, take up the slack, then catches the ball back. Peta, in this situation, usually tucks the front of her shirt up under her sports bra, but that isn't really an option for Shaney today, Lewis can tell.

"Oh," she says, following the look Lewis doesn't mean at her stomach.

It's a long ragged scar up and down, not side to side and low like a C-section. It's an open-heart-surgery scar, just, too low for the heart, and with an ugly, uneven ridge of scar tissue. Is this and whatever happened to her forehead and eye a matching pair? One really bad night instead of a lot of pretty sucky ones?

Lewis wants to ask about that car crash, or ask if the baby made it, or if they got the guy did this, except what if she was the only one to make it through that wreck? What if the baby didn't make it? What if that guy's still out there, carrying no scars himself?

"Say it," Shaney says about the scar, "go ahead, I've heard them all. Did I go to the emergency room or the butcher?"

She axles the ball between her two bird-fingers, rotating it with her thumbs, keeping it between Lewis and her midriff . . . as much bluff as she has, she still doesn't much want him looking, he can tell.

"Can hardly even see it," he one hundred percent lies. "Did— did everything . . ."

Her eyes flit up to the goal, and her non-answer is all the answer he needs, and her story comes together in his head, glued together from all the other stories he knows: she was young, the emergency room doc was a reject from the American medical system, so she ran from that tiny grave as far as she could, which ended up being about one tank of gas away from her reservation.

"Sorry," Lewis says. Not for seeing, but for whatever happened.

"We're from where we're from," she says back. "Scars are part of the deal, aren't they?"

Lewis steps out onto the court proper, wading into this game.

"So you really want a book?" he asks, still sure this is some complicated joke.

"I *read*, yeah," she says like insulted, shrugging one shoulder, dribbling up to him and then turning around in invitation. One thing all guy ballers can learn from how the girls play, it's that trick right there: giving the defender your ass, so you can protect the ball, slash out either way around them. Problem is, guys always think it's an ego thing, that it's a bigger coup to face up, lock eyes, then juke them any the hell way. And maybe it is. But the guys get their pockets picked more, too.

Shaney presses right up to Lewis, dribbling far from her body so he can't reach around.

This would be a bad time for Peta to come strolling up, he knows. He might as well be leaning around a barely halter-topped girl in the bar who's pretending not to know how to play pool. Peta won't be walking up, though. She's not off work for hours yet, and even then, it's a ten-minute hike in from the park-n-ride, her work duffel slung over her shoulder, her ear protection slung around her neck, the world so quiet to her, probably, after planes throttling up around her all day.

Peta.

Lewis vows to keep her name in his head for the next few minutes.

Shaney leans right like she's going to use her left to throw the ball ahead, a long dribble that gets her into layup territory if she glides a bit, underhands it, has that kind of touch, but then she's twisting left already, and Lewis, like always, like with Peta, falls for it. Shaney eels past, has had a coach really make her get her footwork right, and the net's already spitting the ball down.

"I had to hold my pants up," Lewis calls out.

"No you didn't," Shaney says, and bounces the ball into the garage, well away from both Harleys: the dying dog and the parked Road King. "Now, book me, officer."

It takes a second for Lewis to get that. And he's fully aware she just smuggled "handcuffs" into his head. He leads her in all the same, one hand clutching his sweats, and when he makes the turn up the stairs, Shaney's still back at the kitchen table.

"Blackfeet?" she's saying.

She's almost touching the rolled elk hide on the table, and she either just said her name for Lewis, or she's asking if this hide is from the reservation.

"What?" Lewis says, stopped with his non-sweats-hand gripping the newel post at the turn upstairs.

"I didn't know," she says, looking across to him with new eyes. "You're a—you're a bundle holder? They let it come all the way down here?"

From the look on his face, she explains: "It's like a pipe holder. Just, with a bundle."

"Oh, that's just—" Lewis begins, doesn't finish. "I didn't really grow up traditional."

"Think tradition found you just the same," she says, impressed, and almost touches the outermost brown hairs, then draws back like afraid of what might happen, what might pass from this Blackfeet bundle to her Crow self.

It's just an elk hide, Lewis doesn't say. Mostly because now she's drifted over to the couch, can see the masking-tape insult to all elk on the carpet of the living room. She looks from it to him then back, and, without saying anything, she's there, has the masking tape, is tearing off a few long strips, affixing them to the side of the couch. They look like long, careful shavings of wood, curling up.

Lewis doesn't say anything, just steps over like caught, a hundred possible explanations swirling through his head, all of them built to fail.

Moving deliberately, Shaney applies the long strips to the carpet, not adding to the elk, but giving it some insides—that inward-going tube of an arrow Lewis has always seen on lodges and in ledgers, that ducks back from the mouth to the stomach, for reasons he's never had clue one about. Why would the esophagus and stomach be more important than the heart, the liver?

"Now it's right," Shaney says.

It is. It was a smushed sheep before. Now it's . . . not so much a young cow elk, but a shape that somehow represents a young elk better than even an actual young elk, lying right there.

"How'd you know?" Lewis asks.

"You asking that because I'm a girl?"

"It was just a blob with legs," Lewis tells her.

Now she's looking to the ladder, to the nothing happening on the ceiling.

"My books are—" Lewis tries, but this isn't a library visit anymore.

"Why do this here, by the couch?" she asks just generally, coming back around to fix him in her thirsty eyes. She opens her hand to the masking tape elk, leaves her fingers spread like that.

"Wherever I did it, that could be the question," Lewis says, stalling.

"But you did it *here*, not anywhere else," Shaney says back, not pushing this time, but eliciting.

"It's stupid," he says, sitting down on the third step of the stairs. "Just something I thought I saw the other day."

She leans back onto the arm of the couch, her eyes still locked on him, says, "Which was?"

"It's not like in the books," Lewis says. "When you—when you see something that doesn't fit, like."

"Like a werewolf digging through your trash," she completes for him, hauling his current book up from the coffee table and showing him the cover, which is . . . a werewolf digging through a dumpster, trash strewn all over the alley.

Lewis nods, even more caught, his hands cupped over his mouth, his breath hot on his palms.

Is he really about to tell her? Does the hot girl from work get to know what his wife doesn't?

But she knew how to finish that elk on the floor, didn't she? That has to mean something. And—Lewis hates himself for saying it, for thinking it, but there it is: she's Indian.

More important, she's asking.

"It was the winter before I got married," he says. "Six—no, *five* days before Thanksgiving, yeah? It was the Saturday before Thanksgiving. We were hunting."

"We?" Shaney prompts.

"Guys I grew up with," Lewis says with a shrug, like they're not the real focus. "Gabe, Ricky, Cassidy—*Cass.*"

Shaney nods like he's doing good so far, and looks over to the masking tape elk again, kind of for both of them it feels like, and then Lewis is talking, is confessing, is saying it all out loud for the first time, which must mean it really happened.

THAT SATURDAY

The sky was spitting these hard little snowballs that kept catching in Lewis's girly eyelashes that he always thought were maybe just normal eyelashes.

"Wearing mascara now, princess?" Gabe asked all the same, bumping over into him. "Gonna bat your eyes, bring all the big bulls to your door?"

"You should talk," Lewis said, lifting his chin to Gabe's own frosted eyelashes.

Off-rez, people always used to default-think that Lewis and Gabe were brothers. Gabe, at six-two, had always been a touch taller, but otherwise, yeah, sure. In John Wayne's day Lewis and Gabe would have been scooped up to die in a hail of gunfire, would have been Indians "16" and "17," of forty. Cass, though? Cass would have been more the sitting-in-front-of-the-lodge type, the made-for-the-twentieth-century type, maybe even already wearing some early version of John Lennon shades. Ricky, he'd be Bluto from *Popeye*, just, darker; put him in front of a camera, and all he could hope to play would be the Indian thug off to the side, that nobody trusts to remember even half a line. Of Lewis and Gabe and Cass, though, he was the only one who could struggle out a sort-of beard, if he made it through the itchy part, and didn't have a girlfriend at the time. "Custer in the woodpile" was the excuse he would always give, smoothing his rangy fourteen hairs down along his cheeks like Grizzly Adams.

Gabe leaned across to Lewis, making smoochy lips, saying, "A little flirting would probably work better than what we're—" but then Cass, ahead of them at the truck, raised his left hand, silencing them.

"What you got?" Ricky asked, coming back.

He was always ranging out to the side, sure they were just missing a whole herd, that all the elk were single-filing it past just out of sight, ducking their heads down so their racks wouldn't crest over the snow.

"Shh," Cass said, coming down to one knee to read sign like a real Indian.

Tracks.

Elk had been nosing into the bed, probably remembering that some trucks carry hay, and hay never gets *all* the way gone. Not without elk that are tall enough to lean over the side of the truck, that have long enough necks to even get under the toolbox for every last straw.

"Heavy guys," Gabe said, lowering down to insert a trigger finger into the deep hoofprint. He had some complicated method where a bull weighed this much if it was up to his second knuckle, that much if it was halfway past that, but Lewis never bought it.

"Told you they were up here," Ricky said, looking all around like these elk might be turned around at the tree line like a stupid whitetail, to twitch their tails and watch.

"Up here" wasn't *high*-high, snowmobile or horse country, but halfway there, anyway, just down from Babb, over toward Duck Lake. With the weather moving in, the elk should have been filing down from the timber, to wait the big snow out. The idea was to meet them halfway.

"This is some *bull*shit," Cass said, his usual call, and Ricky responded with his obligatory line, "Literally," toeing over a fresh black mound, the pellets more tapered at one end, not both. Nine times out of nine, that'll mean "bull," not "cow."

"They're playing with us," Gabe said, reseating his rifle strap on his shoulder.

"Catch me if you can," Lewis said for the bulls and then lined up on the walking-away tracks, his eyes going downhill with them, downhill, to—

"Shit," Cass said, turning around to kick snow.

"They know," Ricky said with a chuckle, impressed.

"Tricksy, tricksy . . ." Lewis said, smacking his gum too loud, and Cass cut his eyes over at him, not sure he'd heard that word right but not wanting to ask, either.

Gabe didn't say anything, just kept watching where the big bulls had gone—where they *were*.

"Anybody pack some grey braids in with their bear kit?" he finally said with his trademark grin, the one that usually ended up either getting beat in by the end of the night or looking out through bars. Sometimes both. A hundred years ago he would have been the guy always trying to get a raiding party together to sneak over the line, have some fun, come hell-for-leather home in the morning with half of America massed up right behind.

"*No*, man," Ricky said, his eyes hot so he could really mean this, really drill it in. "If we get caught over there, it's—"

"Then let's not get caught, what say?" Gabe said, looking from face to face like polling a jury.

"We can't," Lewis said to Gabe about the off-limits section. "Ricky's right, if Denny catches us again, then he'll—"

"It's not fair though," Cass whined, flicking something off the end of his finger and watching it fly. "That section's reserved for elders, but what if none of the elders are even hunting it, right?"

"Old guys get up early," Gabe threw in, like just seeing this brilliant point. "If they were going to hunt their section today, they'd already have been and gone. We'll just be cleaning up the ones they weren't going to shoot. No big. Cassidy's right."

"Cass," Cass said.

"Whoever he is today, he's right," Gabe corrected, setting his feet to take Cass's elbow.

It wasn't that the elders' section was all the way off-limits, it was that only elders—plus one and only one—could use trucks to get in and out. Anybody younger was supposed to hoof it, which would be a two-hour walk in at least, and it was already an hour and a half after lunch, with the sun going down just after four, and taking the thermometer with it.

"Elders aren't the only ones with empty freezers," Cass said with an obvious shrug. "Anyway, it's my truck. You three bail, I take the heat."

When Ricky didn't say anything, Lewis just looked away, down to the elders' section again.

It *was* some good-ass country around Duck Lake, no two ways about that. And Gabe knew every logging road, every two-track, every old game trail that'd been widened out by four-wheelers and chain saws. And it does suck to be the only Indian without an elk.

"Last day of the season . . ." Gabe pled to all of them.

Technically it wasn't, but it was the last time they could come out for a whole Saturday like this together. There would still be lunch breaks on their own, though, eating and driving down some road somebody maybe saw an elk walking alongside. There would still be being late *to* work because of a set of deep tracks crossing from ditch to ditch. But Lewis heard what Gabe was saying, what he was arguing: the last day of the season, the rules are different.

Anything goes. Whatever fills your freezer. You've put in enough days out in the cold and the snow that you feel like the elk owe you, almost.

Included in that are any moose or mulies you might jump along the way.

"Shit," Lewis said, because he could feel himself starting to cave.

"That's back where you found Junior, enit?" Cass said to Ricky, but Ricky was watching the trees again, always seeing an ear twitch where there were no ears.

Cass was talking about when Ricky found Junior Big Plume floating facedown in Duck Lake, and was reservation-famous for the weekend.

"Shut up," Ricky said, his hunting face all the way on, which was pretty much just a cigar-store Indian mask. Still, Cass let it drop.

Gabe took advantage of the silence to take a long read of all the faces, all the eyes, all the weak, weak spines. "Well, the elk aren't going to shoot themselves, gentlemen," he finally said, satisfied with what he'd seen, evidently. He hauled his rifle around to clear the chamber, Cass's rule since the new hole in the front floorboard of his truck, the hole Gabe insisted Cass would thank him for come summer, which is right where Lewis would like to freeze-frame that day, just stop it completely, hang it on the wall, call it "Hunting" or "Snow" or "Five Days Before Turkey and Football."

But he can't. The rest of the day was already happening, had already pretty much happened right when Gabe kept looking downhill, to where he said the elk were.

"Was he right?" Shaney asks, her legs tucked under her to the side like a traditional.

Lewis chuckles a sick chuckle, says, "About the elk not shooting themselves?"

Shaney nods, and Lewis looks away, says Ricky was right too.

"About what?" Shaney asks.

"Getting caught."

Since Cass's squarebody crew cab didn't have a winch, each time he couldn't tell where the road was and slogged out into the soft stuff, everybody had to pile out again, take turns on the stretched-out come-along, the other two digging with planks and trying to do some magic or other with the jack, one person behind the wheel to feather the accelerator and work the shifter, keep the truck rocking back and forth.

Four separate times at least, certain death loomed, but either that wobbly high-lift sliced down into fluffy snow instead of crunchy skull, or the come-along hook snapped back over the cab of the truck, instead of through any faces.

It was so funny even Lewis was laughing.

It didn't feel like anything could go wrong.

Sure, yeah, he wanted an elk and wanted it bad, but all the same, this was what hunting is about: you and some buds out kicking it through the deep snow, your breath frosted, your right-hand glove forever lost, your Sorrels wet on the inside, Chief Mountain always a smudge on the northwest horizon, like watching over all these idiot Blackfeet.

At least until they got to where it happened.

It was a steep hill, maybe a half mile in from the lake. The big snow was already crowding in, pushing the wind ahead. That's the only thing Lewis has to explain how the elk didn't hear Cass's Chevy struggling through the snow. The squirrels had been chattering about it, the few birds that were still out were annoyed enough to glide to farther-and-farther-away trees, but the elk, maybe because of that wind in their faces, they were oblivious, just trying to chomp whatever they could, since it was all about to be buried.

Looking back, Lewis tells Shaney that the one thing that could have maybe saved them was some horses, the wild ones that were always showing up in the least expected places all over the reservation, their eyes wide and crazy, their manes and tails shaggy and tangled. If four or five of them had pounded through on some important horse mission or another, that might have spooked the elk, or at least got them listening closer, smelling harder, paying better attention.

But there were no horses that day. Only elk. What happened was the same thing as had been happening the last half mile: Cass lost the road again, in spite of Gabe guaranteeing that it turned here, here, *here*. Instead of trying to back up and find the road again, though, Cass drove *into* this wrong direction, his foot deep in the pedal, the wheels already churning for purchase, the only thing keeping the truck going its own sagging momentum.

"Going for the record, going for the record here . . ." Gabe said, lifting his butt off the seat like he was the thing weighing them down, and, in the back, Ricky rocked forward, trying to help the truck along. Sitting beside him, Lewis wondered what the penalty was just for *being* in the elder section. But he knew: nothing, so long as you're not rifled up. If you are carrying, though? Denny throws the key away.

"We're gonna make it, we're gonna make it!" Cass said, one hand on the wheel, the other to the four-wheel-drive shifter to tap the transfer case into high should they be so lucky as to need it. What he was doing, not exactly on purpose, was driving from one part of an S-curve in the road to the other, snow flying every which direction, the tires spinning great white rooster tails of it up and over, some of it probably not even landing, just hitching a ride on the wind, to sift down over Cutbank or Shelby—

somewhere so far away from this as to, right then, just be a legend, pretty much.

"Shit, shit," Lewis said, hooking a second hand through the grab strap, straightening his legs against the floorboard even though he knows that's the wrong way to take a jolt. It was just instinct to brace himself, though. Three times already they'd barely missed a lichen-shadowed boulder left behind by some glacier twenty thousand years ago. They had to be owed one right in the grill-teeth sooner or later, right?

Instead of that granite stop sign, what they almost drove onto and down *into* was open space.

Cass didn't have to hit the brake, he just had to stop gunning the truck forward.

"What the hell?" Ricky said, not able to see from the backseat. Lewis, either.

The engine sputtered out, dropping them into a vast silence.

"Good one," Cass said, disgusted, trying to clear his side of the windshield, finally cranking his window down instead, and Lewis was just thanking any gods tuned in right now: they should be a smoking wreck at the bottom of this drop-off.

"Shh, shh," Gabe said to them all then, and leaned forward over the dash, looking down and down.

And then.

"What?" Shaney asks.

Then Gabe reached over for his rifle, his fingers coming into place on the pistol grip one by delicate one, like all four at once might be too loud.

What Lewis remembers clearest about the next sixty seconds, maybe closer to two impossible minutes, is the way his heart clenched in his chest, the way his throat filled with . . . with terror?

Is that what too much joy and surprise can ball up into, when it comes at you all at once?

There was the instant sweat, his head full of sound, his eyes letting in too much light for his head to process. It was like . . . he doesn't have words for it, really. "That fight or flight rush," he tells Shaney, only, running wasn't even a distant option. It was what he'd always imagined war to be like: too much input all at once, his hands acting almost without his say-so, because they'd been waiting for this moment for so long, weren't going to let him miss it.

Gabe either.

He popped the handle of his door, rolled down into the snow smooth as anything, his rifle whipping out after him.

Following his lead, nobody said anything, just fell in, Ricky coming out his door, Cass trying to jam the truck into Park so it wouldn't roll over the rock lip it was teetering on.

The door on Lewis's side opened like a whisper, like fate, and when he committed his right foot down to the powdery surface that ended up being two feet deep, he just kept falling, his chin stopping a hand's width into the powder the front tires had churned up. His forward motion never faltered, though. He crawled ahead like a soldier, pulling with his elbows, his rifle held ahead to keep the barrel clear.

And—that was when the frenzy washed over him.

He'd seen big herds in the Park, over at Two Dog Flat, had seen them in spring over by Babb, bounding across the road at night, but this many huge perfect bodies against all that stark white was something he'd never seen this close before. At least, not with a rifle in his hands, and no tourists around to snap pictures.

Gabe's rifle going off was distant, was down at the other end of some long, long tunnel.

Lewis, knowing that this was how you got to be a good Indian, finally remembered how to jack a round in. Once it was seated, he pulled that Tasco up until it cupped his right eye, and he was firing now as well, and firing again, just waiting to pull the trigger until he could see brown in the crosshairs. Just anywhere *near* the crosshairs—how could he miss?

He couldn't.

Three rounds, then he was rolling over, digging in his pants pocket for shells, and the elk, trained in the high country, the sharp drop in front of the truck throwing the sound every which way, their first instinct was to crash uphill, to what was supposed to be safety.

On the other side of the truck Ricky was screaming some old-time war whoop, and Gabe maybe was too, and so was Lewis, he thinks.

"You couldn't hear if you were or not?" Shaney asks.

Lewis shakes his head no, he couldn't.

But he does remember Cass standing behind his opened door, his rifle stabbed through the rolled-down window, and he's just shooting, and shooting, and shooting, only stopping to thumb another round in, and another, one of them launching onto the dash and clattering the whole way across, hissing down into the snow by Lewis.

"We could have fed the whole tribe for a week on this much meat," Lewis says, his eyes hot now. "For a month. For the whole winter, maybe."

"If you were that kind of Indian," Shaney says, getting what he's saying.

"There's more," Lewis says, finally looking to the masking-tape elk on his living room floor.

In the hollow deafness after all this, the four of them stood there on that rocky ledge, the snow skirling past, the weather almost on them, and Gabe—he always had the best eyes—counted nine huge bodies down there in the snow, each probably pushing five hundred pounds.

Cass's Chevy was a half-ton.

"Shi-*it*," Ricky said, breathing hard, smiling wide.

This was the kind of luck that never happened, that they had only ever heard about. But never like this. Never a whole herd. Never as many as they could bring down.

"Okay there?" Gabe said across to Lewis, and Cass reached up with the side of his finger, dabbed at Lewis's right eye.

Blood.

Before, when he'd had scope-eye as a kid—when the scope had recoiled back into his eye orbit—he'd felt that shock wave move in slow motion from the front of his head to the back. It makes your brain *fluid* for a slowed-down moment, leaves you scrambled, and because of that you can never remember what exactly it is you're doing to make this scope-eye happen. Except the obvious: pressing it right up to your eye, pulling the trigger.

This time Lewis remembered every shot, the lead-on-meat slap of every slug, but never even felt the force of that sudden recoil going from front to back through his head.

Five years after this a dentist will look at his X-rays and trace out the bone evidence of this trauma around his right eye and ask was it a car wreck, maybe?

"Almost," Lewis will tell him. "But it was a truck."

The last time he saw Cass's Chevy, it was up on blocks by a barbed-wire fence over at a high place north of Browning, the windshield caved in, the hood yawning open like a long scream. The engine must have been good enough, otherwise it would have still been there. The wheels and tires had been yanked as well. After Lewis left that part of the country for what he secretly knew was going to be forever, the first cinder block holding that truck up went soon enough, he imagines, a rust-coated brake drum crumbling down through that stony grey, making the truck look like a horse kneeling, and after that it would have been fast. The land claims what you leave behind.

That day with all the elk, though, back then the Chevy was still on its first or maybe second life, was young and hungry, was telling the four of them it could carry as many elk as they could pile in. Realistically, even just three elk in the back of a half-ton is pushing it, is going to have that truck sitting down on its springs, the nose pointing at the sky, the front brakes useless.

And that was if the stupid come-along was going to cooperate, help get those heavy bodies up the slope, and if four Indians without gambrels or cherry pickers could somehow get the second and third elk in on top of the first.

"And that's when it started snowing heavy," Lewis tells Shaney, touching his face with his fingertips like feeling those cold dabs again.

She doesn't say anything, is just watching, soaking all this in. Not because she wants to know, Lewis doesn't think, but . . . is it more like she knows he needs to say it? To have told *some*one, at least?

"Old-time buffalo jump!" Gabe called out then, and he vaulted right the hell off the ledge, slid on his ass down into that jumble of dead and dying elk.

Lewis and Ricky and Cass picked their way down after him, unsheathed saws and knives, and got to work. Inside of five minutes it was clear this was going to be a haunches-only affair—already big wet flakes were finding their way into the red body cavities, dissolving instantly against that steamy heat. But pretty soon the flakes were going to start winning that little war, no longer melting but piling up, making these carcasses look like giant stuffed animals slit open, all their batting leaking out.

Gabe and Cass doubled up on the one bull that fell, trying to keep his cape intact, since Gabe knew a back-alley taxidermy guy who'd do a mount for meat, so long as he picked the cuts. Ricky was on a monologue about how this Thursday, Thanksgiving, was going to be an *Indian* holiday this year, with the four of them bringing in a haul like this.

"Thanksgiving Classic," Gabe said, giving what just happened a proper name.

Cass whooped once, setting that name in place.

Lewis whipped his hand over his head about the cow he'd just dressed out in record time—it's a rodeo thing, is deep in his DNA—and moved on to the next, the young cow, but when he dropped to his knees to make that first cut from her pelvis to her sternum, she found her front legs, tried to climb up out of the snow.

Lewis fell back, called over to Cass for a rifle. He never once looked away from this young elk, though. Her eyes, they were—don't elk usually have brown eyes? Hers were more yellow, almost, branching into hazel at the edges.

Maybe it was because she was terrified, because she didn't understand what was happening. Just that it hurt.

The shot that brought her down had caught her midway through the back, from the top, and taken her spine out. So her rear legs were dead, and her insides were going to be a mess as well.

"Whoah, whoah," Lewis said to her, feeling more than seeing Cass's rifle plunk into the snow just short of his right leg. He felt down for it, that young elk still struggling, blowing red mist from her nostrils, her eyes so big, so deep, so shiny.

"And I couldn't find a *shell*," Lewis says to Shaney. "I thought I was out, that I'd used my last up by the truck, when everything was crazy."

"But you had one," Shaney tells him.

"Two," Lewis says back, looking down at his hands.

This close he didn't need the scope or a sight.

"Sorry, girl," he said, and, careful of his swelling-up eye, lined the barrel up, pulled the trigger.

The sound was massive, rolling up the slope and then crashing back down.

The young elk's head flopped back like it was on a hinge, and she sank into the snow.

"Sorry," Lewis said again, quieter, so Cass couldn't hear.

But it was just hunting, he told himself. It was just bad luck for the elk. They should have bedded down with the wind in their favor. They should have pushed through to some section the hunters didn't have access to—that *trucks* can't get to, anyway.

After the shot, Lewis looked behind him for some buckbrush or something to hang the rifle from, but then a sound brought him back to the young elk.

The sound was the crust of snow, crunching.

She was staring at him again. *Not* dead. Her breath was raspy and uneven, but it was definitely there, somehow, when no way should it have been. Not after having her back broken, half her head blown to mist.

Lewis took a long and involuntary step back and fell, jammed the butt of the rifle down just ahead of his ass so he could be sure where the barrel was going to be, because he didn't want it driving up under his head, trying to separate his jaw from his face.

She was trying to stand again was the thing, never mind that the top of her head was missing, that her back was broken, that she should be dead, that she had to be dead.

"What the hell?" Cass called over. "My rifle's not *that* off, man."

He laughed, leaned back down into the big cow he was insisting was his. Lewis had his right leg straight out in the snow, was feeling in all his pockets for one more shell, please.

He found it, ran it into the chamber, working the bolt back and forward to be sure the cartridge seated right. This time, talking to the young elk the whole while, promising her that he was going to use every bit of her if she would just please *die*, he nestled the barrel right against her face, so the bullet would come out the lower back of her skull, plow into her back where she'd already been shot once.

Her one yellow eye was still watching him, the right one haywire, the pupil blown wide, looking somewhere else, someplace he couldn't see without turning around.

"So that's where I put the barrel this time," Lewis says to Shaney. "I figured—I don't know. That first shot must have glanced off her skull, right? Looked worse than it was. So this time I didn't want to give it any chance to bounce off. The eye could be like a tunnel in—*in*to her."

Shaney doesn't blink.

"You were gonna be a tough one, weren't you?" the Lewis of back then said, his lower lip starting to tremble, and then he pulled the trigger.

Cass's rifle bucked free of his one-handed grip and the young elk fell *again*, and what he was saying in his head, what he was telling himself even though he was Indian, even though he was this great born hunter, what he was telling himself to make this okay, to be able to make it through the next minute, and the next hour, it was that shooting her, it was just like putting one in a hay bale, it was just like snapping a blade of grass in a field, it was like stepping on a grasshopper. The young elk didn't even know what was happening, animals aren't aware like that, not in the same way people are.

"You believed that, too, didn't you?" Shaney says.

"For ten years," Lewis says back. "Until I saw her again, right over there."

"Still dead?" Shaney asks, sitting on the second step of the stairs now, her hand on the knee of his sweats, and that's how she is and that's how Lewis is when Peta walks in the front door.

FRIDAY

When the Thunderball Express slams past at 2:12 in the morning, Lewis's half-asleep mind turns those slamming wheels into thundering hooves, going up and down faster and faster into some muck, until he sits up hard from . . . *what*?

His knee-jerk thought is that the train threw one of those grey rocks into the fence, knocked another slat out, left it spinning on the cross-board like a cartoon, but it wasn't the train at all, he realizes. It was a . . . *chain*? He sits up when that word connects to what's right under the bedroom: the garage. The sound that shook him awake was the garage door chain in its long greasy track, the little motor grinding and pulling.

And the garage door would only be going up because someone pushed the button. And Peta's not on her side of the bed, is she?

Lewis sits up, his feet to the carpet now, his head trying to swim back to functional. When he can balance enough, he steps into those same useless sweatpants, feels his way across the bedroom to stumble down the stairs, the same ones Peta caught him and Shaney on. Doing nothing, but still, right? Lewis made sure Shaney left with an armload of books, a whole series, to prove to

Peta why she'd been there, but the whole time, stacking them up in Shaney's arms, it felt like an overcorrection, like trying to hide a body on the lawn by covering it with eight other bodies.

And Peta bought it, too, that was the thing. There was that moment when it all could have gone the other way, sure, but the reason it didn't, she told him later, it was his eyes. Lewis hadn't even been there on the stairs, not really.

All the same, Lewis knows it might have hurt Peta less for Shaney to have been just stepping back into her jeans. That would have been better than Lewis telling another woman something so intimate, so personal, so private. And that he'd been telling the elk story to another *Indian*, which Peta could never be no matter how fast she ran, no matter how high she jumped, that was maybe the final cut. The deepest, anyway. The one she was probably still nursing.

Thursday, the little him and Peta saw each other, she was cordial but not really herself. Not like she had something to say so much as she didn't have anything to say. And now she's gone from the bed at two in the morning, when she's a sleeper who treasures every minute she can get until that five o'clock alarm.

Coming down the stairs, holding on to his sweats, Lewis overshoots the step-off at the bottom, falls ahead into the living room, tight-wiring it around the edge of the masking tape, and, because it's not on any human schedule, that stupid spotlight in the ceiling flickers. From Lewis's stumbling footfalls? Is *that* what makes it come on? Or are the aftershocks from the garage door what's flickering it on?

Before the mystery of that spotlight, though, there's the mystery of the wife.

Lewis pulls the door to the garage in kind of reverently, and the light built into the garage door motor is still on because it's only been about forty seconds since the door came up. Sitting on the pad of concrete out at the soft edge of that light, her knees to her chest, arms hugging them, white-blond hair cascaded down her back, is Peta in her sleep shirt, her ankle socks, her breakfast scrunchy around her left wrist, ready for cereal.

She's been crying. Lewis doesn't have to see her face to know. He can tell just from the curve of her back.

He steps down onto the cold smooth concrete of the garage to pick his way through to her, and that's when he sees it.

Harley, but not. Not anymore.

That good dog from his childhood, that got its head kicked in by a horse? That's the closest thing to this. To what's happened to Harley. Except that was just one fast kick, there and back in a snap, so nobody watching the parade even knew what had happened for a breath or two.

This—this is a dog that got ran down *by* a horse, and the horse had some serious score to settle, went down and came up over and over, slamming that dog into nothing, into a red chunky smear, teeth here, flash of bone there, matted fur all in and among.

The vomit's coming up and out of Lewis's mouth before he even realizes it. It's hot, thin, and already on his hands, like keeping it from splashing down onto the floor of the garage is suddenly the most important thing. Once he feels it stringing out between his fingers, he really gags, is shambling for the outside, losing everything under the basketball goal, his sweats around his ankles.

It's probably not a good look, but Peta's not looking, either. When it's over he yanks his stupid sweats up and pushes his forehead into the flaky paint of the basketball pole just to have something solid to hold on to.

"I don't understand," he says.

"He's dead," Peta says, kind of obviously.

Yeah, *but*, Lewis doesn't say.

If the door was only open *four inches*, like he's been leaving it for air circulation, then . . . then: "What could have done that?"

Peta looks over from her grief hole, says, "Should we call your coworker about it?"

Lewis deserves that, he knows. "Coworker" is what he was calling Shaney for the few minutes after hustling her out the door with her armload of books.

"No, let's not," he says, cleaning his hands in the dirt. "I don't even have her number."

Except, he realizes, he does, doesn't he? In the work directory thing, the brand-new one.

"What could have even done that to him?" he says, settling down beside Peta.

She scooches over like giving him room. Like there's limited space on this two-car-wide pad of dribbled-in, oil-stained concrete.

No: like she doesn't want to be touching him.

"It wasn't his fault," Peta says, staring off into the nothing all around, "he was just a dog," which—is that an answer, really?

Without meaning to, Lewis clocks her socked feet.

No blood, no gore.

No hooves, either.

But the door, it was only up *four inches*. And Peta had to *raise* it to come sit out here and think. The only explanation is that it was either one of the two of them stomping Harley, or it was some-one . . . some*thing* else.

Lewis cranks around, heart thudding in his chest, and stud-ies the dark cave of the garage for a tall, top-heavy form standing flat up against a wall, hidden just nearly enough, her yellow eyes drinking the light in.

It wasn't horse hooves that did that to Harley, he's sure. It was an elk. How he knows is that it's after midnight, meaning it's tech-nically *Saturday* now—it's exactly one week before the ten-year anniversary of the Thanksgiving Classic.

"I don't know if we should be here anymore," he says.

Peta doesn't look over.

"All new houses take some getting used to," she says, always the rational one. "Remember that one with the attic?"

The place Lewis was so sure was haunted. The one where he nailed a board across that attic door up in the ceiling, in case anything wanted to crawl out, stand by the bed on his side. Or on any side. *Indians are spooky* had been his explanation to Peta. It's pretty much all he's got now, too.

"I can't sleep," he says.

"You were sleeping a few minutes ago."

"Why are you up?" Lewis asks, watching the side of Peta's face.

"Thought I heard something," she says, shrugging one shoulder.

"Harley?" Lewis says, because it's the obvious thing.

"The stairs," Peta says, which instantly sucks all the heat from Lewis's body.

He breathes in, breathes out long and shaky.

"I didn't tell you the whole story about that . . . *hunting* thing because I didn't want you to have to have it in your head," he says.

This gets Peta looking over. A mealy-mouthed excuse like this, it deserves her full attention.

"You don't like to hear stuff about . . . animals," Lewis adds.

"It's about you," she says back without hesitating. "It's who *you* are."

"I didn't tell her the end of it," Lewis says, his voice barely more than a creak.

Peta's still watching him. Waiting.

"You sure you want to know?" he asks.

"Who are you married to?" she says back. "Her, or me?"

Lewis nods, taking that hit, and wades into it one more time, starting with how, when he split that young elk open, when he carved into that elk who didn't know when she was dead, what spilled out into the snow were her milk bags. They were light blue, muscular and veiny, the ductwork still attached and ready.

She was too young to be pregnant, probably couldn't have carried full term all the way to spring, and it was too early for a calf to be this far along anyway, but still—*that's* why she was fighting so hard, he knew, and still knows. It didn't matter that she was dead. She had to protect her baby.

And that baby, that embryo or fetus, that *calf*, it was still rounded like a bean in there, its head shape ducked down into its chest like it was going to look up at him from its mother's gore, like it was going to wobble up onto four spindly legs, walk away, grow bigger but never actually develop, so it'd end up being a seven-hundred-pound big-eyed, smooth-skinned fetus, always looking for its dead mother.

When Cass wasn't watching, which was the whole time, Lewis used the butt of the rifle to scrape a hole in the frozen dirt, and nestled that unfinished, only-wriggling-a-little-bit elk calf into the ground, covered it as best he could, and then—never mind that storm swirling in, dumping load after load of snow—insisted on dressing this young elk mother out right, and all the way.

Nothing was going to spoil. No part of her could go to waste.

To do it right, he hacked a thick branch from the brush, split her sternum with just the knife—she wasn't even old enough to need the saw—then cracked the pelvis like prying a butterfly's wings apart, jammed the branch into her chest to prop her open. To be sure to get every bit of her ruptured guts, the last little bit of her lungs, he even crawled in like a kid with his first elk, scooping and pushing, and when he finally rolled out, dislodging the branch, Gabe was standing there watching.

"Just the hindquarters today, Super Indian," he said with a smile, a big brown leg Fred-Flintstoned over his shoulder, the black hoof cupped in his hand, blood dripping down the back of his jacket.

Lewis didn't take Gabe's bait. Just kept working.

The next part of his promise to the young elk was the skinning, which was a job he really needed to hang her up for, from a stout rafter in a shop, the radio playing over on the workbench. What he *had* was a trading-post knife that was too sharp at first, then too dull, and by the end of the job Gabe and Ricky and Cass were all standing there watching, the snow coating their shoulders, not even melting in their hair anymore.

And Lewis was maybe crying by then, he admits to Peta. He doesn't say it for pity, just because not saying that part would feel like lying.

"What did Gabe and them say about that?" Peta asks, her hand to his forearm now, because he's trying not to cry *here*, he's trying not to be that stupid, that needy.

"They were my friends," Lewis says, sputtering now and trying to just keep it in. "They didn't—they didn't say anything."

Peta reaches up to his forehead, delicately removes a flake of paint from the basketball pole, and then pulls him to her chest, her palm to his cheek, and this, her, it's home, and it's not haunted, not even a little. This is where he wants to live forever.

But he *still* hasn't said it all, about that day.

What he didn't get to before turning into a blubbering excuse for a grown-up is the four of them struggling that young elk up the hill, finally just using the junk come-along as a cable after digging the truck out, never mind that this ledge is the exact point on the reservation where all the wind gathers to sweep down like the end of the world.

Against all rationality, and though each step uphill takes about twenty steps in total, the young elk makes it all the way up, and in one piece, the four of them sweating in the freezing air. And neither Gabe nor Ricky nor Cass even asks Lewis why this is so important. They don't blame him, either, when Denny Pease is waiting by the truck on his game warden four-wheeler, looking from face to face like impressed that they thought they could get away with something of this magnitude on his watch. It's just as well. The snow's too deep, is coming down too fast. Without Denny's radio to call in more help, the truck doesn't make it out, Gabe and Cass and Ricky and Lewis don't get found until spring, and Lewis never meets Peta, never gets Harley, never goes to work for the post office, never builds his Road King.

The condition Denny lays down that day, it's that the four of them can either throw their honorable kills back down that slope and pay the fine for what they've done here, multiplied by *nine*, not counting any elk that ran off shot, are out there dying now, or they throw all this meat back down that slope and then cash out once and for all, never hunt on the reservation again. Happy early turkey day, turkeys.

It's a small price to pay, really. It's not like Lewis has the nerve for shooting big animals anymore. Not after having gone to war against the elk like that. That craziness, that heat of the moment, the blood in his temples, smoke in the air, it was like—he hates himself the most for this—it was probably what it was like a century and more ago, when soldiers gathered up on ridges above Blackfeet encampments to turn the cranks on their big guns, terraform this new land for their occupation. Fertilize it with blood. Harvest the potatoes that would grow there, turn them into baskets of fries, and sell those crunchy cubes of grease back at powwows.

Even after taking Denny's option two—I will hunt no more forever—all Lewis could think about, standing there, was that young elk he'd spent so much time on. She was freezing solid on the ground between them all, skinless, surrounded by sawed-off legs.

"Can we at least keep her?" he asked Denny, Gabe already rushing to the ledge to sling his elk haunch out into open space, the storm swallowing it whole.

Like a ritual, Cass stepped forward, hurled his leg down the slope, and then Ricky did it, his going the highest before disappearing, all five of them tracking its descent until they couldn't.

Denny looked over to Lewis about his question, then down to the young elk, all her muscles showing, a hole blown in her back, her head mostly gone, and Lewis, in the driveway well after midnight, shudders against Peta. Not because Denny shrugged a what-the-hell about the young elk, but because Harley's dead, isn't he? And not just dead, but killed, in a way that had to be terrifying. It should have been *Lewis* under those flashing elk hooves, Lewis knows, it should have been *him* paying for that young elk. Not Harley.

"I don't understand what's happening," he says into Peta's chest, his hand gripping hard on her leg. All her running muscles are still there, are there forever, probably.

"Something must have got in," she says back, about Harley.

She's right, of course, but the real question isn't what got in, it's *when* did it get in.

Lewis's breath hitches and he stands all at once, faking resolve, is already at the side of the house, digging for a shovel.

Peta stands at the edge of the concrete watching, her elbows in her hands, parentheses of concern around her eyes.

"I'm sorry," she says. About all of it—the elk, Harley. Maybe even Shaney.

When Lewis comes in thirty minutes later, Harley poured into the hole he dug that was bigger than it needed to be, a blanket and a sleeping bag or two packed in all around him to keep him warm, he steps out of those useless sweatpants, balls them into the kitchen trash, and what he sees nestled in there is a ball of crumbling masking tape.

Peta peeled the elk up from the living room floor. *Good*, he tells himself, standing there naked, chest heaving, *good*.

Just, it doesn't feel good.

SATURDAY

To keep his hands busy, maybe occupy his mind if he's lucky, Lewis puts the Road King up on the stand, is going to take it down to the frame again, clean and detail every bolt thread, check and double-check every connection, blow every line out twice, make it brand-new, cherrier than cherry.

He's just gone what he thinks might be a full five minutes without images of Harley cycling through his head when two of Great Falls' best show up, doing that thing where they park their patrol car across the bottom of the driveway. Lewis keeps on tracing the throttle cable he's tracing, like that's the only thing he's interested in today. The cops walk up spaced out wider than a single shotgun blast. The reason for their spacing, Lewis knows, is that he's sitting in the dark of the garage, shirt off, hair over his face, and he didn't walk out to meet them, is making them come to him.

"That really your name?" the first officer asks.

"Like, on purpose?" the second adds.

"What's this about?" Lewis says, hands in clear view up in the frame of the Road King. Though of course, should they pop him in the back with their .40-calibers just because, then their report could be all about how it looked like he had a gun tucked up under the tank.

"This is about your killer dog," the second officer says.

"What'd he do?" Lewis asks.

"According to emergency room personnel," the first officer states, looking at his notebook like reading it but of course he's not, "a dog at this address bit a man on the face."

"Silas," Lewis says with a shrug. "That's between me and him, isn't it?"

"Not when the hospital gets involved," the second officer says. "We have to see if the animal qualifies as a menace, a threat to public safety."

"Aren't you people cops, not dog cops?" Lewis says, standing, each of the cops taking a tactical step back, their right hands suddenly loose by their sides.

"We're the *police* asking to see your *dog*," the first officer says, that thing rising in his voice that isn't so much saying this call can go bad, but that he's kind of hoping it will.

"You really want to see him?" Lewis asks.

Where he leads them is the tamped-down grave on the back side of the fence, close to the tracks. He explains to them that he buried Harley there because he liked to bark at the train. They ask what happened to him. Instead of telling them that an elk from back home followed him all the way down here, is apparently on this big revenge arc, and instead of telling them option *two*, which is that there was something in this house before he even got here, and it's using his own memories and guilt against him, Lewis just shrugs.

What he also doesn't tell them is that there's always the chance that he's just flat-out losing it, here. That all the bad medicine from that hunt's built up all these years, has turned into something that's messing with his head from the inside. Or maybe that repetitive scope-eye he got that day in the snow was worse than he thought, it kicked something loose in his brain, something that's just now blooming.

"Do you not want to tell us because you put the dog down yourself, and don't want us checking serial numbers on any unregistered weapons?" the first officer asks.

"You don't have to register hunting rifles," Lewis says. "Do you?"

"You shot a deer rifle this close to other houses?" the second officer says, real concern in his eyes.

"Elk rifle," Lewis corrects. "And no, I didn't shoot it this close to other houses. He hung himself from the fence, trying to get over."

"'He,'" the second officer prompts.

"Harley," Lewis fills in.

"Like your bike," the second officer says.

Lewis doesn't dignify this.

"The one you're taking apart as well," the second officer says.

"What are you saying?" Lewis asks.

"What are you doing?" the first officer says right back.

Lewis thrusts both his hands up through his hair and like that both cops have drawn, are in that shooting crouch they like.

Going slow, finger by finger, Lewis lowers his hands back to his sides.

Dealing with cops is like being around a skittish horse: No sudden movements, nothing shiny or loud. Zero jokes.

Still, Lewis leans forward, shakes what hair he has to show there're no weapons there.

"You'll dig him up?" the second officer asks, holstering his pistol.

"I can," Lewis says, toeing at the loose dirt of the obvious mound.

"You're supposed to have a permit to bury on private property," the first officer says. "Otherwise everybody buries their pets down at the park, or in their neighbor's lawn, because they don't want to mess their own grass up."

Lewis looks up to the tracks on their long spine of gravel-skinned earth, says, "Think BNSF cares?"

"We'll make the necessary inquiries," the first officer says, his pistol holstered now as well.

"Fine," Lewis says.

"We might need to see the animal, too," the second officer says. "To confirm."

"That he's dead?" Lewis asks.

"That you're not hiding him," the second officer says.

"Unless you want to grant us permission to inspect your house," the first officer says.

Lewis hiccups half a laugh out, shakes his head no-thank-you to that home inspection. Just on principle.

"He was a barker," he says, about Harley. "You'd have heard him when your car pulled up."

"We'll be back soon," the first officer assures Lewis. "Either with the proper documents to perform a comprehensive search, or with the railroad's reply."

"Or to dig my dead dog up," Lewis adds, stupid Indian that he is.

"That, too," the second officer says, and then the three of them are walking back to where this started.

Lewis sits back down on the purple milk crate beside the Road King.

"Shouldn't you be at work?" the second officer says in farewell, his chrome shades already back on.

Lewis shrugs, is leaned down into the frame of the Road King again, rolling a vacuum tube for pliancy.

"Anything you want to tell us, sir?" the first asks.

"I miss my dog, yeah," Lewis says, and like those were the magic words, the patrol car is easing away. They're coming back, though. Because cops are exactly what Lewis needs in his life. His thinking is already twitchy enough without having to act all law-abiding for them.

He goes inside for a sandwich, eats it standing over the sink so as not to crumb the place up, and when he comes back to the Road King, two of the books he loaned Shaney are on the purple crate, like she showed up in the garage while he was leaning against the kitchen counter shaking Fritos into his mouth from the bag. He picks the two paperbacks up, studies the spines. The first two in the series. He grins a little, maybe the first time he's smiled in two or three days. He wishes he could go back, read them all over again for the first time. He wishes he had the concentration for reading at all, right now.

Instead, what he can't stop thinking, it's why now? Why did this elk, if it is an elk, why did she wait so long to come for him? Was it so he could have time to cobble a life together, get people and things he cares about, so she could take them away the same way he took her calf from her? But why start with him, not with Gabe and Cass? Not that he wishes any kind of ill on them, but if she's from the reservation, well: That's where they are, right? Why trek all the way down here first? And Ricky doesn't factor in, since he died just a few months after Lewis left, and it wasn't anything out of the ordinary, just another Indian beaten to death outside a bar.

The only part that makes sense, Lewis supposes, it's starting with the dog. It's what serial killers and monsters always do, since dogs bark the alarm, dogs *know* there's some shape standing over there in the shadow.

But how, right? *How* did she do it?

Does she, like, inhabit random people to do her bidding or something? Could she have snagged some kid bopping down the road after lights-out, gotten him or her to weasel through that four-inch space under the garage door and go to town on Harley with a mallet?

But none of Lewis's mallets have heads that big. And what happened to Harley *looked* sort of like elk hooves.

Lewis stands, studies the garage with this possibility in mind. What else could have done this to Harley, right?

"Post driver," he says, drifting over to it in the corner. It's the kind you need two hands and your whole body for. The kind that should be over in the corner with the T-posts, since that's what it goes with.

Lewis doesn't want to lift it, see the business end, but he has to.

It's clean, pristine, even has delicate flakes of rust-backed paint just hanging on, flakes that no way could have stayed there while crushing a dog to death with ten or twenty heavy blows.

A quart paint can, maybe? Those are hand-sized, could do the job. Lewis inspects all of them as well, even the ones that are light, obviously dried up. Nothing.

"You're being stupid," he tells himself, and sits down hard on the concrete step leading up to the kitchen door, pulls the mallet from its hook on the side of the rolling tool chest, bounces its butt between his feet.

The mallet is clean, too. For a mallet.

Of *course* an elk can't "inhabit" a person. That person would fall over onto all fours and probably instantly panic. Unless she's like that shadow he saw in the living room. Woman body, elk head, no horns.

That's all he's really got, though: a shadow he probably saw wrong, and something he thought he saw through the spinning blades of a fan.

Those two cops would love him to come in with that for evidence, or as explanation.

And thinking about it isn't making it go away. Lewis chuckles at himself, shakes his head, and drops the mallet handle-first into the closest receptacle, which is one of the cheapo rubber boots Peta always keeps by the door of all the houses they've rented since moving out of her aunt's basement. The boots are big enough that either Lewis or her can pull them on, wade out into the snow for the mail, then slip them off, not track slush in.

Lewis is so used to these boots by now that he doesn't even see them, not until they're in motion. From the mallet he dropped into the right one.

He pushes away just on instinct—boots don't move on their *own*—then comes back closer to be sure he's seeing what he's seeing.

The motion is ants. The boots are coated in small black ants, summer ants, even though Thanksgiving's just next week. Halloween ants, maybe? Is that a thing? If not, it should be, once he realizes what the ants are after: Harley. What's left of him, smushed into the tread of the rubber soles, smeared on the toes because it wasn't all stomping, evidently. There was some kicking, too.

Lewis shakes his head no, please no, and backs away, out into the light, then feels his way around to Harley's grave. Lewis is breathing deep but he's not going to cry. He's a stoic Indian, after all. When he was a kid, he thought that was the fancy word for "stone-faced," which he figured was some connection to Rushmore, since he knew it wasn't supposed to look like that.

That was back when he was stupid, though. Before now, when he's even stupider.

Except—what he's thinking now. No.

Last night out here in the dark, when he kept asking Peta about Harley, about how that could have happened. Could she have just been seeing a dog that finally died from its injury? Had Lewis seen something completely different? Did his questions even make sense to her?

He thinks back through what he can dredge up of her answers, to see if they track with a Harley that *wasn't* stomped to mush.

On his knees back by the fence, he claws the earth open with his desperate fingers, breathing fast. He pulls up the blanket with the ducks on it and the sleeping bag that tapers at the foot end, and one Star Wars sleeping bag deeper and it's going to be Harley.

But then Lewis doesn't pull that field of stars away.

Does he even really want to know? Will seeing Harley smashed to pulp prove anything about who was wearing those boots? Is that even for sure dead dog *in* the tread of those boots? What if Peta was hauling the trash out from the kitchen and it burst, and she had to wade through it? Halloween ants would go for that just the same, wouldn't they? If there is such a thing as Halloween ants?

What he's really afraid of, though, he knows, it's that Harley will just be dead from being strangled by his collar, from hanging on the fence.

And now the ground is trembling with Lewis's chest. The train's coming. The train's always coming.

Lewis closes his eyes against the screaming wheels and the sparks, but then a rock chip catches him on the arm and he falls away slapping at it, and that's when he finally looks at the train rushing past. Not at the different-colored cars, not at the graffiti smearing past at sixty miles per hour, but at the space *between* the cars, that space that's full full full full, then, for a flash, for a slice of an instant, empty.

Only, it's not.

Standing out there in the yellow grass is a woman with an elk head, and—no, no.

Lewis stumbles forward, the train cars whipping just past his face now.

Is she wearing a thick brown jacket with reflective stripes? Like the kind the ground crew of an airport wears?

"It can't be," Lewis says, and the moment the train's gone he's scrambling up onto the hot tracks, but of course the grass over there is just grass again, like nobody was even there.

SUNDAY

For once, Lewis wishes he were at work. Because the only other option is faking sleep until Peta's gone to her shift. For maybe thirty seconds he felt her standing in the doorway with her morning coffee, watching the mound of covers he was trying to make rise and fall like completely normal, non-mechanical breathing, but at least that kept her from asking him why he was acting like such a weirdo last night, cooking alone out on the grill like some backyard warrior, then staying in the garage with the Road King until late.

Are you pissed about something? she might have asked, if she'd seen an eyelid flicker.

The answer he had ready was *No*, and *Harley*, but then she bought his sleeping ruse, he guesses.

Well. If she's Peta she bought it.

If she's something else, well.

The dots he's trying and trying not to let connect in his head are that Peta showed up *on* the reservation, didn't she? And it was the exact summer *after* the Thanksgiving Classic, when he was all busy flipping the whole place off with both hands, denying it his sacred presence from here on out. Maybe that's the answer for why this is starting with him, not Gabe or Cass: because he was the first to leave.

As for the case against Peta, or for her *not* being Peta, it doesn't help that she's a vegetarian, either, Lewis has to admit. Which is what you call a person who doesn't eat meat. What you call an animal that doesn't eat meat, that's "herbivore."

Elk are herbivores. Grass-eaters. Vegetarians.

And: maybe she wasn't lying when she said it was her past making her not want to have kids? Only, the past she meant was the one where she already lost a calf?

Moments after the front door shuts and locks, Lewis covers his face with his pillow, screams into it.

If it's her or if it's not her, either way, one fact is that *somebody* in those boots stomped Harley dead. And he definitely for sure saw a woman with an elk head through the boxcars flashing past— maybe even flashing past at the same flicker rate as the ceiling fan?

It's too much to hold in his head all at once.

He loves Peta, and also he's terrified of her.

Worse, there's no proof either way. No way to tell.

Lewis smushes the pillow up his face, pushes it behind him, and, with his ears cleared now, hears a telltale creak on the stairs. As if, say, someone didn't actually just leave. As if someone just shut the door and locked it from the *inside*.

Slowly, deliberately, the most distinct footfalls he's ever heard are coming up the stairs, but each light *thunk* is preceded by a draggy *whisk*. Because an elk will feel forward with its hooves, right? Find the leading edge of the next step before actually taking it?

Lewis rolls over fast, his bare back to the door, and stares at the curtainless window, trying to memorize each waver and imperfection in the glass so he can clock the reflection when it comes. And his right ear, the one that's up, dials down as sensitive as he can get it. The kind of sensitive that can hear a large set of nostrils breathing his scent in, should that happen.

A tear spills from his left eye, soaks into the pillow.

Is she there now? And if she is, then which her is it? Peta-Peta, or Peta with an elk head?

When one of the ripples in the window glass finally smears with color, with motion, Lewis breathes in deep, says, "Hey, forget something?"

No answer.

When he breathes his next breath in, it's thready, unsteady, isn't a breath he can trust not to explode into a scream.

"Or was it—?" he says, rolling over fake-groggily like he has an end to that sentence.

The doorway's empty.

Lewis closes his eyes, opens them, doesn't let himself rush to the window to see who, or what, might be walking away.

It's too early for this shit.

He brushes his teeth and pees at the same time, spits into the toilet and sort of on his hand, and makes his way downstairs, taking the steps slow, trying to memorize each creak. It's hopeless, though. Each stairstep makes one sound in the middle, a completely different sound eight inches over. Of course.

At the kitchen table he stands before the elk bundle—the hairy burrito—for maybe thirty seconds, finally pushes a finger into it. It's mushy and rough at the same time, smells like some soft cheese that was on the table at a party once, that he knew better than to eat.

"Cheese," though. Now he's thinking cheese.

It'll wreck his digestion, but, figuring that's the least of his concerns right now, he makes a grilled cheese for breakfast, just staring down into the yeast-craters in the toasting bread while it cooks in the pan.

Because he's such a good and considerate husband, he eats it over the sink. Either that or he's kind of scared of the living room. His big irrational fear now is that that spotlight in the ceiling's not broken, it's just waiting for him to be the right kind of alone, so it can shine down like a UFO beam, a woman with an elk head materializing in it. Or it can shine down on Peta when she's standing right there, that light showing her true form.

Which is just *Peta*, Lewis insists to himself, raising the last triangle of the grilled cheese high to slam it down through the rubber flaps of the disposal, as if a grilled cheese can be the deciding gavel. It sort of works, but the crust breaks away on the backswing, lets that last good bite go flying. Trying to imagine either him or Peta finding a moldering hunk of bread and, worse, cheese behind some jar or can next week, he flips the light on, hunts the lost bite down.

Instead of finding it, he sees a paperback on top of the refrigerator. Not either of the two Shaney left in the garage, which he already put up, but the third in the series. Already. Beside it is Peta's thermos, the one she takes to work, that she can never find, that she evidently didn't find this morning, either. The thing with her is she's tall, so when she comes home she sets stuff in the first place she sees, which is generally somewhere high. The top of the refrigerator, this time. The book must have been out front somewhere, the porch, maybe.

"You can bring them back all at *once* . . ." Lewis says to the idea of Shaney, taking the book down from its perch, and, as if by design, the guilty last bite of grilled cheese is right there behind it. Lewis pinches it up like it's gross, like he wasn't just eating it ten seconds ago, and delivers it to the sink, the headline scrolling across the back of his forehead: INDIAN MAN FIRST IN HISTORY TO PICK UP AFTER HIMSELF.

He smirks about that, kind of stupidly proud, and takes the stairs two at a time up to the linen closet that's his new bookshelves.

Before filing the book back in the stack, he fans the top corner to make sure Shaney isn't a page-folder. She isn't—this alone pretty much means she's a good person—but he does catch something. He flips through again, slower, and doesn't see whatever it is again until . . . the inside of the back cover.

"Seriously?" he says.

She *writes* in books, apparently. In *borrowed* books. In pencil, and light like she maybe meant to erase it, but still, right?

Screw it, Lewis tells himself. Who cares? They're mass market, not collectors', and the story's still the same, and it's not like she's putting happy faces or question marks in the actual margins. But now Lewis has to flip through to be sure there's none of *that* going on, and, even while doing it, he's wondering if he's doing it to have something to rib her about at work. Which sounds a lot like flirting.

But it's not that, he insists. This is book-policing. And it's his book anyway. He can look through it all he wants.

Flipping through, he finds himself sitting down against the wall, back in the world of this story again. It's the series about that stone the elves didn't want, but didn't want *found*, either, because it can destroy the whole world. So they hide it in a magic fountain. Which is also, Lewis forgets just how, twinned with the wishing well in the mall that one doofus works in . . . Andy? Yeah, Andy. Of course "Andy." Andy the This, Andy the That. And then all the magical creatures are trolling the mall for the stone their magical radar is telling them is here somewhere. It's kind of hilarious, and has more sex scenes than really make sense either for such an actiony story or for a story in a place as public as a mall, but that's magical creatures for you.

"Did you like it, at least?" Lewis mumbles, flipping to Shaney's notes.

She's not jotting stuff down about the novel, though. She's still thinking through the masking tape on Lewis's living room floor.

What makes this elk so special? is the first note.

Under it she's drawn three lines, like giving herself room to figure this out. But they're blank.

Peta could have answered it, though. Because Lewis told her: this young elk had been pregnant, and farther along than she should have been for November. He thought that was what gave her fight, but what if—what if every great once in a while an elk *is* special, right? What if there are wheels within wheels up there on the mountain, where ceremony used to take place? Was that unborn elk supposed to, Lewis doesn't know, grow some monstrous rack, be a trophy for some twelve-year-old's first kill? Was it supposed to be the big elk an old man chooses not to shoot on his last hunt? Was it supposed to clamber up onto a certain stretch of blacktop, wait for headlights to crunch into it? Was it supposed to find new and safer grass for the herd? Was it not even about the calf, but the mother?

What process had Lewis broken by popping this elk back in illegal country?

"You're thinking crazy," he tells himself, just to hear it out loud. He's right, though. These are the kind of wrong thoughts people have who are spending too much time alone. They start unpacking vast cosmic bullshit from gum wrappers, and then they chew it up, blow a bubble, ride that bubble up into some even stupider place.

Elk are just elk, simple as that. If animals came back to haunt the people who shot them, then the old-time Blackfeet would have had ghost buffalo so thick in camp they couldn't even walk around, probably.

But they killed them fair and square, Lewis hears, and in Shaney's voice, he thinks. Probably because he's reading her writing.

Shaney's next question, still in her voice, is, *Why now?*

Lewis is the only one who maybe knows this answer.

It has to do with her meat, doesn't it? All that meat he gave away door-to-door on Death Row, which is where the closest-to-death of the elders get to live.

It's not out of reach to think that one of those elders he gave the meat to is still alive. Some of them old cats can sit in the same chair for ten, twenty years. Or—

That's it, Lewis knows all at once, sitting up from the wall, his face muscles tense from this certainty.

One of those elders *was* still alive . . . until last week, or last month.

This has to be it.

One of those elders finally kicked last week, and way in the back of her freezer, frozen to the side of it after all these years, there was one last packet of that meat left. Because it was locked in ice, her old fingers could never pry it free, and the reason none of her kids or grandkids ever mixed it into Hamburger Helper or cooked it up with taco seasoning, it was that raccoon stamp.

If you don't know the story of the meat, if that elder couldn't remember the kind young man assuring her it was elk, then what you think, with a black footprint like that on the white paper, it's that somebody's ground up some raccoon from somewhere—the road south, probably—and left it in this freezer like a joke, like a dare.

No, nobody ate it. Nobody would.

But now, with that elder dead, another family's getting that house, right? Which means new furniture, new appliances. Out with the old freezer, in with the new one.

The meat finally thaws, gets tossed. For the birds, for the dogs. And that last packet of meat, it was Lewis's one chance, wasn't it? He'd promised the young elk that none of her would go to waste. But now some had.

That's why now, Shaney. Shit.

The moment that packet of raccoon-printed meat hit the ground, started to thaw, the ground hatched open back in the elders' hunting section. What clambered out, just like a monster movie, was the ghost elk, the one he'd had to shoot three times.

At first she's wobbly on her legs, but with each step south, her hooves are more sure.

Peta didn't stomp Harley, *she* did, this ghost elk. After . . . what let her in, though?

"That I was still thinking of her?" Lewis says in the hallway.

His memory of that young elk, his guilt over her, that was the tether she pulled herself back with, wasn't it? That's why she's starting with him, not Gabe, not Cass: because they don't remember her. She's just one of a thousand dead elk to them.

It's all making sense now. Without Peta here to talk him down, this is all making *perfect* sense, actually.

Shaney's last note is only half formed, still in its egg of parentheses: *(ivory?)*

Shit. Of course. Lewis stands, paces back and forth, slapping the paperback against his thigh, pushing his other hand through his hair.

Shaney knows elk as well as he does, doesn't she?

The thing with elk is that their canines, they used to be tusks, thousands of years ago. They're shorter these days, but are still ivory. That's why they look good polished up and sewn to a traditional dress. If Lewis and Gabe and Ricky and Cass had been thinking that day in the snow, their pockets would have been clinking with elk ivory, to trade back in town.

What Shaney is saying with that *(ivory?)* is that there's a way to tell who the ghost elk is.

Check the teeth.

Lewis holds his left hand out. It's shaking. He drops the paperback, grabs his left wrist with his right hand to steady it. When that doesn't work he retreats to the garage again. By the time Peta gets home hours later, he's got the Road King down to smaller and smaller pieces, arrayed all around him like an exploded diagram from a repair manual.

She stands out there under the goal and studies him—he can feel her. She's studying him and she's trying to make sense of all these parts, all this grease and oil. All this effort. A husband who doesn't go to work anymore, and refuses to talk about it.

Finally she sets her duffel down, tosses her ear protection on top—she's superstitious about them, won't leave them at work—and uses her foot to flip the basketball up to her hands.

She spins it backward, dribbles it twice.

"Real leather," she says, impressed. "Where's it from?"

Lewis looks from it to the street, realizes he has no idea. Shaney was just shooting with it. He never stopped to ask if she'd brought it.

Like he can say that now.

He shrugs.

"Make it take it?" Peta says, chest-passing the ball at him, which is practically a skills challenge, what with how he has the garage booby-trapped. But that's Peta.

Lewis catches the ball the same as he had to when Shaney zinged it at him—what is it with the women in his life? After rocking back and almost falling off the purple crate, he chocks the ball under his arm to clean his hands on his pants legs and eases out under the floodlight with her, dribbling once like testing is this ball up to his exacting standards.

"Eleven?" she says, coming around to place herself between him and the rim, palms up, eyes ready even though she has to have been awake going on twenty hours.

No way is she anything but herself.

Lewis smiles his best Gabe-smile and looks up to that orange rim like asking Peta if she's sure about this, asking if she really thinks she's ready for what he's about to bring.

She is, and then some.

They trade buckets until they're both slick with sweat, and Lewis never stops to think that she's going easy on him, that she's letting him feel like he has a chance.

What he's doing specifically, for the first time in days it feels like, is *not* thinking, just stopping on dime after dime, faking to make airspace, running through the tall grass and junky lumber for the ball again and again. It's one hundred percent exactly what he needs, and would have never known to ask for.

By the end he's laughing, she's laughing, and then they're in each other's slick arms, and he's guiding her back onto the mound of blankets and sleeping bags whose sweat lodge dreams are over, and the door is lowering over them as they add their clothes to the pile, and the world is kind of perfect.

MONDAY

It's lunch by the time Lewis gets the drive belt back onto the Road King. The bike is still a skeleton, but now it's a skeleton with an engine that cranks and can blur the spokes of its rear wheel. No forks or bars, no seat or pegs, and the throttle is just a cable, but this is something, he tells himself. It's a sign that he's climbing back to his life. Once the Road King's back together enough, then he can finally ride in to work, provided he still has a job. There's a lot of steps to getting fired from a federal job, though.

Lewis might can stop them by sitting in the big office and taking his medicine, promising to be a model employee from here on out, offering to take all the shit details, covering for whoever needs it, coming in on holidays, on snow days, whatever it takes.

The best excuse he'll have for his prolonged absence will be Harley, but that's also the most embarrassing excuse: a dog. Is he really that fragile? Is he going to lodge a complaint about "Chief" next? Will his new name around the post office be "Kid Gloves"?

It's not supposed to be easy, though, he tells himself. It's not supposed to be easy or comfortable or fun or any of that. And if it ends up with him keeping his job, maybe even getting his own route someday, well, then it'll have been worth it. Sorry, Harley. You deserved better. But right now it's about proving to Peta that he's not stalling out in the middle of his life. Right now it's about showing her that she's not going to have to carry him from here on out. She would, Lewis knows, she'd do it for as long as she could, but the strain would show. She's pretty much superhuman, and would never complain, but they're supposed to be a team, too. He delivers the mail, she brings the planes in, and they meet at the end of the day over tofu and beans, compare notes, and, like last night, work out their kinks on the court. And also on the floor of the garage.

The more Lewis thinks about it, tightening this bolt, wiping that smudge off, no way can it be Peta, right? If she were really this "Elk Head Woman" he's making up, which isn't even a Blackfeet thing so far as he knows, then why would she have saved him from bashing his head in on the hearth when he fell off the ladder? Answer: she wouldn't have. That would have been just what she wanted. And it would have been the perfect accident, giving her an excuse to go up to the reservation for the funeral, look across the grave to Gabe and Cass right there, like they know it's their turn.

No, Peta's Peta, Lewis decides.

But the only reason he thought she wasn't?

Shaney.

He stands to find a cable clip he knows is in the garage *some-where*, probably within arm's reach, and manages to kick a housing into the torque wrench he has leaned against the front tire, and it all clatters down like misshapen dominoes and Lewis just stands there, unable to take his frustration out on any of this because that'll make even more of a mess.

Shaney, though.

What if that elder whose freezer got cleaned out didn't die a week or two ago, but a month or two ago? Shaney could have heard it hit the ground, clawed up from the pile of weathered bones at the bottom of that steep slope, and walked on wobbly legs down across half of Montana, finally got steady enough that she was able to stride right through the front door of the post office, fill out a federal application.

And it makes sense that when that elk took two-legged form, human form, that person might have skin to match Lewis's own. He doesn't know why he didn't see this before.

The clincher comes when he's back in the house, cleaning a grimy washer in the sink, trying to use the dish brush as little as possible, since Peta doesn't like grease showing up in the kitchen. Which Lewis completely understands. So he's just brushing the washer lightly, with the very tip of the blue bristles, not the white ones.

Walking back to the garage turning the washer back and forth to see if it's possible anymore to tell which side had been facing out, his heel on the floor shakes the house in the way it needs for that spotlight in the living room to jiggle on in his peripheral vision.

Lewis freezes, half afraid to look directly at it, since he's trying hard for this episode of his life to be over.

For it to really be over, though, he has to prove he's not scared anymore, doesn't he? He makes himself look.

On cue, like it's shy, the light sucks back up into the bulb.

Lewis stamps his heel on the kitchen floor again. Nothing.

"Such bullshit," he says, shaking his head at the stupidity of all this, haunted houses and ghost elk and Crow women, and then, not wanting to in the least but making himself, because he *doesn't* need to be handled with kid gloves, he looks up, through the spinning blades of the fan instead of at them. The angle from the kitchen is bad, so he feels safe, but still, there's the chance he's going to see a woman-shape up in the far corner, trying to skitter out of view.

Nothing.

He lets himself breathe out, rubs the coolness of the washer against his chin, and tracks down from the fan to . . . where he saw her first. The couch, the carpet there.

"Oh shit," he says, letting the washer fall and not bothering to go after it.

Why didn't he see this the other day? It's so obvious.

When—when Peta was helping him re-create the conditions of what he thought he'd seen, he'd climbed the ladder, he'd looked down through the fan blades at the carpet, and . . . he'd also looked down at Peta, on the couch, looking back up at him, not judging, not having to suppress her smile, just playing along with her losing-it, spooky-Indian husband.

That's not the important part, though. The important part is that, through the revealing blades of the fan, through that flickering that strips away fake faces or whatever, she'd been *herself.*

"I'm sorry," Lewis says to her. For avoiding her the other night. For even allowing the possibility that it could have been her.

It was never her. That's just what he was supposed to think— that's what Elk Head Woman wants, for him to tear down his own life. That way she doesn't even have to do anything, can just sit back and watch.

She's devious like that.

And . . . using the same logic he used to indict Peta—that she'd shown up the summer right after the Thanksgiving Classic— Lewis realizes it can't be any accident that the day Shaney showed up at his house, delivered by *him*, Harley was already most of the way dead.

If he hadn't been, then he would have gone for her throat, wouldn't he have? He would have ripped her mask off, shown her for what she was.

Shit.

It's like rebuilding a carburetor. You seat that last jet and then realize this thing can breathe on its own now.

Like to confirm that, when Lewis steps outside to just not be in the house for a minute or two, the fourth book in the series is there, balanced on top of a stray beer can so anybody leaving or coming home has to trip on it, find it.

Lewis stares down at the book for maybe twenty seconds before nudging it over with his toe, like there might be something ready to spring up from the can. The book falls open-faced on the rough concrete, the can doing its tinny roll for a foot or so, until it finds a pebble to stop against.

Lewis kneels, saves the book from the scratchy concrete, and flips to the inside back cover first thing, for the next note.

It's blank, doesn't even have erased pencil marks.

Lewis studies the street and across the street, and both ways as far as he can see.

Shaney must be close, right?

Nothing moves, though. No big ears flick back in the trees, no large black eyes blink, no hooves shift weight.

Lewis takes the book back inside, sits at the kitchen table with it, and interrogates the cover, the spine, flips through the pages.

"Why the books?" is where he finally lands. That's the part that doesn't track, that's the thing niggling at his mind, trying to poke holes in his theory, his suspicions. If—if Shaney *is* this young elk reborn or not yet dead or come back for unfinished business, then why is she interested in a fantasy series about a jewelry store worker trying to save the world from itself?

Lewis scans the back cover to be sure he remembers this one right. Yep. It's the installment where the usher at the movie theater, the one who's more than she seems, figures out that the food court is actually the front gate of the fairy prison. It's maybe the best book in the series, really. It ends with Andy on a woolly

mammoth, rampaging through the makeup and perfume department of one of the pricey department stores, and then it has that
epilogue—rare for an installment in a series—where the dwarves
discover carbonated drinks, and you can tell from the glimmer in
their eyes that this is going to be trouble.

None of which applies in any remote way to the Thanksgiving
Classic, to hunting in general, to the post office, to Gabe and Cass,
to Peta. At least not in any way Lewis can track.

He shuts the book, ditches it on the stairs so he can grab it next
trip up.

So it's Shaney, then. If it's not Peta, and it's not, then Shaney's
the main and only one left. And maybe she didn't crawl up from
that killing field up on the reservation, maybe she had a whole
real life before . . . before she stopped being herself, opened her
eyes, and looked around with a different set of instincts. Maybe
she was up in Browning for Indian Days, or maybe she clipped an
elk on the interstate down here, or maybe she just signed on to the
wrong job, took a cigarette break on the wrong stoop by the load-
ing dock, breathed in more than smoke.

The how doesn't really matter. What does is that she's coming
for him. And that she's been trying to set Peta up, meaning Peta's
a target as well.

Lewis shakes his head no about that.

This ends here. Or, it ends where he wants it to end, not where
Shaney wants it to.

To be sure, though, beyond a shadow, he has to somehow get
Shaney into his living room one more time. He has to get her in
his living room *while* he's up on the ladder, so he can look down at
her through the spinning blades of the fan.

And it's probably best to do this when Peta's not around. Meaning tomorrow, when she's at work.

It's leaving himself vulnerable, Lewis knows—it won't look

good if Peta walks in on them alone in the house *again*—but if Peta's piddling in the kitchen while Lewis relays some made-up work news or whatever, then Shaney's defenses will be up, and her real face might not show.

No, her real *head*.

But what will get her over here tomorrow, right?

The one thing Lewis maybe has going is that he's half sure that on Tuesdays, Shaney doesn't go in until noon. And that he, of course, won't be going in either. For the moment, there's more important things.

He paces and paces the house, looking in every corner for a reason to get Shaney over here. Something work? Indian? Basketball? Should he act like he's ready to go the next step with her? Does he need some help keeping his sweats up? Would she even be interested, or has he been reading her completely wrong?

No, he finally figures out—not that he's been reading her wrong or right—but, none of those options. There's a better way to get her into his living room.

Silas.

He was the gift Shaney didn't know she was giving him.

That's the way it always is in fantasy novels, isn't it? The evil wizard or dastardly druid builds his own doom into his plan, like he knows he really shouldn't be doing this, or like there's some magical realm rule where he has to leave a single scale off the dragon's belly, to give the puny crew a one-in-a-thousand chance.

Harley biting Silas is that missing scale, that chink in the armor, that one chance he has in a thousand. Lewis thinks it through once, twice, and nods the third time through, when there aren't any red flags.

This can work.

He digs around for the work directory, can't put hands on it, so just calls the post office, talks Margie out of Shaney's number because he's coming back to work but his bike's all taken apart, and she lives out by him, he can catch a ride with her.

Ten digits later, Shaney's phone is ringing.

"Blackfeet?" she creaks after his *Hello?* Lewis listens for rustling in the background to see if she's alone.

"Hey," Lewis says. "Silas is back in the mail room, isn't he?"

"Frankenface?" she says.

Lewis winces, is responsible for that.

"We were kind of short handed," Shaney goes on, coughing like a smoker.

"Sorry about that," he says.

"What already?" Shaney says. "It's my day off, man."

"Thought you were off Wednesday," Lewis says like the question it is.

"Missing two people, schedule's fried," she says back.

"But you go in tomorrow, right?" Lewis asks. "Silas, his build, his bike—he was supposed to get a bracket from me the other day, right? When Harley . . . you know?"

"He's not supposed to ride for two weeks," Shaney recites. "Wind can blow his stitches out."

"But he can still tinker around in the garage," Lewis says. "This'll help, it'll be good."

"A bracket?" Shaney repeats.

"For his headlight," Lewis tells her. "I was thinking you could bring it up there to him, maybe."

Long pause, in which Lewis imagines Shaney shying away from the bright window by her bed.

"Think it's going to take more than a new headlight to get that bike in shape," she finally says.

"It's a start," Lewis says.

"I'll have to leave an hour *early* . . ." Shaney says, playing up the groan.

"Thank you, thank you," Lewis says, and gets off the phone before she can tell him to leave it on the porch like she's been doing with the books.

For two hours, then, Lewis wears out the carpet, going back and forth, gesticulating, orchestrating, framing ideas between his held-out fingers, trying to figure everything through from each possible angle. He tries to work on the Road King, get it closer to ready to maybe *really* go back to work, but his mind is too jumpy, won't settle down. By midafternoon he's got the tape measure out, is duct-taping a free-throw line on the driveway. His rule is he can't quit until he makes three in a row, no iron, no backboard, but about fifty tries in he's counting trash, because, he tells himself, this is basketball, and basketball is made of trash. Still, he can swish two easy enough, just, the third always back-irons out at some crazy angle, like the world is laughing at him. Maybe it's for the best, though. This way he'll still be shooting when Peta walks up, and maybe they can pull a replay of last night, happy ending and all, he'll even use the same stupid joke about it not mattering they don't have any protection out in the garage—Indians like to go bareback anyway, yeah?

Just like always, Peta will grin and pull his mouth to hers.

It's looking good for a repeat—well, him being out there when she walks up, anyway—except then she's calling, is having to cover some no-account's shift again. Some no-account like Lewis, she doesn't say. Some no-account who just doesn't show up, doesn't even call in.

"Fine, cool, great," Lewis tells her, the phone going from side to side of his head because he can't find the best way to hold it, can't figure out what to do with his hands in the moment, or this whole day. But it *is* good, her pulling an extra shift, maybe edging into some overtime. Money's about to be tight once his next check's docked, if there even is a next check, so any way to earn a bit more's pretty much just what the doctor ordered.

"Love you," Lewis says into the phone. "Anything I can do, bring, be?"

It's his usual sign-off.

"Just yourself," Peta says like always, and they hang up together.

An hour later he's warming a can of chili for dinner, eating it with a whole tube of crackers, all the crumbs raining down into the sink. By nine he's nodding off at the kitchen table, and by ten he's in bed trying to read the fourth book in the series, a longneck leaning cold against his right side.

Peta says it's a bad habit to get into, drinking at lights-out, that your body can forget how to go to sleep on its own, and Lewis is sure she's right, but she's not here, either, and this whole "sleeping" thing seems to always be about to happen instead of actually happening, anyway. The pages gather in his left hand, thin out in his right. He'd forgotten how fun this mall is, and what a good contrast this magic is with the commerce going on around it. It's cool how the seasons and the decorations are always changing, kind of giving a theme or motif to each installment, and it's hilarious how these pagan characters both recognize and are seriously insulted by all these holidays—especially the elves. But they're insulted by everything.

Inside an hour, finally, gratefully, Lewis starts to lose the line between reading and sleeping. Because Peta isn't here to reach across, guide the book off his chest, careful to save the page, Lewis tells his distant index finger to be a bookmark, and then, right before the nothing of sleep, he asks himself what's he going to do when Shaney's elk head shows under the fan, and he's up on the ladder.

He'll know at last, but what will he *do*?

He mutters an answer but his lips and mouth and voice belong to someone else at this point of almost-sleep, and his ears can't make out the words, quite.

He feels himself chuckle with satisfaction all the same.

TUESDAY

Lewis is standing on a five-gallon bucket, looking over the fence at what used to be Harley's grave. Something's dug him up, scattered the blankets and sleeping bags across the train tracks.

Lewis insists on that: something dug him up. Otherwise Harley struggled out of the dirt himself and walked up the railbed, that Star Wars sleeping bag holding on until it snagged on the grabby edge of one of the wooden ties.

Peta was already gone by the time he got up, so she didn't have to see this. What's she made of, Lewis wonders for the fiftieth time, that she can crawl in at one in the morning, be gone again before sunup? Can't they just shut the airport down, let her catch a couple more hours' sleep? But it's good she's not here, too.

Shaney's coming over.

Lewis eats toast and a candy bar for breakfast, candy bar first because it makes the toast taste better.

Something definitely dug Harley up. That's the only way it could have gone. Coyotes, probably, but a badger will scavenge as well. He doesn't want to picture the long-headed shape of a woman out there on her knees at three in the morning pulling the ground open, but not wanting to have to see it just cleans the focus on that image up, pretty much.

Lewis is puking into the sink before he even realizes he's gagging. It's not from nerves about Shaney, he tells himself. It's from thinking about what Harley must look like now.

When he's done throwing up he turns the disposal on and a chunk spits back up at him and he falls down in the kitchen trying to get away.

"You're doing great," he tells himself from the floor. "You're completely ready, Blackfeet."

It's the first time he's ever called himself that.

He hand-over-hands his way back to the kitchen table, where at least he probably can't fall down. Not as far down, anyway. Well, not from as high.

His fingers busy themselves smoothing down an unruly tuft of the elk hide.

It still doesn't smell right, but it doesn't smell like cheese anymore, so that's some kind of progress, right?

10:40 already. If Shaney's shift starts at noon, and for some reason stopping by here means leaving an hour early, which has to be a lie, then she should be here in the next ten, fifteen minutes, Lewis calculates.

Enough time to unroll that hide. Not for the nicks he knows he left all over and through it, so it would probably only be good for a few pairs of gloves, nothing of size, but because . . .

Maybe some elk *are* special, right?

What if it wasn't that she was carrying a calf early? Or, what if she was carrying that calf early because she needed to get it birthed before . . . before some Gabe or Cass or Ricky or Lewis poached her in late spring, or some shed-hunter popped her with the handgun he only carries for bear?

What if she needed to get that calf out because she was already scheduled to die, so she could get skinned?

In the museum, behind glass, there's an old winter count, drawn on . . . it's probably buffalo, Lewis imagines. But why not elk?

And who's to say it's all drawn, either?

It could be that, back when, the people would bring any hides or skins that looked different in to the old-time version of a postal inspector. Because maybe some hides, some skins, right when they peel back from the meat, there's already some markings there, right? A starting point, maybe. A story of things to come. Pictures of the winter yet to come.

That day in the snow, the Thanksgiving Classic, there'd been too much blood and hurry to wipe the skin clean.

But there's time now.

Lewis clears the table and unrolls it delicately, like parchment.

The back side of the skin is black with freezer burn or something, Lewis isn't sure. He tries to wipe it away with paper towels but it's in the pores like ink, which he guesses either blows his big theory or proves it, only what this skin is tattooed with is a storm so bad it eats the world.

"Little late," Lewis says down to the young elk. Could have used this kind of warning about 1491 or so.

There is something, though. In the last roll, which would have been the first when it was being rolled up, is that trading-post knife that he thought he'd lost.

He'd put it in here, really?

For what reason?

Lewis extracts the knife. The blade that's on is the short skinning one with the curved nose. The handle still fits perfect in his hand, too, which is why he bought it in the first place. Oh, the adventures he thought they were going to have.

Instead, that was the last day he ever hunted.

He sits back in his chair, studies the ladder he's already got set up half under the fan, already test-leaned over to see if it lines up with the dent in the wall. *Thank you, Peta.* Even when she's not here, she's saving him.

10:55. Shaney should be here by now.

Lewis stands, studies the living room all over again to see what he's forgetting.

Nothing he can think of.

When things are simple, there's not a lot to keep in mind.

He crosses to the front door, cocks it open, then comes back to the living room, looking from the Road King's headlight bracket on the floor and up to the fan, confirming the angle one last time. It's dead-on. The elk was right here.

And she's about to be again.

Lewis puts one foot on the lowest step of the ladder and reaches up for the red-handled screwdriver on the fourth step, at eye level.

He can't just be standing on a ladder for no reason, right?

It's 11:05 before tires crunch up in front of the house.

"Okay, then," Lewis says, and nods to himself, steps up the ladder until the spinning blades of the fan are at his hips again.

His angle down onto the headlight bracket on the floor is perfect.

Shaney doesn't step on the beer can on the porch, just knocks on the door. It creaks in with her knocking, because Lewis left it slightly ajar.

"Blackfeet?" she calls.

"In here," Lewis calls back, the screwdriver handle clamped between his lips muffling his words, the strain of keeping both hands busy at the little spotlight compressing his breath.

"Say what?" Shaney calls back, leaning in, it sounds like.

"In here!" Lewis says, louder, hopefully clearer.

She steps in timidly, like this might be a trap.

"What the hell are you doing up there?" she says from the edge of the living room.

"Stupid light," Lewis says, and trying to speak around the screwdriver means losing grip *on* that screwdriver. It tumbles down behind him, bounces into the corner.

"Smooth move, Ex-Lax," Shaney says with a smile.

"There's the bracket," Lewis says, nodding down to it, and then realizes that, without a screwdriver, why's he up on the ladder anymore? Why isn't he climbing down *for* the screwdriver?

But he can't leave this step of the ladder—he has to look down through the fan, see Shaney's real self.

His hand, moving on its own almost, rounds to his back pocket, comes back with the knife from the elk hide. He looks at it like just seeing it, doesn't remember having grabbed it.

With this round-nosed skinning blade, though, it's a putty knife, an art knife, the widest flathead. He swallows it into his hand, works it up into the space between the spotlight's buried can and the crumbly ceiling.

"Need help?" Shaney asks, and Lewis looks to her, shakes his head, and finally sees her for the first time. She's dressed for work, just normal clothes, same flannel as ever, but her hair's still done from, he guesses, the night before. It's spiral-curled but still forever long, over half her face.

No, Peta does not need to come home, find Shaney here looking like this.

But it's fake, too, Lewis reminds himself. She's showing him what he wants to see, she's making herself up like this specifically to get to him.

"So when are you coming back?" Shaney asks. "There's a pool at work, you know?"

"Tomorrow," Lewis says, straining with the fake adjustment he's doing on the light. "Day after."

"Make it Friday and I'll split the take," Shaney says.

"What's the pool up to?" Lewis asks, because he's no dumb Indian.

Shaney just smiles, nods across to the headlight bracket, says, "Frankenface will know what this is?"

"His name is Silas," Lewis says.

"Past tense," Shaney says, and, stepping down into the living room at last, she reaches over to the bank of switches, turns the fan off, finding the control first try.

Lewis's heart drops. His face goes numb.

She knows exactly what he's doing.

"I'm saving your life," she says, and is to the couch now, is squatting down, knees together, to collect the bracket.

Lewis zeroes in on her through the fan but the blades are already sagging, losing their speed, the rate of flicker slowing, slowing.

Through them like that, Shaney's just Shaney.

"No, no, turn it on," Lewis says, pleading, holding hard onto the ladder. "The—the switches. When the fan's off, the power comes on for this light."

"What kind of bullshit wiring job is that?" Shaney asks, looking from the fan to the light in disbelief. But, using up the rest of the wishes Lewis has left for his whole life, the bulb in the spotlight flickers the slightest bit. Just the filament glowing on for a moment, but it's enough.

Lewis looks from it down to Shaney and she shrugs, cradles the bracket, careful of the bolts he intentionally left hanging, and crosses to the switches, turns the fan back on. It whirs back up like sad to have been turned off after such a long and constant run.

"Oh, hey," Lewis says, pointing with the knife to the carpet in front of the couch. "That fall out?"

The fan pushes Shaney's hair across her face but she clears it, looks down to the bracket, touches the three bolts in the outer ring, shrugs up to Lewis.

"There, there," he says, still pointing, and she steps across, her legs coming into the tunnel of vision the spinning blades are carving, but then, her face just out of it, she looks up, says, "You trying to see down my shirt, Blackfeet?"

She looks down to her own chest and, instead of pinching the flannel together at her throat, she pops it out, lets it slap back, then looks up to Lewis with a little bit of devil to her eyes.

"No, no," Lewis says, coming a step down the ladder to see her face through the blades, but, at this angle, at this getting-there speed, it's just Shaney.

Shit.

Shit shit shit.

But still, that she knew not to step into that space? That she knew to turn the fan off?

"If it's a loose *connection*," she says, "you have to, like, jam something in right there." She points with her free hand to the spotlight, and because he's the one faking this repair job, Lewis has to play along.

She steps ahead, to see the light around the fan, and Lewis takes a step higher, high enough to work the blade of the knife up beside the can.

Just like she said, the little spotlight glows on, holds steady.

"Pay me later," she says, already turning around, drawn by the elk hide on the table.

Lewis climbs down, follows her.

"What happened to it?" Shaney asks, still almost touching it but not quite.

"Neanderthals," Lewis says, the funniest joke.

Shaney just looks up at him, squinting.

In the fourth book, the one she just returned, there's Neanderthals slouching around the mall with their heavy spears and heavy brows, and it's kind of the running joke. Every time there's the next version of "Cleanup on aisle nine," Andy shakes his head, spits air, and says, *Neanderthals*, like they were put in the mall specifically to ruin his life.

Lewis swallows hard, a thrill rushing through him, all the way to his fingertips.

"You're kind of weird, you know?" Shaney says.

"Me and Andy, yeah," Lewis says.

While it might be possible to somehow forget "Neanderthals," each installment in the series is Andy the Something: *Andy the Water Bringer, Andy the Giant Slayer, Andy the Unemployed.* The fourth one is, of course, *Andy the Mammoth Rider.* No way could she not know who he's talking about, here.

Shaney holds Lewis's eyes for a moment like checking if he's for real, then makes the turn to the front door.

"Wait," Lewis says, his heart pounding in his chest, his face heating up with possibility. "That's the wrong one," he blurts, making this up as he goes.

Shaney looks down to the headlight bracket she's holding.

"I think about anything will match his bike," she says.

"I've got the right one," Lewis says. "It's just out here, I just saw it . . ."

Shaney just holds him in her stare, like waiting for him to draw the curtain on whatever charade or joke this is going to be.

"You can go out this way," Lewis says, stepping past her for the garage door, not giving her a chance to say no.

He grinds the big door up, which brings the light on, then he just stands there inspecting all the parts strewn across the concrete and boxes and old towels.

"What happened?" Shaney says, impressed.

"It always gets like this," Lewis tells her, trying not to let on how fast things are cycling through his head. It's like that flicker rate he needed to see through to the real, it's behind his *eyes* now.

He's afraid to look directly back at Shaney. Instead he jogs three steps ahead, knocks on the basketball to get it dribbled up.

"Forgot your best friend the other day," he says, and underhands it across to her, hardly even a pass at all. Instead of one-handing it to her hip like he knows she can do, she steps to the side, lets the ball lob on past, still watching him like trying to figure him out.

"Oh, oh, you'll like this," he says, stepping across to the Road King.

"I've got to get to work, Blackfeet," Shaney says back, trying to pick a path to freedom.

"Just wait, wait," Lewis says, and comes around to the other side of the bike, the side without the purple crate. He crosses the poles, throws some sparks, but pulls the current before the engine can start up, so that it sounds like a failure, like it choked down. "Shit, shit," he says, shaking his hand like he got burned, and leans over to look inside. "Oh, of course," he aha's, and, without looking up, does his right hand to pull Shaney over.

She approaches slowly, uncertainly.

"I've heard a motorcycle before," she tells him.

"New pipe," Lewis tells her, and is still guiding her closer, closer. "You've got to—" he says, finally looking up. "Here, here," he says, taking the headlight bracket from her, setting it down wherever on his side. "This vacuum hose right here, just plug it so I can turn the engine over. Should start right up."

Shaney inspects the Road King like for safety, says, about the rear wheel and all the dangerous possibilities there, "How about just show me when you've got it together, yeah? I promise to be real impressed."

"I want you to tell Silas," Lewis says then, like embarrassed to be admitting it. "Don't tell him this part, it's still secret, but I ordered him the same exhaust. As, you know, apology. Just tell him how throaty this sounds."

"I don't have to actually hear it to—" she begins, but Lewis is already leaning over, guiding her finger-finger to the open end of the vacuum tube, its junction right there, which would be so much easier to stopper it with.

Is this the first time he's touched her skin to skin? It might be, he thinks.

There's no sparks, no flood of memories or accusations rushing in, no replay of four Indians pouring lead down a slope.

"You're making me late, Blackfeet," Shaney says, and Lewis, coming back to his side, realizes he *can* see down her shirt for a flash.

She sees him seeing, says, "All you had to do was ask, yeah?"

"No, it's not like—" Lewis starts, and then they both turn to the basketball, slowly rolling down the slope of the garage like the biggest, softest, most drunk pinball.

"This better not get me dirty," Shaney says over the wide tank, her eyes locked on his, like she means the exact opposite.

"I know who you are," Lewis says back right as the engine cranks over, and that narrows her eyes because she couldn't have heard that right, and, just like that last day hunting, this is the moment where he could back out, this is where he could stop this from happening. He could break the connection, kill the bike, make like he said something else—*Watch out for your hair*, yeah. That would be the perfect thing to have said.

Except that's exactly what he doesn't want her doing.

She killed Harley, he makes himself remember. She killed Harley and she's trying to turn Peta against him. And the final way he can tell she is what she is, the thing that gave her away for sure, even more than the basketball, it's that she doesn't know about Andy the Mammoth Rider. The books were just props to her, just excuses to be over here, turning the wheels of her plan. If she really *had* read book four, then she would have ridden that emotional roller coaster Lewis and the rest of the world had to ride after Andy "died" at the end of book three, and then was a no-show for the first half of book four. He wasn't pulling a Gandalf, though, was just trapped in the fizzy world inside the fountain drink dispenser, waiting for the right set of circumstances to get born into the world again—which turned out to be a mammoth one of his ancestors had driven over a cliff, except that mammoth had fallen into a pool that was right where the fountain was. So, when that mammoth fell *again*, like happens when time is a cycle, the elves carved Andy up from its belly. At first he was just a skinny mammoth fetus, but then he grew into himself over the course of a single day, rode that dead mammoth's mate right through the makeup and perfume department, became the true champion and savior he was always meant to be. It wasn't the kind of return a person forgets, especially if she just read it.

"You know who I *am*?" Shaney says over the scream of the *un*mufflered four-stroke, still holding that dummy vacuum tube shut with the pad of her index finger, and that's all she gets out before this thing is happening.

The drive belt is on Lewis's side of the bike—Shaney isn't stupid, *Elk Head Woman* isn't stupid, she would have clocked that danger, that little conveyor belt of instant death—but he started it in first gear, meaning that naked rear wheel he's already got in place, *it's* spinning as well, is an instant silver blur.

It takes maybe half a second for those chrome spokes to grab her long spiral curls, crank her head both up and to the side, her neck obviously cracking. But her hair's still pulling, still winding into the spinning spokes, the *flickering* spokes. An instant after her neck breaks, the top of her head scalps off and her forehead tilts loosely down into the rear wheel, the spokes shearing skull as easy as anything, carving down into the pulpy-warm outside of her brain. It's greyish pink where it's been opened, and kind of covered with a pale sheath all around that, the blood just now seeping into the folds and crevices.

Lewis backs off the throttle, lets the starter wires go.

Silence. Just that bare wheel winding down. Shaney's throat is still sucking air in, her eyes locked on Lewis, calling him *traitor*, calling him *killer*, calling him "Blackfeet" one last time. Then she falls back, slumping into the sleeping bags and random parts, her left foot twitching, a line of saliva, not blood, threading down from the corner of her mouth. But there is bright red aerated blood—a spattery stripe bisecting the garage, going from floor to wall to ceiling then down the other wall again. It's a line between who Lewis used to be and who he is now.

He stands, pushes the button on the wall.

It's time to lower the door on all this.

STILL TUESDAY

Lewis never built the sweat he wanted, but if he stands in the up-stairs shower long enough that it's all steam, he can pretend, can't he? The blood and brains Shaney splashed on his face swirls down the drain, is gone forever.

Her little yellow Toyota truck is still pulled up outside, but once he's clean he can drive it wherever, walk back, no witnesses. *Yes, Officer, she stepped by for a part, but she left with that part. The proof of that is—hey, that part's not here, right?*

Easy as that.

Now the next ten years of his life can start, finally. Payment came due for that young elk, for all *nine* of those elk—ten if the unborn calf counts—but, this far from the reservation, he just managed to duck paying it.

As for what to do with Shaney herself, his first instinct is to bury her with Harley, but the cops are going to be digging there before too long, and the noon train's coming through anyway, and he doesn't need an audience for that kind of work.

No, for once in his life he's going to be smart about a thing. And he's not even really a killer, since she wasn't even really a person, right? She was just an elk he shot ten years ago Saturday. One who didn't know she was already dead.

Still, his soapy hand, when he raises it into the stream of hot water, it's trembling, won't stop trembling. Twice so far he's ripped the shower curtain to the side, sure he saw a shadowed figure standing out there, sure he'd heard a door creak, or footsteps. *Hooves.*

It's just nerves, he tells himself. Any first-timer would be having the same exact panic attack now.

He puts his face into that scalding water some more, promises himself not to crank his brain up, but it cranks up anyway, can't stop dwelling on how could it be that Shaney didn't seem comfortable around a basketball, didn't automatically catch it like any real player would have to, just let it slip past like an object, not a thing she'd sweated countless hours over.

But, *could* she still be that same player she was before? Did she sidestep that pass because she was holding a delicate bracket? Did she dodge it because, unlike him, she's not obligated to catch a ball she didn't ask to be thrown?

It doesn't matter. What does is that she didn't know the books.

Lewis steps out, towels off, his shape blurry in the mirror.

She didn't know about the books, he repeats in his head.

Meaning?

Meaning she was Elk Head Woman.

Because?

Because she was lying.

That means she's a monster?

Lewis squats down in the hall, his face in his hands, his head shaking back and forth to resist this line of reasoning.

No, he finally has to admit to himself.

It doesn't mean *for sure* she's that monster, but added together with the basketball being so alien to her, and her knowing where to stand in the living room, and to turn the fan off, and, and: What about how she wouldn't touch her own hide on the kitchen table?

Lewis stands nodding.

That, yeah.

She could have been lying about the books just for an excuse to break up his marriage, because that's what she does, that's the *human* thing she just does, but touching the skin she'd worn the last time she was alive, that probably would have made her relive her first death all over again, wouldn't it have?

Lewis nods. It would have, yes. Definitely.

Oh, and also: She was lying about having to leave an hour early, wasn't she? What she really wanted was more time alone over here *before* work. And Lewis can prove this.

He calls work again, gets Margie on the line again.

"You must really want to hear my voice," she tells him.

"Shaney," he says, switching ears like that can get across how much he doesn't have time for small talk, "she—she never showed up, but if I run I think I can catch her, but I don't know her address—the flower farm, right?"

It's stupid, nobody lives over there, it's probably not even zoned for residential, but it was the first sort of close place he could dredge up.

Margie's silence means she's weighing this for the bullshit it is.

"Please, please, Jerry'll kick my ass if I'm not there," Lewis adds, bouncing up and down like that can help make his case.

It's that easy to get an address.

Moments later, still in his towel, he has the fold-out map of Great Falls spread over the back of the elk hide, his hair dripping all over the red and blue lines.

"No way," he says when he finally finds Shaney's place.

She *did* have to leave an hour early, because she *does* live all the way on the other side of town—Gibson Flats. That's not even really Great Falls at all, is it? But, at the same time, she *did* really leave with the books. And they *have* really been showing back up, haven't they?

Lewis plunks down into a chair, his eyes lost.

Finally, an explanation bubbles up.

It's thin, it's anorexic, but: What if she read the first chapter or two of book one, and it wasn't for her, was just stupid elves in trench coats, halflings at the hot dog stand, so she drove the whole long-ass way over, dropped all ten books off on Lewis's porch?

That would explain her not knowing about the story, the people in it.

But, then, who found that stack? Who's been parsing them out one here, two there? And why?

To make you do what you did, Lewis hears in his head, in a colder voice than his own.

He stands breathing hard, shaking his head no.

She *was* Elk Head Woman. She had to be. She was—she's the only Indian in his life down here, right? Lewis *sees* other Indians out and about, but that's always just a nod without stopping. No, if it's going to be anybody, it's her.

There is one last way to tell, though, isn't there? One way she wrote in the back of the third book?

Lewis goes to the corner of the living room behind the ladder, comes back with the red-handled screwdriver.

Next, the garage, the mound of sleeping bags and blankets.

He pulls them back from Shaney, tries to close her eyes that won't stay closed.

Not gagging even a little, he threads her scalped hair up from her mouth where he'd stuffed it, thinking that had to be some old-time Indian shit. That she didn't fight back when he was burying her in the sleeping bags and blankets, that meant it worked, the hair in the mouth.

This next part, though. Getting her hair into the spokes of the Road King, that was easy in comparison. This is a lot more involved.

But Lewis has skinned out he doesn't know how many elk and deer. Once even a moose, right? He's even delivered an embryo or a fetus up from a pregnant young elk, one he didn't tell Peta was still kind of struggling in its thin, veiny bag.

He can do this.

First is opening her mouth with his fingers, then it's forcing his hand in as deep as he can and pulling down hard, breaking the jaw at the crunchy-wet hinge so he can have the kind of access he needs. So he can see her top row of teeth.

Elk Head Woman told him what to look for, didn't she? She told him how he'd know her.

(ivory)

He positions the screwdriver between a canine tooth and the next one over and jams the red handle with the heel of his hand, driving it in deep enough to lever out the canine he needs, bloody root and all. Because she's fresh, the tooth doesn't want to let go.

It does, though. Along with the one he was using for leverage.

Lewis rattles them in his hand, considers it lucky to have accidentally pulled two. That way he can compare them: normal and ivory.

Except both of these are the same.

He gets some carb cleaner, sprays them down because there's got to be ivory in there somewhere. When there's not, he closes his eyes, falls to his knees on the sleeping bags.

Next he's laughing to himself, and sort of crying.

Work didn't *have* to be so short-staffed, did it?

NATIVE AMERICAN MAN SINGLEHANDEDLY TAKES DOWN USPS.

He's trying to work a grin up about that headline when he finds his eyes fixed on the stomach of Shaney's flannel shirt. Because that's not where the blood and damage is, it's as safe a place as any to concentrate on, maybe even better than most. But . . . no. No no no.

He can *untuck* that shirt if he wants, can't he? He can untuck it, pull it up to check if she's got that long vertical knot of scar tissue. If she does, if she *was* field-dressed, then—then she was definitely Elk Head Woman.

Unless she got butchered on an operating table. Unless some drunk IHS doctor scarred her for life, made her into a woman always trying to get eyes to focus on her chest, not below that.

Lewis shakes his head no, doesn't want to have to do this, doesn't want to have to know either way. What if she doesn't have that scar at all, right?

Still, he owes it to her, even has his hand to her stomach, his fingers bunching the flannel up into his palm, is *going* to look around, face this truth. On the count of three. Now on this next count of three.

What saves him—who, *who* always saves him—it's Peta.

The front door opens, then closes.

Shit.

Fast, fast, he gets Shaney buried again. He can still make this work. Peta doesn't have to know. That's hydraulic fluid splashed all over the ceiling and walls. It smells like opened body because of Harley.

It takes thirty seconds to stop hyperventilating, and then another full minute to clear his eyes.

Nodding to himself for strength or something like it, Lewis walks into the kitchen, ready to jerk his head up like surprised by Peta being here, unloading her lunch box. She's not at the counter like always, though. To find her he has to look up, and up.

She's . . . now *she's* on the ladder?

"You figured it out!" she says, her whole face a smile, like the last two or three back-to-back shifts don't even matter, suddenly.

"What?"

"The whole *thing's* loose," she says, and wiggles the knife jammed in alongside the light.

The bulb flickers on, goes back off.

A warm smile crosses Lewis's face.

He did fix it. This is the perfect gift, the best surprise. He is a good husband.

Smiling like it was nothing, he walks past the table, into the living room, and only slows when he catches the way Peta's looking him up and down, slow and unsure.

"What?" he says, and only then does he look down to his hands, wrist-deep in Shaney's blood. It's probably splashed onto his chest and face, too, from the tooth extraction, and it's not hydraulic fluid—the Road King doesn't *have* this much hydraulic fluid.

The red against the white of the towel is unmistakable.

"Are you ok—?" Peta says, eyes fixed on him, stepping down the ladder without looking, probably concerned that he's hurt himself bad enough to go into shock, and that's how it happens, that's *why* it happens: because she's worried he might be cut somewhere. The left toe of her work boot that she's no longer paying attention to, thick for safety, misses the next rung, and her other foot was already shifting, and she knows better than to clutch onto the sides of the ladder because that just means bringing it down with her, and there's already one gouge in the wall.

Just from instinct, probably, her hands slash up, to try to find something to hold her.

What she finds is the handle of the knife jammed in alongside the spotlight's can. She brings it down with her, and, instead of bursting across the room to tackle her into the wall like a good husband would, Lewis stands there clutching his towel, watching this happen in what feels like the slowest motion ever.

Anybody but Peta would fall down into the rungs, get tangled up, break their fall with their basic awkwardness.

She used to be a pole vaulter, though.

She knows to push off, to arc away.

It's beautifully executed, and, being her, she even manages to fling the knife to the side so it won't impale her on landing like Lewis guesses he was expecting, since everything else is already going wrong.

Peta's used to falling onto huge mats, though. Not the sharp brick corner of the fireplace hearth, back-of-the-head first.

The cracking sound of her skull opening up is distinct, and permanent, and looking away doesn't help Lewis process it, or accept it.

Just like with Harley, he doesn't rush up to hold her in these last moments.

He just stares, shocked.

Her body spasms and her breath hitches for maybe ten seconds, her eyes locked on him like trying to communicate something, like . . . like trying to relive the last ten years with him? Like, now she can go back to sitting at that picnic bench in East Glacier and start the two of them all over again, live it right up until now. What *was* she drawing that day? Was she drawing her dream house, complete with fireplace and a little apron of brick before it, "hearth" labeled above it? Did she know all along this was what was going to happen, but then did it anyway, because these ten years were worth it?

"Peta," Lewis finally says, seconds and a lifetime too late.

The corners of her mouth grin just a little and then, like has to happen, her hips die down with the rest of her, like electricity's leaving her body, is running into the ground or wherever it goes.

Lewis is still just standing there.

Peta's blond hair is staining red, spreading out into the pale carpet. It's not a stain he's getting out. No, they're not getting the security deposit back.

"Hey," he says when he can, once he's sure it's too late, once he's sure she's not going to be answering.

Her pupils are fixed and dilated, her mouth open in a way she'd never let it hang in life.

Ten years, Lewis says to himself.

They made it ten years.

That's a pretty good run, isn't it? For an Indian and a white woman, especially when she outclassed him so much, and when he had all the usual baggage?

And—and maybe he *was* thinking right all along, he tries hard to believe. Maybe she appeared the summer after the Thanksgiving Classic for a reason—because she wanted to move from place to place with him, get him to invest his whole life in her, then stage a grand death scene like this, one he'd never be able to shake, would always be running from.

Wouldn't that be the best revenge? Death is too easy. Better to make every moment of the rest of a person's life agony.

Like with Shaney, though, there's a way to check. A way to know.

Lewis steps up onto the ladder to pull the knife from the wall where it stuck. Because the way he broke Shaney's jaw open let her teeth cut into his wrist like a bite from the wrong side of the grave, for Peta he grabs her chin from the outside, sets his knee against her forehead, and cracks the hinge that way.

Her teeth come out so much easier. All of them, like they were just waiting, were hardly in there at all. Maybe that's a difference between white people and Indians?

Lewis lines all her teeth in a rough crack of grout between the bricks of the hearth.

None of them are ivory either.

He sits back, hugs his legs to him, resting his chin in the cradle between his knees.

This is a thing he did, a thing he's definitely done.

Planes are probably going to be crashing into the terminal for months now, and mail's going to be piling up on the dock at the post office.

In addition, two women are dead who probably didn't have to be.

Lewis stares into what would be the fire if the chimney weren't boarded up—the lease says no open flames, only gas grills—and then he has no real choice but to smile when the light in the ceiling flickers on, even without its can being pressed to the side.

It's shining its bright little spotlight down on Peta. On her . . . stomach? Her belly?

Because everything means something now, what Lewis flashes on is that up-and-down scar that either is or isn't on Shaney's stomach in the garage.

It's a scar he knows for sure Peta doesn't have. But still, he's thinking of it for a reason, isn't he? Or, the world showed it to him in the driveway that day for a reason.

Soon enough, that reason pushes against the tight fabric of Peta's uniform shirt.

Something's struggling under there. Something's moving.

It's like—it's like when Andy was trapped in the belly of that dead mammoth, but for Lewis, for this, it's not a mammoth in there, is it?

"Indians like it bareback," he hears himself recite, and chuckles about it.

Some of his salmon *were* pretty good swimmers.

Sure, it's only been, what? Two nights? That's plenty, though. Nine months would be a luxury, an indulgence, would take so long he'd probably forget. And anyway, Peta would be all falling apart by then.

Forty-eight hours to gestate feels just about perfect, to Lewis.

He can even see some tiny limb pushing against Peta's skin now. Something in there suffocating, drowning, fighting to live.

His plan, only half formed but that's how he does it, had been to stand after a few more minutes, stand and feel his way outside, flop over the fence, sit between the two rails of the train tracks, wait for the Thunderball Express to come, deliver his judgment at sixty miles per hour, its air horn filling the whole world with sound.

But this is something new, something unexpected, something wondrous.

Lewis never thought he might be a father.

There's still hope, isn't there?

This can all still work out.

Using the same dull knife he used to pry Peta's teeth out, the same one he used to carve open that young elk ten years ago, he slits the tight skin of Peta's swelling-up belly.

A thin brown leg stabs up and he grabs on to it, traces it to its terminus.

A hoof, a tiny black hoof.

Lewis nods about the rightness of this, pulls that leg gently, his other hand ready.

Two days later, his elk calf wrapped in its mother's ten-year-old hide, he wakes under a rock ledge that's partway between the rent house in Great Falls and the reservation he still calls *his* reservation.

Shaney's yellow Toyota truck is two or three miles back on the plains, tucked just in from the gas station where he's pretty sure someone called him in, from all the headlines that made the rounds Wednesday: NATIVE MAN ON KILLING SPREE, TWO DEAD SO FAR, BABY MISSING.

The story on 12b is him, here, sleeping in the cold like the bow-and-arrow days. The story on 12b is how he looks up into the huge white flakes drifting down out of the sky, just like the Thanksgiving Classic.

He raises his face to those cold wet flakes, closes his eyes, holds this elk calf he's been calling his daughter close to his chest. She hasn't been growing as fast as Andy, and she hasn't moved since stabbing that leg up into the air, but she will, he knows. He just has to get her home, to land she knows, to grass she remembers. He'll watch her grow for the rest of the year, keep the coyotes and wolves and bears away, and, when she can, he'll let her go on her own, stand there crying from sadness, from happiness. And then it'll all be over. Indian stories always hoop back on themselves like that, don't they? At least the good ones do.

Lewis smiles, pulls her tighter, breathing heat down onto her thin ears, and on the ridge above him there's four men sighting down along the tops of their rifles. He looks up to them, his lips moving, trying to explain to them what he's doing, how this can work, how it's not too late, how they don't need to do this, it's not like the papers have been saying, he's not that Indian, he's just him, locked into the steps of this story but finding his way now, finally, making it all work.

When they shoot is when he finally feels what he's been waiting for, what he's been gambling on, praying for: long delicate legs against his chest, kicking once, twice, again. That small head nuzzling up into his neck, and the long lashes of big round eyes brushing his cheek as they open, and then closing against the mist of blood that, for the moment, is its whole world.

Her name in Blackfeet is Po'noka.

It means elk.

THREE DEAD, ONE INJURED IN MANHUNT

Four Shelby men were attacked last night, following the apprehension of the fugitive Lewis A. Clarke (see Wednesday's edition), who had apparently been fleeing back to his tribe's ancestral reservation. Clarke was the main suspect in the brutal murders of both his wife and a federal coworker.

Reports indicate this group of four hunters had been out all day, aiding in the search for Clarke. Representatives for the highway patrol say that while armed citizen patrols of this sort might seem helpful, staying off the roads is actually more beneficial to recovery and apprehension efforts.

Reports that these four Shelby men were actually the ones to find Clarke, now deceased, are unconfirmed.

According to sources at the hospital, who were able to speak to the lone survivor before surgery, the four Shelby men had in the back of their truck both Clarke and the deer or elk calf he had apparently been carrying for reasons unknown.

At some point in the drive back to town, according to this survivor, someone stood from the bed of the truck while it was moving. It was a girl of twelve or fourteen, Indian. Presumably she had climbed into the truck earlier, when it was going west.

When the driver of the vehicle slowed to keep her from falling or blowing out, and alerted his three cab mates to her, the survivor says the girl "rushed forward over the toolbox" and "through the rear window" into the cab, which is where the eyewitness testimony ends.

Anyone finding an Indian teenager perhaps hitchhiking or loitering is advised to alert the authorities.

Names of the dead and injured are being withheld until families of the slain can be notified.

More on this story as it develops.

SWEAT
LODGE
MASSACRE

FRIDAY

The way you protect your calf is you slash out with your hooves. Your own mother did that for you, high in the mountains of your first winter. Her black hoof snapping forward against those snarling mouths was so fast, so pure, just there and back, leaving a perfect arc of red droplets behind it. But hooves aren't always enough. You can bite and tear with your teeth if it comes to that. And you can run slower than you really can. If none of that works, if the bullets are too thick, your ears too filled with sound, your nose too thick with blood, and if they've already gotten to your calf, then there's something else you can do.

You hide in the herd. You wait. And you never forget.

What you do after you've made your hard way back into the world is stand on the side of the last road home, wrapped in a blanket torn from a wrecked truck, your cold feet not hard hooves anymore, your hands branching out into fingers you can feel creaking, they're growing so fast now. The family of four that picks you up is tense and silent, neither the father nor the mother nor the son saying anything with their mouths, only their eyes, the infant just sleeping. They make room in the backseat because if they don't stop, someone else will, and the father driving the car says that that never ends well for starved-down fourteen-year-old Indian girls wearing only one thin blanket.

You're fourteen, then. Already.

Just a few hours ago you're pretty sure you were what he would have called "twelve." An hour before that you were an elk calf being cradled by a killer, running for the reservation, and before that you were just an awareness spread out through the herd, a memory cycling from brown body to brown body, there in every flick of the tail, every snort, every long probing glare down a grassy slope.

But you coalesced, you congealed, you found one of the killers about to spark life into the body of another, a life you could wriggle into, look out of. He had to be groomed first, though, groomed and cornered and isolated.

It was so easy. He was so fragile, so delicately balanced, so unprepared to face what he'd done.

You settle into the soft fragrant backseat of the car taking you the rest of the way home. The father behind the wheel turns the radio knob constantly backward and forward, looking for a song that may not exist, and the mother beside him, holding the new calf—baby, baby baby *baby*—to her chest, she's staring out the side window, maybe at all the dry grass slipping by.

The boy in the backseat with you smells like chemicals. They steam up from his skin and his eyes are wet and mad behind his waist-long hair, and in him you can sense all his ancestors before him, and you're surprised he doesn't recognize you for what you are.

You say something to him in your own language, this mouth and teeth and throat and tongue not made for the shape of these words, and the boy just stares at you for a long moment, says, "What are you?" and then rotates in the seat, away from you.

So he does sense you. Just, not in a way he can acknowledge.

Good, good.

If you can't interact with him, then interact with the grassland sweeping past with so little effort. Lean over to the center of the backseat to see the white mountains rolling up. It feels like you're rushing, like you're stretched out and running. You can't help but smile a bit from the feeling, from the velocity. It's your first smile in this face. On the last hill down to the town, though, your smile droops when the necessary memory rises, from seeing the train tracks from far away and above like this.

The memory is an old one, not your generation but a few before, a thing that happened right there to the south, just past where the last fence is. The memory is of how the herd came down here in the night. How they found good grass closer and closer to the buildings, where nothing much ever grazed, and then they kept eating and eating, bloating their sides out because they needed this to get through the winter that was coming.

But then the hunters stepped out onto their porches, saw tall brown bodies in the waving yellow, and reached back inside for their rifles.

They approached on their bellies all morning, and the herd knew they were there, their smell so tangy, their crawling so loud, but the grass was good and the horizon was open on the other side from the hunters. The herd could run as one when they needed to run, could dig in with their hooves, bunch their haunches and burst away, move like blown smoke across the rolling prairie, collect in a coulee they knew. The water that ran through that rocky bottom was already trickling through their heads. From its taste they knew exactly where it came from in the mountains, and its whole story getting here.

They didn't know about trains, though. Not like the hunters did.

When the locomotive and all its boxcars thundered through, the scent hot and metal, it was as if those tracks in the grass had stood up. They became a flashing moving wall of sparks and wind no elk could run through (one tried) and the screeching and tearing of those great metal wheels covered the boom of the hunters' rifles firing again and again, until the sound of the rifles and the sound of the train were the same sound, and in the backseat of this impossibly fast car you reel from the acrid taste of this memory, causing the chemical boy in the backseat to pull away from you even more, but it was fair, what happened that day, and it had been the herd's own fault.

You run when you first taste hunters on the air, don't you? When you first even *think* that might be their ugly scent. One more pull of grass isn't worth it. Even if it's good and rich. Even if you need it worse than anything.

Knowledge of this day lodged in the herd, got passed down like what headlights meant, like how those blocks of salt aren't for elk tongues in the daytime, like how the taste of smoke means to walk somewhere else slowly, head down, feet light. The price of the knowledge about trains had been high and the coming winter harder, as less hooves means more wolves, but the herd didn't feed down near town anymore, and they didn't trust the metal tracks anywhere they encountered them, knew they could stand up into a sudden wall.

Instead they kept to the high country, the lonely places where the air tasted of trees and cold and the herd, the places the trucks never lurched into.

Until one did.

In the backseat of this speeding car you thin your lips, remembering that day as well.

An elk mother, cornered, will slash with her hooves and tear with her mouth and even offer the hope of her own hamstrings, and if none of that works, she'll rise again years and years later, because it's never over, it's always just beginning again.

The father lets you out in the parking lot of the grocery store, where you've told him with this new voice that you can call your aunt, but you're really only there to dip into another car that's not even locked. You stand from that car with a duffel bag of clothes, never mind the starving dogs circling around now, snarling and tearing at the air, the wiry hair at their spines maned up, tails tucked over their soft parts.

You snap your teeth back at them, watch them roil with spit-flecked rage, writhe with desire they want you so bad, want you gone even worse.

Town is such a funny place, isn't it?

You can't rid yourself of the annoyance of these dogs without drawing more annoyances, though. But you won't be here long.

It's another thing the herd's always known: never stay in one place. Keep moving, always moving.

First, though, one of their calves is sitting in eighth-grade geography—*girl*, girl girl girl, not "calf." And this girl has this certain father you remember, and that father, he has a friend you remember as well, from looking up a long snowy slope, their monstrous forms black against the sky.

For them, ten years ago, that's another lifetime.

For you it's yesterday.

THE GIRL

Her name is Denorah. Her dad used to tell her she was supposed to have been *Deborah*, since that was the name of one of her dead aunts, but his handwriting had never been so good, and then he'd smile that sharp-at-the-right-side smile that had probably been killer in high school, a hundred thousand beers ago.

Her dad is Gabriel Cross Guns. He's the one who shot the hole in your back, took your legs away.

In Denorah's eighth-grade geography right now, six days before Thanksgiving turkey, Mr. Massey is saying that all of the details aren't in, that it might have been highway patrol that shot that Native American man just off the reservation, that it doesn't have to have been vigilantes or militia, even though this state is stacked deep with the second, all of them hoping to be the first.

"*Native American?*" Tone Def says back to Mr. Massey. "I thought he was Blackfeet."

"Tone Def" is Amos After Buffalo's hip-hop name.

The class falls in behind him against Mr. Massey. Not because they care, but because it's fun to harass the white teacher.

Tone Def Amos—the name he's earned—stands up from the

desks, calls out about is there really some big *difference* between state troopers and idiots with guns anyway, at which point Christina or one of them over by the window says back that this dead Indian who nobody on the reservation really remembers anyway, he killed his wife and gutted the baby from her and pulled all her teeth out, didn't he? Does it matter who shot him down for that? And now voices are rising and more kids are standing and a couple are crying already just from the tragedy and drama of it all and there's probably not going to be any geography going on today.

Denorah pages her spiral notebook over to a blank page and tries to think if she really even remembers this Blackfeet who got shot. His name, sure. His name was a joke, except this joke had been by the dead Indian's parents, who probably came up with it down the hall in history class. But it's hard to tease what she actually remembers apart from what she's been told twenty or thirty times.

There *is* this dim sort-of image of her dad and Cassidy, as he likes to be called now even though it's a girl name. They're crossing the living room before dawn on a Saturday, and Denorah's sleeping on the couch, just a kid, not even in kindergarten yet. At the door are two not-yet-dead Indians: the joke-named one just shot down over by Shelby, and Ricky Boss, who she's pretty sure died from getting beat up outside a bar over in North Dakota. Unless that was somebody else. But she's pretty sure about the North Dakota part.

Anyway, Denorah remembers this early morning living room not because it was the Saturday before Thanksgiving, and not because her real dad and Cassidy were being too loud with their hot-hot coffee. It's not because the knocking at the door woke her from sleeping on the couch, either. Her real dad long-stepped past her to keep the door quiet, Cassidy right behind. It was Ricky Boss and that other dead one, Lewis, with rifles slung over their shoulders and sleep in their eyes. The only reason Denorah has any of this left ten years later, now, it's because when Ricky Boss was slurping from his coffee, the steam like a veil in front of his eyes, he was looking straight through it at her on the couch, like he knew what was going to happen that day, hunting, and wanted instead to just stay inside, drink the rest of his coffee.

It was something she would have tried to draw, once upon a time. When she used to draw.

It had started in sixth grade, the drawing, two years ago, before she got serious about basketball. It was right after the museum visit. A class project. It didn't matter that they were all drawing just in spiral notebooks. Miss Pease, who's her aunt now, explained how, back when, ledgers were the spiral notebooks of the day.

Denorah would never admit it no matter what, but she'd believed Miss Pease that day. Sitting in the second row, she hadn't even had to close her eyes to see the picture of an old-time lodge, inside it all manner of things for sale: beaver pelts, pipes, braids of sweetgrass, hunks of boiled buffalo meat with brown-colored ropy string through them (for hanging on pegs), pounded-flat strips of pemmican (yuck), beaded bags like at the trading post for tourists, where the flaps are big to show off the beadwork, and, way back in the corner, a stack of blank ledgers. She knew she just had to put her finger on the fast-forward button of that picture, keep it pressed until that lodge grew shoulders, squared up into a building, a store, one with a school supplies aisle. Now the ledgers are spiral notebooks, just like Miss Pease was saying.

It felt magical in class that day, opening her spiral up to that new blank page, that modern-day ledger. She imagined it being in a museum, even pictured a class of sixth-graders single-filing it up to the glass display case someday, to see how the old ones used to do it, back when spiral notebooks were everywhere, back in that handful of years when Indians only had reservations, before they got all of America back.

The assignment was for class to draw their favorite holiday. It was supposed to be Christmas or Thanksgiving or the powwow from the summer like everybody else was doing, but what Denorah drew is from when her sister's team went to regionals in basketball the year before, the holiest day of all in her family, even though they weren't completely a family yet, since her mom and new dad were only dating.

This is the day her big sister, Trace, who's her new dad's daughter he already had, scored ten just in the first quarter, then eight in the second, and came back from halftime to go six for twelve, then in the fourth, when it was down to the wire and the whole gym was stomping and screaming, when the other team had figured out how to swing a double-team over to her if she so much as touched the ball, she passed out of it every time, to whoever had to be free, and racked up nine crushing assists in a single quarter. The other side was chanting, *Indians go home, Indians go home*, but Trace was home, all of this was home, no place more than a basketball court in the last thirty seconds.

What Denorah drew at the bottom right of the blue-lined page she'd quartered up into panels that day in sixth grade, it was her sister at the end of that game, the one free throw she had in the whole second half, a technical for illegal defense, only the way Denorah drew her arms, it isn't proper form at all. Her big sister's got her arms up and out like she's holding a bow, like the ball balancing in the cup of her outstretched fist is an arrow, one she's aiming up at the whole world.

She rode that historical free throw, that game, that *win*, to a full-ride four-year college scholarship down in Wyoming, and Denorah talks to her every week on the phone, big sis to little one, no "step" between. When she was done with her ledger art that day, when it got Miss Pease's "B–" scrawled top-right—"Is this really *Indian*, D? Shouldn't you do something to honor your *heritage*?"—

she mailed it to Trace, careful to fold along the panel lines, and Trace said Denorah got it just right, that's just how it happened, thank you thank you, Denorah should keep practicing, she's better than any twelve-year-old has any right to be, she'll tell her coach, she'll make her listen, this is A-plus work. A-plus *plus*.

It's two years after that B minus, though.

Denorah hasn't drawn probably since last summer. Not since her hands got big enough to make a basketball look like it's going one way when it's really going a completely different way.

She really is good. That's not just something her sister tells her. Coach says it after practice, to Denorah's new dad, and when he's home from his busy time in a couple of months, he's promised they're going to go up to the gym every night and run drills, work on her left-side attack—so long as she keeps her grades up. Because they don't just hand scholarships out.

New dad: "And why do you need to be sure to go to college?"

Same daughter: "Because you can't eat basketballs when you grow up."

Even though secretly she kind of thinks she can.

But still, she won't get good enough to live on basketball if she doesn't run all those drills, and she doesn't get to run those drills if she doesn't maintain a solid B average.

In the left-hand margin, Denorah pencils her grades in with the lightest pencil. It's her way of reminding herself that they're not stable, that they can change in an instant, with the least quiz:

> *Pre-Algebra: B–*
> *Biology: C+*
> *English: B+*
> *Geography: A*
> *Athletics: AAA+*
> *Health: ?*

So, health, once that six-week unit kicks in, can make all the difference, Denorah maths out. She draws three hearts by "Health" like hit points and shades in the first one, half of the second one. She pretends the red margin line on the left side of the page is a pole and draws some dramatic shade coming down from it. She thinks about how a good point guard holds the defender's eyes with her own, to keep that defender from watching the ball. She remembers back when spiral notebooks were Big Chief tablets, and how she used to think those came from Chief Mountain, and that her reservation was the only reservation that got them. She tunes in to Mr. Massey, trying to defend both the highway patrol *and* the Shelby vigilantes, trying to flip this turtle of a discussion onto its back to see the real issues scratched on its belly, but there's nothing there Denorah hasn't heard in her first three classes already, so she closes her spiral notebook and holds it closed, looks out the window at the storage trailer with the big dent in its side, from when a senior tried to push it over with his dad's truck and got expelled, joined up with the fire crews, and burned up before he even would have graduated.

But . . . what?

There's a figure standing there in the ragged shade of that storage trailer. A pair of eyes that blink once and resolve into a blank face so much like Denorah's, the long hair not braided, a bright white scrimmage jersey, gym shorts, knee socks—*My workout gear from the car?* Denorah thinks, leaning closer to the glass to see.

You look right back at her, your hair lifting all around your shoulders.

She doesn't know you yet, no.

She will.

DEATH ROW

Gabriel Cross Guns, right before lunch.

While his daughter he hasn't seen in going on two weeks is flinching back in her seat in geography, drawing her teacher's attention, he's raising a dusty rifle from the front closet of his dad's living room and trying not to make a big production of it.

The rifle's an old Mauser that his dad used to load with bird shot, so it could be a real mouser. The baseboards of the living room are pitted and scored from it, and there's a crater near Gabe's right eye that's not acne, but a ricochet that he was never sure if it was a pellet or salt or a shattered fragment of mouse bone or splinter of wood or what, just that it stung and it was close enough to his eye that he'd slapped at this sudden dab of pain without thinking, and probably just succeeded in pushing it in deeper, meaning he's got some salt or lead or some baseboard or some rodent in his face. It's a dot in his life he's always touching. It makes him feel like Cyclops from the X-Men, like he can place his finger to that dot, that button, that release, and glare a ruby optic blast at whatever he wants, blow it so deep into next week that nobody'll ever catch up with it.

He hasn't read comic books for years now, though, is only thinking about them from a couple of weekends ago, from a smoky couch he was sitting on that he's pretty sure Ricky's little brother died on back when—drowned, technically. Gabe was sitting on the couch because he'd woke on it with his boots on, and when he sat up he'd had to carefully extract his arm from deep between the cushions, down where the lumpy-flat mattress was folded over three times.

His hand had come up from that with a comic book, and he'd wondered if it was worth anything at the pawnshops in Kalispell, and thinking about pawning shit got him thinking about that old Mauser his dad always said he was going to sell if he needed some quick cash. It's supposed to be a historical gun, from World War I or World War II, that he'd inherited from one of *his* uncles, who got it on the actual battlefield.

Gabe wonders if shooting years of bird shot through the barrel at mice has worn the rifling down. To find out, he jacks the breech open, holds the butt to the light coming in through the front window, and looks down the barrel from the front.

As if he can tell whether the rifling's worn down or if it's at factory specs, yeah. What was he thinking? It's old anyway, right? Being wore down is what an eighty- or whatever-year-old rifle that's maybe from an actual German in an actual war is supposed to be, right? Anyway, the crispness of the rifling won't be what sells this rifle. What sells this rifle will be this goofy forestock that tapers up nearly to the end of the barrel and has what looks to be hand-carved checkering scratched in.

Gabe shoulders the rifle all at once, tracks an imaginary antelope bounding from right to left.

"*Lead it, lead it . . .*" he says, left eye closed, right sighting, then comes to a sudden stop on his dad's bored-with-this face.

His dad palms the rifle away, runs the bolt back to be sure there's no live round.

"Think I'm stupid?" Gabe says, turning sideways to get past his dad to the refrigerator.

"You can't have my uncle's war trophy," his dad says.

"Don't want it, it's too old," Gabe says back, twisting the top off a stubby bottle of V8. He doesn't like the way it coats his mouth like cold spaghetti sauce or the way it clumps down his throat like throw-up he's having to swallow, isn't even that fond of the way it pools in his stomach and boils in his gut, but, technically, it's not food, and he's supposed to be fasting today, for tonight's sweat. The rocks are already all heating up in the fire. By dusk they'll be crawling with red heat, ready to shatter if the handler isn't careful, and—Gabe hasn't told Cass this yet, and he probably won't tell Victor Yellow Tail, who's laying down a cool hundred for the sweat—but these particular rocks, they're from a scattering of old tipi rings he found way back in Del Bonito in August. Meaning they won't be the first Blackfeet to use them, ha. Maybe it'll make them better or hotter or someshit, right?

Anything helps.

It's not the first sweat he's thrown, but it's the first one he's thrown in honor of a friend just gunned down the day before.

As to what Lewis had been doing to get himself shot, that's the big mystery. Going crazy from marrying a Custer-haired woman, Gabe figures but knows better than to say out loud—yet. Give it a few months. Give it a few months and that'll be the joke going through the reservation.

The best jokes are the ones that have a kind of message to them. A warning. This one's warning would be to stay home. To not go postal.

It's what Gabe thinks he's maybe going to do right now, with his dad following his every step like Gabe's sixteen again, is only swinging by to thieve anything not bolted down.

"For recycling," his dad says, about the plastic bottle Gabe just banked into the white trash can by the back door.

"Oh yeah," Gabe says, casing the interior of the fridge some more, "Indians use every part of the V8, don't we?"

His dad grunts, settles the Mauser into the corner by the door, and canes across the linoleum, reaches into the trash for the clear plastic bottle.

Gabe shuts the refrigerator in frustration.

"How long since you've even shot a mouse?" he says. "That rifle's just sitting there. You know it."

"What are you wearing that for?" his dad says back.

The black bandanna tied high on Gabe's left arm, with the knot on the outside because that makes it look more like a headband, just, on his arm.

Gabe stands to his full height, always feels more traditional when his back's straight like a ramrod—well, when it looks like he's got a stick up his ass, anyway.

"You heard about Lewis?" he says to his dad. "You remember him, Lewis?"

His dad lowers his face as if rattling the right tape into some slot in his head, then comes up with an old-man smile, says, "Little Meriwether?"

"Still not funny," Gabe drolls. "Highway patrol shot him yesterday, yeah? Here, here, here," making up the bullet holes as he goes.

He watches his dad for a flicker of reaction but instead his dad says, "Didn't he die already once?"

"What? No. That's . . . you're thinking of Ricky, Dad. Ricky Boss?"

"Boss Ribs Richard," his dad says, putting faces with names.

"Lewis was trying to come home at last," Gabe says.

"For Thanksgiving moose?" his dad says with a smile.

Oh yeah: Turkey Day's not even a week out, is it?

"Is everybody wearing those on their arms?" his dad asks, circling his own left bicep with his hand.

"He was my friend, Dad. Cass is wearing it, too."

"Just the two of you, then?"

"Lewis had been gone a long time already."

Gabe's dad looks out the kitchen window, at the wall of the house right beside his, maybe. Who knows what old men look at?

"Do mice even come out in winter?" Gabe asks.

"It was my uncle Gerry's rifle," his dad says back.

"He's not coming back for it, Dad."

"He used to shoot prairie dogs with it," his dad goes on, a smile ghosting his lips up. "But only the ones who were wearing those German helmets."

Gabe has to spin away from this.

"His wife is dead, too," Gabe says. "Lewis's, I mean."

"Field-dressed her," his dad adds in.

So. The headlines are even circulating over here on Death Row, then. Great. Wonderful. Perfect.

"They don't know what happened yet," Gabe says.

"Meriwether . . ." his dad says then, casing the refrigerator himself now, probably taking inventory for whatever Gabe might have palmed. "He was selling that raccoon meat that one time, wasn't he?"

"I don't even know why I come over here," Gabe says, brushing past his dad, pushing through the front door he'd hung himself one many-beers day. It's not his fault it's crooked, though. Whoever framed the doorway must not have had a square. Or maybe it's whoever poured the foundation's fault. Or whoever came up with the whole idea of "doors."

He roars his truck to life and backs out without looking, finds the three unbroken teeth in his transmission that still allow first gear, and touches two fingers to his eyebrow, saluting his dad bye, if he's even watching.

Two houses later he pats the Mauser nosed down into the floorboard on the passenger side. His dad didn't even see him snag it when Gabe had brushed past. In court-mandated substance-abuse counseling once—completely unnecessary, but slightly better than ninety days in lockup—Neesh had explained to the ten little Indians in group about counting coup. How that's what all of them were sort of already doing, did they know that?

Twenty bored eyes looked back at him.

Counting coup, he explained, using his ancient-old hands to form each word, act out what he was saying, counting coup was running up to the baddest enemy and just tapping them, then getting clear before that enemy could bash you with anything.

That, he claimed all reverentially, was what each person there in group had already done: rushed up to overdoses, to freezing while doped up, to crashing a car because of impaired reflexes, to vomiting in their sleep and drowning—addictive behavior was the *big*-time enemy, couldn't they see? And the fact that they were all here meant they'd already ran up to it, had already counted coup on it, and gotten away with their lives. The question now was whether they would come back to the tribe proud of how close they'd got, or if they'd go back again and again, until the enemy got its hook into them all the way, left them in a ditch somewhere.

Gabe has always remembered that. "Counting coup." It's kind of what he lives by, isn't it? With wives and girlfriends, with jobs, with the law, with how much gas is left in the tank, and now with this: he'd counted coup on his dad, had actually been brushing right past him while his other hand snaked the rifle, swinging it forward with his left leg until the butt could catch on the steel toe of Gabe's boot, just like Denorah's foot had back when he'd taught her cowboy dancing.

But he knows better than to think about her.

Not because he doesn't want to, but because he won't stop, will have to go out and find something *to* stop his thinking. Either that or show up at Trina's front door again, apologizing, begging, asking her to give Den something from him. Maybe just a bottle of Sprite with a chance to win under the cap.

At which point the lecture comes, about how he can't keep showing up like this, about how she's at practice but don't go back there, about how don't call her that, it's *Denorah*, not Den, okay?

Better yet, don't call her at all.

Gabe pats the rifle, rolls it over so the hand-carved checkering won't rub away against the seat.

Snow swirls across the blacktop and, screw it, Trina can't tell him what to do. D's his daughter, too, isn't she?

Gabe hauls the steering wheel over, takes the turn that leads down to the school. Just to drive by. She knows his truck. Everybody knows his truck. They should invite him to drive it slow in the parade, let him rain candy out the window.

On the way down to the school, though, his mind churning through who might even have cartridges for a rifle this old and weird, he sees a girl walking on the opposite side of the street, away from school.

"D?" he says, letting his foot off the gas.

She's wearing a scrimmage jersey and shorts, probably for the game tomorrow, but has her hair down, like Denorah never wears it since she got all serious about ball.

That can't be her, can it?

Gabe coasts past and just glances over. In case it's not her, the last thing he needs is word getting out that Gabriel Cross Guns is creeping on the junior high set.

Is it her, though? And, shouldn't she be cold?

Right when he's cranking his window down to see better, you raise your face, level your eyes at him through your black hair blowing everywhere, and this is the first time you've seen him since that day, the air full of sound, your nose breathing in just blood, your calf gasping inside you, your legs gone.

Don't look away.

Make him be the one to break eye contact.

Listen to his truck accelerate away.

It doesn't matter that he saw you now, either. The next time he lays eyes on you, you'll be taller, different, better. Already these stolen clothes are getting tight.

SEES ELK

Cassidy is changing his name again.

From here on out, as long as it lasts, he'll be *Cashy*, he thinks.

It's payday in the Thinks Twice household. Or, the Thinks Twice camper, anyway. Not that Thinks Twice is his born name either, it's just what his auntie Jaylene always called him like to remind him what to do, but, in his head anyway, it kind of stuck.

In addition to his check, cashed and still in big bills, Gabe's sliding him forty just for rehabbing his old sweat and keeping the fire stoked all day. In the old days, which means up until last month, forty dollars extra would have pretty much turned itself into a cooler of beer. Just, *poof*, Indian magic, don't even need any eagle feather fans or a hawk screeching, just look away long enough for it to happen.

Since Jo, though, Cassidy is a new man. Gainfully employed—even more legal once he takes the driving test—home by an hour after dark most nights, up with the sun like there's this big long string tied between him and it. Who'd have thought a Crow would be the one who finally stepped in, saved his lame ass? Never mind all the sage around the camper, all her smudging. There *was* something bad following him, Cassidy finally had to admit, but it wasn't anything Indian. Or, well, it was pretty Indian, he guessed: a bench warrant. But it wasn't even for anything bad, was just an unpaid ticket, which can happen to anybody.

Still, he can tell Jo's waiting for the other shoe to drop. At the high school basketball games he hauls her to so she can start knowing everybody, he can tell she's always looking around, watching for a ten- or fifteen-year-old with pale eyes like his, even though he guarantees her he never slipped any past the goalie, that he would have heard *all* about it if he was owing anybody child support.

What he figures is that he's shooting blanks, just like all the Indians when they're fighting John Wayne, and what he blames for *that*, or thanks, is uranium in the water. Gabe and Ricky and Lewis had grown up down in Browning, which, the water's not perfect there, but you can usually drink it anyway. Cassidy has been living on his dad's place in East Glacier most of the time, though, where the water's cloudy with who knows what-all. It is kind of weird, though, he's always thought. Of him and Gabe and Ricky and Lewis, they've altogether only had one kid? He figures Lewis and that blonde he'd run off with might be waiting till the time was right like white people do, or maybe she already had some before Lewis, didn't want any more, but that *Ricky* never threw any kids before he died—it's not like he was ever careful, right? The only one of them to leave a kid behind so far, though, it's Gabe, and that was, shit, what? Fourteen years ago already? It's really been that long since him and Trina? At least he did it right, though. Denorah Cross Guns can flat-out *ball*. She's the one Jo's always standing up for at the games and telling to shoot, shoot, that this game is hers if she wants it.

She's right, of course, the girl has Trina's drive on the court, not Gabe's interest in what's happening behind the gym, but still, the first time Jo came up out of her seat like that, not looking around for permission or to see if she was the only one who could see the magic happening at the top of the key, Cassidy knew she was going to be all right here. It's so stupid, too: Jo was just a random Crow girl he got to talking to at the powwow last summer—well, her and her cousin, whatever her name was. They'd been doing a thing of standing up in front of tourists' cameras right when they were about to take the perfect shot of the grand entrance, and they weren't doing it to protect the Blackfeet or anything, they were just doing it for the hell of it. Cassidy had liked that, had scooted over to stand up with them, and then, before he even really knew it was happening, he was driving down to her rez every other weekend, then every weekend, then every day if he could get away. And then, after her big fight with her mom, and after her cousin moved down south, taking away Jo's couch, Cassidy was coming back with Jo's stuff mounded in the bed of his truck, a borrowed horse trailer dragging behind.

So it was all on accident, him and Jo, but at the same time it feels like it was meant to be. It's like he walked into the best thing ever, and all he was doing was screwing around at the powwow. But maybe that's the way it works when it's real?

Cassidy rolls the doubled-over pad of cash in his front pocket and considers going into the camper to wake Jo just to be sure she's there, that he isn't just dreaming all this, but . . . she works nights, is a stocker, the one and only Crow to ever work at the new grocery so far—she needs her sleep, he knows. Instead he goes to the camper of the old truck, where the dogs sleep. They won't miss the pile of sleeping bags and blankets and old jackets for one night, will they? For one sweat?

Maybe he'll buy them forty dollars of dog food.

Well, twenty.

He hauls an armful of the blankets out and down and drops them to the dirt, finds a corner here, an edge there, a sleeve poking out like it's reaching up to get saved. One by one Cassidy separates them all and shakes them out, then carries them to the frame of the old sweat. The poles are still good, are from some kids' tent he guesses, propped up with forks of tied rebar at the four points. Not four for any bullshit Indian reason, but because, first, the day Cassidy had put this together, he'd only been able to scavenge eight pieces of rebar, two per prop, *X*'d like he was doing, and, second, the tent frame was made to hold a kid's *tent*, not forty-odd pounds of dog bedding.

Too, it's good that Gabe wants to do this in winter. In summer, because of Cassidy's great idea to dig the floor of the sweat down a foot and a half, it's sometimes soggy. Frozen like this, though, it'll be perfect. Anyway, it'll be good to sweat the past year out. Reset, like. The old-time Indians had it right, Cassidy figures.

At the frame he tightens all the shoestrings holding the poles and rebar together, then shakes each blanket and sleeping bag and jacket out before draping them across the white plastic skeleton of the sweat, saving his prison brother's old Army coat for the flap. The sleeping bag with the silvery insides flashing in the sun spooks the horses and Cassidy notes this, reminds himself to keep this one free, that maybe it'll scare the magpies, too. Last summer they stole threads from his favorite shirt when it was hanging on the line between the camper and the pens. Somewhere back in the trees there was a nest with colorful accents, he figured, which was great and all, but not at the cost of his favorite shirt. Now, to protect Jo's clothes that he should probably be taking down so they don't smell like smoke, he's got Christmas tinsel strung up all down the wire. So far the magpies just think it's pretty. They squawk their thanks to him for dressing the place up, keeping things interesting.

When the sweat's together—it looks like an igloo made from homeless dudes—Cassidy goes to the tack shed, roots around, comes back with a mallet and enough junky tent stakes to be sure no flaps blow open tonight except the door flap. But the door flap is a greasy old BDU jacket with a rock in its pocket to keep it down, so that should be good.

Next, what should have been first: sweeping out the floor. If he'd done it before, he could have used a normal broom. Now he has to use the broken-off head of a broom, and a tray like from a cafeteria. Zero clue where that's from, but it works.

Slapping the tray on the side of the pen spooks the horses again, too.

"What's with y'all fraidy-cats today?" Cassidy says to them.

The paint whinnies back, stomps her front hoof like trying to pull the ground between them closer, and Cassidy ducks back into the lodge for one last sweeping. A little extra dirt doesn't matter to him, but it's the Yellow Tail kid's first sweat, so he's probably going to have his face right down by the ground, just trying to breathe. *Heat rises, kid. Way it is. Sorry.* Maybe this'll clean him right up, though. It's a different kind of getting baked, right?

"Here all night," Cassidy calls out to the horses and the dogs, and parade waves to them all. The paint swishes her shampoo-commercial tail back at him. The dogs are pretending to be guarding some other camper, it looks like. One they'd be more proud to be associated with.

Cassidy turns around to take his world in. For miles around there's just yellow grass and crusty snow and, in the folds of the hill where seeds can blow and water can flow, clumps of trees. The only thing keeping this from being 1800 or all the centuries before are the utility poles hitching the power cable out to the camper. Well, he supposes the camper's not very pre–white people, either. Or the horses.

He's always kind of wondered about the dogs, though. Back when, dogs would sometimes pull little travois, wouldn't they? He's pretty sure he's seen drawings. But, wouldn't those dogs have pretty

much just been domesticated wolves? At the same time, though, all
the dogs living on the streets in town, they may have started out as
Saint Bernards or Labradors or Rotts or whatever, but, to grit out
the winter, to fight it out over every scrap, they bush their coats up,
they bare their teeth first thing, and their ears aren't as floppy as
whatever line of lapdog Frisbee-catchers they come from. It's like,
living like they do, it's turning them back into wolves.

Case in point: Cassidy's three women, each faster to snap at
your hand than the other. The black one with the blaze, Ladybear, is the mom of the two others. There used to be a boy dog he
called Stout, because he was, but the problem with the males is
that they're never content to hang around the camper. Stout went
out on self-imposed patrol one day, which Cassidy figured was
really just looking for women in heat or something to fight, and he
must have found one or the other, because the next time Cassidy
saw him was when him and Jo were trotting the horses a couple
miles off, just killing the afternoon. Stout was a mat of ratty hair
and a few bones.

"Always wondered where he got off to," Jo'd said, her paint
dancing and spinning under her.

"Not far," Cassidy said.

That was probably only a couple of months after she'd moved
in, when he was still trying to prove to her that he was a Real
Indian. Exhibit one: I ride my own horses on the same land my
ancestors did.

Whatever. It had worked, Cassidy supposes. Never mind she
was twice the rider he was, and probably three times the Indian.

Not that she could come into the sweat tonight. If it was just
him and her, sure, always, forever, please. Gabe had read in one of
his books that women and men didn't mix in the sweats, though,
and anyway: the kid. Cassidy still remembers his own first sweat. It
was bad enough sitting in all that dark heat with a bunch of naked

uncles. Add a woman into that mix—especially one like Jo: two unfair inches taller than Cassidy, curvy, solid, long black hair—and it wouldn't have been ceremonial anymore, it would have been about how, *Look, I'm tough, this heat isn't anything, I can take it longer than any of these old-timers.*

He probably never would have sung, either, if there'd been a woman there. Yeah, sweats shouldn't be like the bar, he figures.

But now that it was built, they could heat up the rocks whenever they wanted, get clean, screw whatever book Gabe had. What, were the Indian police going to thunder down from the sky on lightning bolts, write Cassidy up for letting a woman into the sacred sweat lodge?

If they did, he'd ask them about their dogs, maybe. And also what they did for water for the sweat, back in the pre-bucket days.

In town, Cassidy could just run a hose over, snake it under a blanket, spray the rocks when they needed more steam. This far from town, though, all high and lonely, water was in the five-hundred-gallon tank behind the pens, and cost a tank of gas to drag all the way here.

What did the old Indians use?

Probably they built their sweat lodges by creeks, Cassidy figures, or where the snow was melting downhill. *His* solution is . . . that old green and white cooler that doesn't have a lid anymore, that he's been using for the dogs to drink from.

"Sorry," he says to them, tumping it over.

Miss Lefty bats her tail once against the dirt in response. Her name is Miss Lefty because that's a funny name for a dog.

Cassidy scoops the cooler into the tall snow living in the shade behind the horses' lean-to. Their ears are all directed right at him.

After working the cooler into the sweat, all that's left is a shovel for Victor, tonight's designated rock handler. Cassidy jogs around back of the camper, not sure where he last saw the shovel but sure he can't use the wide flat one they muck out the stalls with. He's not a hundred percent on board with keeping every part of a ritual intact, but he is against the shitty end of that shovel being anywhere near him.

Jo's around back of the camper, it turns out, wetting the air needle with her lips to push it into the basketball, shoot a few thousand on the little court maybe a camper's length past the outhouse. Really it's just the foundation left over from a house that used to be here, that blew away. All Cass had to do was grind down all the water pipes level with the concrete and screw an old backboard to the utility pole the tribe left behind, that he spent a whole day digging the hole for, and another day getting to stand up straight.

Jo's sitting on the little weight bench Cassidy liberated from one of his kid cousins, her foot stepping on the bicycle pump's base to keep it from tipping over into the dirt.

She jabs the needle in, tries to hold the ball between her knees while she works the air pump's squeaky plunger. Cassidy wants to step over, help with either the ball or the pump, but one thing about Jo is that she'll either do it herself or she'll go down trying.

"Couldn't sleep," she says, checking the pressure.

"Who needs sleep when there's basketball?" Cassidy says.

"Macaroni's cooking," Jo says, tilting her head inside.

"Hot dogs?" Cassidy asks.

"Once you cut them in," she says back, then, about the lodge: "Who for?"

"Lewis," Cassidy says. "You know—that guy. One I grew up with, got himself shot yesterday?"

"That how y'all do it up here, throw a sweat? This a Blackfeet wake or something?"

"Just a remembering. It was Gabe's idea."

"Gabe," Jo says, flat as it's possible to say a name.

"Also there's this kid," Cassidy adds.

Jo nods, meaning he doesn't need to take her through it again: Victor Yellow Tail's kid needing something traditional to maybe ground him, keep him from burning out on dope and 90 proof.

"Almost forgot," Cassidy says, "payday," pulling the cash up from his pocket enough to show some thick green.

"My man."

Soon enough Jo's involved trying to grease the bicycle pump's plunger, so Cassidy steps into the camper to cut hot dogs into the macaroni, cube some Velveeta in—smaller the better, so they'll melt. He walks a bowl out to her, spoon already in, the cheese thick enough that the spoon isn't even tapping into the side of the bowl.

"Needs ketchup," she says after her first bite.

They're sitting by the fire now, away from the smoke.

The dogs still haven't moved, know this lunch isn't for them. The horses are lined up against the fence, their jaws on the top rail, tails swishing like cats.

"We should run them guys tomorrow," Cassidy says about her paint and the sorrel. The mouse-colored gelding isn't broke enough yet, maybe never will be.

Jo looks over, waits until Cassidy's chewing a big bite before saying, "Aren't you not eating today or something?"

Cassidy chews, swallows, says like a question, "I did skip breakfast, yeah?"

"You never eat breakfast."

"But especially not today."

Jo shakes her head, spoons another bite in, says, "Where you gonna stash that drug-dealer roll?"

"The safe, I figure," Cassidy says, and as one they look over at the truck he dragged up a few months ago. It wasn't stealing, he assured Jo, it wasn't even salvaging—it was *his* truck. Just, he'd walked away from it for a few years. But it had been a good pony once upon a time, deserved to rust into the ground close to people instead of out by itself.

The safe he's talking about is a powder-black thermos he's got shoved up inside a rotted-out glasspack up under the truck, rotted out because when he'd pulled the engine forever ago, he'd left the headers mouth-up to all the rain and snow the sky could funnel down into them. The result is an exhaust system no one would ever try to spirit away, as it would crumble in their hands. Besides, anything worth stealing off that truck, making it work on some other truck, it was taken years ago.

And, an actual safe, tucked under the bed in the camper, or in a high cabinet, or hidden in some clever cutout? That would be exactly what anybody breaking in would key on, carry off to crack open in their buddy's shop. It's not like him and Jo can be at the trailer every hour of the day, and, way out and lonely like they are, the dogs and horses are no way keeping anybody from taking a pry bar to the flimsy door.

But no one would ever look in a trashy old glasspack barely hanging on under a truck with no engine, no wheels, only one vent window, its four drums up on cinder blocks. Already there's six hundred dollars in that thermos in large bills, and, smushed way down at the bottom under that green, a little medicine pouch with a secret ring in it, for Jo.

She struggles another apparently too-dry bite down and hands her bowl to Cassidy, says, "I'm gonna teach you good taste if it takes forever," and steps inside for the ketchup.

Forever, Cassidy repeats, liking that, spooning another bite in. It's not *that* dry.

The paint at the fence shakes her head from too many horse thoughts rattling around in there and Cassidy shakes his head just the same, trying to get a rise out of her. She's smart enough it works sometimes.

Not this time.

She's looking past Cassidy.

He turns, stands slow, dropping his bowl and Jo's both.

"Holy shit," he says, having to move side to side to stay standing, from the dogs rushing this spilled lunch.

He doesn't care about it anymore.

Spread out behind him, just down the slope from the camper, are probably eighty, ninety elk. Maybe a hundred.

They're all looking right back at him, not a single tail flicking, not one eye blinking.

Cassidy swallows hard, wishing more than anything for his rifle.

The name he was born with wasn't Cassidy Thinks Twice, even though that's what he's doing now—*Where's my gun, where's my gun?*—but Cassidy Sees Elk.

Names are stupid, though.

Pretty soon he won't even need his.

FOUR THE OLD WAY

Standing up at Ricky's grave behind the old lodge, sharing an after-lunch beer with him, tipping a bit out for Cheeto, too, what the hell, it's not giving alcohol to minors if the minor's in the ground, Gabe is still thinking about the basketball girl he saw not wearing a jacket, walking in the snow by the school.

What he's talked himself into is that it couldn't have been Denorah. Den's tight-laced like her mom, wouldn't be walking around with her hair just flying around her head like some Indian demon. And it had been school hours anyway, right? One rule about sports that Gabe's pretty sure still holds, it's that truancies mean you can't play. A one-for-one kind of system, each truancy keeping you on the bench for a game, even though there's so many more school days than there are games. It's what Gabe blames for never being the basketball star he's sure he could have been.

He shakes his head no again, that it couldn't have been her. That he's not a bad dad for not having stopped to get her warm, hike her up to wherever she was going. Just, what that means, he supposes, it's that she was some other baller, out in shorts in the cold. Meaning he's just not a good Indian.

But bullshit to that, too.

Gabe cashes his beer and hooks the neck of the bottle into one of the chicken-wire squares of the Boss Ribs family fence.

What if Den's having some big war with Trina, though, right? They are alike, Denorah's like a little clone of the girl Gabe knocked up fourteen years ago—fifteen, really—but that little clone, she's got some Cross Guns in her veins, too. What this means, Gabe knows, it's that she's going to reach an age where she'll want to take the world in her teeth and shake until she tears a hunk of something off for herself. And then, whether it's good or bad, whether it's a scholarship or a five-year bid in state or two kids in as many years, she'll sit in the corner by herself and chew it down, dare anybody to say this isn't exactly what she wanted.

She's going to be like him, he knows. She's got that in her. She didn't get that smile of hers from Trina, anyway. Gabe's seen it when she plays, in spite of the restraining order. The order's not about staying five hundred feet away from Denorah, or even from Trina, though he kind of self-imposes that one for purposes of self-preservation, it's about not coming to any more home basketball games. Because of boisterousness, which is just cheering. Because of fighting, which wasn't his fault. Because of public intoxication, which was only that one time.

With the right jacket and hat and sunglasses, though, he can still slip in with the visitors, so long as he doesn't draw attention to himself. He's pretty sure Victor, the tribal cop slipping him cash for the sweat tonight, has seen him over there all incognito, but Gabe keeps his hands in his pockets and he doesn't explode up out of his seat each time Denorah pulls a no-call, so Victor lets this sleeping dog lie.

It's not easy being quiet, though.

Denorah is a special player, that once-in-a-generation kind. Yeah, he's her dad, but everybody else says it, too, even that newspaper guy. She's got everything her big stepsister had, but Trace, she does it at college with all the basics she's had drilled in, which, as far as Gabe can tell, has pretty much stamped all the Indian out, left it on the practice gym floor.

Den's got those basics down pat, can walk that line in practice day after day just like her coach wants. When the game's down to it, though, when the buffalo chips are down, as Cass used to say when he was still just Cass, when two defenders are ganged up on this little Indian girl straight out of Browning, that's when she'll smile a smile that Gabe has to smile with her.

It's that hell-for-leather look, that come-at-me look, that let's-do-this look.

Instead of passing out of a double-team like she's been told to, what Den'll do is back off these two defenders, look from one to the other, and then get her dribble and her feet just out of sync enough to throw them off balance, giving her room to split them.

Second game of the season, she even threw the ball between a tall girl's legs and caught it before the second bounce, cut for the basket straight as any arrow ever let loose.

That was the game they had to escort Gabe out, disinvite him from the rest of the season. The reason he got kicked out was because her coach had benched her for showing off. For being Blackfeet. It was like—it was like what Gabe had read about in that one book. Those two Cheyenne from the old days who got caught by the cavalry, sentenced to death, but asked if they could die like they wanted.

Sure, the stupid Custers said.

The way those two Cheyenne wanted, it was to die on their horses, with all those soldiers shooting at them as they ran past.

Only, they did it once, and made it through all the bullets.

And then again.

Finally they had to walk slow, give those plowboy soldiers a chance.

That's what Coach had done to Den: made her slow down, when she was faster than any of them, fiercer than them all.

Gabe figures he should maybe slip through town on the way to Cass's, look D up, make sure everything's good, be sure that wasn't her out walking in the cold.

It's the day before their first scrimmage, isn't it? There's really one place she'll be.

"She's good, man," he says down to Ricky, cracking the top off a second beer, killing this one all at once, like old times.

He hooks it into the fence alongside the first one. They look like two bottles in the side of a hamster cage. One for him, one for Ricky.

Gabe opens a third, considers it, the white chill swirling up from that brown neck.

"So ask Lewis what the hell, if you see his ass," he says to Ricky, tipping the first swig out for him, for them, for all the dead Indians. But for Lewis first.

He wasn't the best of them, was maybe the stupidest of them, really, always with his nose in a book, but that didn't mean the staties needed to pop him like that.

But—Gabe squints his face up, tracks a cloud scudding along the treetops, the sky grey and forever behind it—but why would Lewis have been carrying a dead little elk around with him? At first Gabe knew he had to have heard it wrong, but then the paper confirmed it: when the truck Lewis's body had been in back of had wrecked, there'd for sure been an elk calf thrown in there beside him, because he'd been *carrying* it, and it might be some Indian evidence, or evidence of Indians, who knew.

Just, when the emergency responders piled onto the scene of the accident, they were interested in dead *people*, not dead animals that had probably been in the ditch already, as far as they knew. By the time they realized it was evidence, had come back for the calf, the coyotes had probably dragged it off, made themselves a fine meal.

Good for them.

It doesn't explain what Lewis had been doing with the calf in the first place, though.

The only thing Gabe has to sort of explain it is how sentimental or whatever Lewis had got over that skinny elk, that day they'd jumped that herd out in the elder section.

Lewis had known they were just sawing haunches off and running, but he'd insisted on taking all of her, even her head, which he'd just have to throw away in town anyway, right? He'd skinned her too, hadn't he, and carried that rolled-up wet hide under his arm like a football, like he was some Jim Thorpe wannabe? Like this really *was* some bullshit Thanksgiving Classic? Gabe nods, can see it again, Lewis struggling up that long hill, all the odds against him.

What he told them was that he needed her head because he wanted her brains, to tan that hide with. Like he knew anything about leather. Like that hide hadn't been thrown out years ago, like every other hide any of them had ever saved. Like she'd even *had* all her brains in her head at that point.

Good job, Lewis.

Gabe tips beer number three up to him and drinks it down, hooks it in the fence in line with the others. One bottle for Ricky, one for Lewis, and one for himself. They chime against each other once, then still.

He shakes another one up from the little cooler, for Cass, even though he's seeing Cass in a few, here. Four's too many for three-thirty in the afternoon, on zero food, but screw it. He'll sweat it all out come nightfall, and then some.

Was that what Lewis had actually been smuggling home, that old hide? Had Lewis made it down to the city with it, kept it frozen all this time, and had he been trying to bring it back to the reservation now? Did the cops just not know the difference between a thawed-out, ten-year-old skin and an elk calf? Had they shot him enough times that it was all guesswork?

But *why*?

Was Lewis going to hand-deliver it to Denny at the Game Office, say he'd done his penance, could he please please hunt on the reservation again?

You don't have to ask, though, Gabe tells Lewis. *You just have to not get caught.*

The last ten years of his ban, which he guesses is short for *banishment*, he's taken probably twice again as many elk as they popped that day. Well, enough that when he was stashing some of the meat in his dad's freezer in the garage a few months ago—it was that little one-horn that had still been in velvet—he'd had to make room by cleaning all the old stuff frozen to the walls of that freezer.

The reservation dogs had eaten well that night.

Gabe had watched them until they were done, paper and all, and then nodded once to them because they owed him now, didn't they?

They knew. They would remember.

"Tell me when trouble's coming for me," he'd said to them. "You'll know."

And then he'd laughed. Like now.

Gabe has to wait until he can wipe his smile away to drink the top off the fourth beer. He checks the time.

He's just waiting until he's sure where Denorah'll be. Who he'll call *Den* if he wants, and *D* if she's on defense, *Killer* if she's not.

He hooks the bottle in the fence alongside the others, just like it's the old days, the four of them always together, and leaves a drink sloshing in it for the dead Indian hamsters. Halfway to the truck he turns back to the grave, undoes the black bandanna from his arm, and ties it into the fence as well, like a prayer he doesn't know how to say with words. It's about Lewis, though. And Ricky. And how they all used to be.

Easing back down the logging road in first, just riding the transmission, he crunches the clutch and brake in, leans over the dash to be sure he's seeing what he's seeing.

He has to set the parking brake, get out to be sure.

Elk tracks in the snow. A big cow, just walking up the road like following him up to see Ricky, but a heavy cow, too. Gabe points his trigger finger down into the hoofprint and wonders if it's a small horse with elk feet, carrying a rider.

He stands, looks ahead for anything this ridiculous, but the road hooks back to the right almost immediately.

Still. This is a good sign, isn't it? Strong medicine, like Neesh used to say? The sweat's going to be good for the kid tonight. It's going to be good for all of them.

Gabe climbs back into the truck, eases down the two-track, has his eyes on the road enough that he doesn't catch the flash of black in the rearview mirror when a full-grown woman in a too-tight scrimmage jersey steps out of the trees, into the bed of the truck, her long black hair swirling in after her.

It's where hunters carry the animals they shoot, isn't it? It's where they put you, ten years ago. Don't smile too much about this, just work your way under the toolbox.

The night is almost here. It's the one you've been waiting for.

OLD INDIAN TRICKS

It's about form, yes, Coach is right about that, everybody knows that, but what Denorah's big sister taught her, forwarding and re-winding through hours of tape, is that it's also about using the exact same form every single time you step up to the stripe.

And that form, that ritual, it's not just the second and a half or two seconds of your free throw, either.

It starts with how you toe up to the line. For Denorah it's right foot first, right up to the paint, then backing off about a shoelace width because the point will get erased if your feet are illegal. If you're a good shooter that's not the end of anything, as you usually get a do-over in junior high, but if you missed and one of your tall girls hauled the rebound down, has position to slip it back in for an easy two, then, well, then you've screwed things up, haven't you?

So, out at the pad of concrete at the back of her family's two acres at the edge of town, where her new dad's rigged up some floodlights for summer, where she had to measure out and paint the charity stripe herself, Denorah shoots and shoots and shoots, never mind that she can see her breath in the cold.

Eighty-six out of one hundred, then seventy-nine, which gets her breathing hard and mad, then an even ninety.

Because the scrimmage this week is Saturday night—tomorrow night—and there's no practice the day before a game so everyone can have fresh legs and be mentally prepared, today is for free throws.

They've never been Denorah's weak point, but she's also never had a game where she swished every one. So there's room for improvement. Like with Trace, her whole future might come to rest on making one point the easy way, with the whole gym thundering and crumbling around her, the floor beneath her shoes trembling, sweat pouring into her eyes.

Coach never has them do free throws at the front of practice, but the back, so they'll know what it's like to make themselves have good form when they're exhausted, just want to fling the ball up there, say a prayer after it.

But Denorah needs fresh legs for tomorrow, so she's compensating by trying to get a cool five hundred shots in before dark. Or to get five hundred either way, whether she gets to slope down to the house for dinner or ends up shooting right through it again.

Toe up to the line with the right foot, back off a touch for safety, then work the left up until it's dead even with the right. Spin the ball back with the lines going from thumb to thumb and dribble twice, fast and hard with the right hand, using the whole shoulder, elbow straightening out each time. Catch it, look up to the rim, bend the knees, back straight, ass out, and push up with the front of the thighs, extend with the right arm, left hand just there to keep the rock steady, the calves pushing right at the end, when the middle finger of that right hand is gripping on to the rubber of the valve hole, imparting the perfect spin.

Swish, swish, swish.

The machine girl is on automatic, she's locked and loaded, doesn't even need to concentrate anymore. Fouling her in the act of shooting is the same as putting a pair of points up on the scoreboard for her team.

"Bring it," Denorah says, lining up again.

The only thing she regrets about basketball, that baseball and football and even golf have over it, it's that those players all get to wear war paint under their eyes.

What Coach tells them in the locker room before every game, it's that their war paint is on the *inside* of their faces, it's in how they hold their faces, it's in how they look the other girls in the eye and don't look away. Dribbling and passing and shooting are just the parts of the game that get recorded in the stats. There's also who wants it worse.

To steel herself against the kind of bullshit Indian teams always get hurled at them when the game's close, Denorah tries to inoculate herself with all the bullshit that the other side of the gym will be chanting.

> *It's a good day to die.*
> *I will fight no more forever.*
> *The only good Indian is a dead Indian.*
> *Kill the Indian, save the man.*
> *Bury the hatchet.*
> *Off the reservation.*
> *Indian go home.*
> *No Indians or dogs allowed.*

Her sister heard them all in her day, perverted on spirit ribbons, usually illustrated, too. Shoe-polished on the windows of buses, the big one was always, *Massacre the Indians!*

Bring it, Denorah says in her head, and drops another through the net. If the only good Indian is a dead one, then she's going to be the worst Indian ever.

Her promise to herself for tomorrow, win or lose, is to be back out here again right after the game, working on any shot she should have made but didn't.

They don't just give those scholarships away.

Denorah shags the rebound, jogs back to the line without stopping to spin, bank one in from the block. From what would be the block if she'd measured that out too, painted it.

Her dream is to somehow extend this pad of concrete, so there can be a three-point line.

Someday.

Not today.

Today it's just free throws.

Swish, *swish*, a sound in the grass behind her but she can't look, it's probably just Mom, home early from work, and . . . rattle, bounce, clunk.

Denorah starts to spin around to whoever made her miss but reminds herself at the last moment that *she* made herself miss, that *she* let her concentration flag, that *she* didn't follow through on the ritual.

"Hey, Finals Girl," an unhilarious male voice calls out from behind her, moments after a truck engine's been turned off.

Finals Girl.

It's what her real dad calls her when she's on the court, ever since she was his lucky charm when she was four and he was watching her in June, during the NBA finals.

She looks back with just her head.

He's sitting in his truck, window down, one arm patting the side of the door like it's a horse he's riding, not a pickup he's picked back through the grass with.

"The septic's there," Denorah says, nodding to the greasy grass by the scattered pipes he must have just driven on one side of or the other.

"That's why I got four-wheel drive," her dad says, pushing the shifter up into place. "The slop."

He's been drinking. She can tell from his eyes. They're loose in his head, too happy for this early in an afternoon.

"Just wanted to wish you luck for tomorrow," he says.

Denorah looks around for the ball, walks a beeline across to it.

"You're not supposed to be here," she says, and he's already cutting her off by rolling his hand, saying, "Your new and important dad doesn't think I'm a good influence, blah blah blah . . ."

Denorah toes up to the stripe, brings the left foot even, her back to him.

He won't get out of his truck. Not when he might be needing to make a hasty exit.

"You're going to kill them tomorrow night," he says. "We're doing a sweat tonight, to, you know. Like, help the team."

His talking is good, Denorah's telling herself. He's like a whole crowd chanting, *Indians go home.*

Just noise.

Swish.

"That's the ticket," he says, patting his door again in token applause.

"You and who's doing this sweat?" Denorah asks, chancing a look back to him while snabbing the ball from the tall grass.

"Cass," her dad says, then, "you want to keep a song in your head when you're shooting free throws, and always let go on the same beat. Old Indian trick."

It makes Denorah do two extra dribbles, trying to keep music from playing in her ears.

Clunk.

"It's okay, it's okay," her dad says.

Rebound, reset.

Was that nineteen out of twenty or nineteen out of twenty-one? Shit. Twenty-one, then. Losing count never counts in favor of.

"I think it's Cassidy now," Denorah says, just because.

"Little Miss Cross Guns," her dad says back, which is what he calls her when she sounds like her mom to him.

"I see his new snag at Glacier Family Foods sometimes," Denorah says, saying the store's whole name because she likes the way it sounds.

"What do you know about snagging?" her dad asks, not patting his truck now.

"She's in produce now," Denorah says, a grin he can't see warming her lips.

Swish.

"Probably a vegetarian, yeah?" her dad says with a smile in his voice, and that tells Denorah all she needs to know about how much Jolene the Crow appreciates her dad coming out to do sweats with her man.

"Didn't know he had a lodge out there," Denorah says.

Dribble, dribble, find the valve hole by touch. Right when she rocks back to shoot, her dad touches his horn. Still: *swish.*

"Good, good," he calls out.

Returning to the line for number twenty-three, she sees a black hank of your hair breeze up from the bed of the truck and it stops her for a moment, the ball held at her stomach.

Her dad sees, leans out to look back, says, "What?"

"You're not supposed to be hunting," Denorah says, no joke to her voice about this of all things.

"What, you an officially deputized game warden now?" he says, settling back behind the wheel, leaning over to get at something from the floorboard.

Whatever he gets doesn't raise above the level of the door, but Denorah's pretty sure it's cold and beer-shaped.

And? Maybe he's not even lying.

Elk and deer don't have manes. Maybe he's a horse hunter now, she thinks, and has to turn around to the rim so he won't see the smile in her eyes. Just because she can't see him doesn't mean she can't hear a beer cracking open.

Noise, noise. The whole gym going wild.

"This the same sweat Nathan Yellow Tail's dad's making him go to?" she says.

Rattle, rattle, lucky roll.

"We're letting him in, yeah," her dad says like a challenge. Like she should try to call him on his kindness, his manners, on who this sweat is actually for, Nathan or the scrimmage.

"Coach says she sees you at the games," Denorah says, walking to the tall grass for the ball.

No answer.

She looks back to him.

"You look more like your mom every day," her dad says.

Trina Trigo, the grass dancer champion from high school, was even on a powwow calendar from back then. Except Denorah isn't sure if this is a compliment or if she only looks like her mom when she's saying stuff her dad doesn't want to hear.

Line up, draw a bead on those eighteen inches of circular orange up there. Remember that the higher you arc the ball, the more circular that rim gets.

The ball is a touch over nine inches wide. That leaves all kinds of room to play with. All kinds of lucky bounces.

But proper form is where it all starts. More you practice, the luckier you end up.

The ritual, the ceremony.

Dribble-dribble, thighs, extend, spin with the valve hole, hold that follow-through, hold it, hold it . . .

Swish.

Denorah smiles, is the deadliest Indian on the whole reservation.

"Do it again, it's worth twenty," her dad says behind her, low like an invitation he doesn't want just everyone tuning in to.

She turns back to him and he's pushed up against the back of the seat to dig in his front pocket. At least until whatever it is that's cold and beer-shaped and chocked between his legs spills forward.

"You've got twenty?" Denorah says back to him.

"I will tonight," her dad says. "When Officer Yellow Tail pays me."

"So it's like that," she says.

"Gratuity," her dad says. "He's very gracious."

"Double it if I go ten for ten," Denorah says.

Her dad raises his eyebrows, says, "You are my Finals Girl, aren't you?"

She smiles her smile that she knows is his, that she can't do anything about, and dribbles twice, *banks* it in just for show.

"Somebody give the little lady some dice," her dad says.

It's not luck, though. It's skill. It's practice. It's proper form.

"That's one," Denorah says, and turns her back on her dad again, imagines a gym all around her, wall-to-wall white people, all chanting for her to go home, go home.

She spins the ball toward her, dribbles twice, and lines up.

THE SUN CAME DOWN

Cassidy stands from his lawn chair to watch Gabe rattle over the cattle guard. The dogs, tongues hanging long from chasing that herd of elk off, swarm his truck before he's even got the door open, maybe thinking he's bringing those elk back, that he has them all in the bed of his truck.

Dogs are stupid.

"Ho, ho!" Cassidy calls out to them, slapping his thigh.

Gabe kicks his door open to scatter them but they just keep bawling their fool heads off. He wades out holding a rifle above his head like that's what the dogs are after.

"Don't you feed them?" he asks above the din.

"They like *red* meat," Cassidy calls back, making his way over.

"They're scratching the other scratches, man," Gabe says, pushing in between the dogs and the bed of his truck.

"What you got back there?" Cassidy asks.

"Not dog food," Gabe says back. "Unless—they eating spare tires now?"

Before Cassidy can get close enough, Ladybear nips at Gabe's left hand. In response Gabe pops the forestock down across the bridge of her nose. Then he steps into her space, driving her back, his lips thin like this could get serious.

Ladybear whimpers, backs off, the other two following.

"Shit," he says, shaking his hand, opening his door back up to see it with the dome light.

Cassidy leans over to see. Gabe's bleeding from the meat of his left palm. Two neat, welling punctures.

"Got rabies now," Gabe says, wiping the blood onto the saddle-blanket seat cover. "What, they on JoJo's side now? She even got the dogs turned against my ass?"

"Watch out for the horses is all I'm saying," Cassidy says, and returns to the lawn chair. The fire's down to coals mostly.

Gabe steps in, hunkers down into the other chair still holding his hand, settles the rifle across the top of his legs.

"Those rocks working out?" he asks.

"They're rocks," Cassidy says.

"Got water for the sweat?" Gabe asks.

"In there," Cassidy says, pointing to the lodge with his chin. "Got the money?"

"About that," Gabe says.

Cassidy chuckles and shakes his head, turns the bottle of water up and drains as much as he can without drowning. He's not thirsty, but he will be.

"She here?" Gabe asks, tilting his head over at the camper, its windows dark in the gathering dusk.

"Work."

"I've never done one at night," Gabe says then, leaning back in Jo's chair, the chair not quite bending. Yet.

"A sweat?" Cassidy says.

"There's nothing, like, *against* doing it at night, is there?" Gabe asks.

"Let me check the big Indian rule book," Cassidy says. "Oh

yeah. You can't do anything, according to it. You've got to do everything just like it's been done for two hundred years."

"Two thousand."

They laugh together.

Cassidy fishes a dripping bottle of water up from the cooler and spirals it across the fire to Gabe. The droplets spinning off it hiss against the embers, send up tiny geysers of steam.

"So what do you know about this kid?" Cassidy says.

"Nate Yellow Tail? You know. Twenty years ago, he's you and me. He's Ricky and Lewis."

"Half of us are dead, yeah?"

"Either that or one of us here is already half dead," Gabe says, and slings a dollop of water across the heat at Cassidy, to show this isn't completely serious. That it is, but he wants to get away with having said it.

"Maybe it'll be good for him, I mean," Cassidy says. "Help him out, like."

"Arrows are straight, but they have to bend, too," Gabe says, his voice dialed down to Wooden Indian to deliver Neesh's old line. It's what the old man used to always end his group sessions on. There was even a series of posters all along one wall of the substance abuse office, an arrow looking all bowed out at the moment of the string's release, like it's going to crack, shatter, blow up. But it doesn't. It's bent out to the side in the first poster, it snaps back a foot or two from the riser of the bow in the second poster, and then in the rest it's snapping back and following through, bending the arrow the *other* way now, and until the last possible instant before the bull's-eye, it's flopping back and forth through the air like that, trying to find true.

That's how they were supposed to be. It's what they, at fifteen, were supposed to have been doing. They'd been fired into adolescence and were swerving to each side now like crazy, trying to find the straight and narrow. If they did? Bull's-eye, man. Happy days.

If they didn't?

There were examples under every awning in town, drinking from paper-bagged bottles. White crosses along the side of all the roads. Sad moms everywhere.

"He'll sweat it out," Cassidy says. "Sing it out."

"Wish we had a drum," Gabe says.

"I got some tapes."

"Screw tapes, man. This is for Lewis, too, yeah? But don't tell Victor-Vector."

"Maybe don't call him that," Cassidy says.

"It's not bad, is it?"

"For Lewis," Cassidy says, holding his water up in salute.

Gabe lifts his the same, says, "He always was a stupid ass, wasn't he?"

"Smarter than you," Cassidy says. "He got out of here."

"But then he tried to come back," Gabe says, drinking once and swallowing hard. "They didn't shoot him until he tried to come back."

"He was just running for home base," Cassidy says. "They'd have shot him if he'd stayed where he was just the same."

"Why you think he did it?" Gabe says. "His wife, that Flathead girl?"

"She was Crow, man."

"Serious?"

"He probably couldn't have told you even while he was doing it, yeah?" Cassidy says, studying the clarity of this bottled water.

"Still," Gabe says, draining his, dropping it into the fire. The plastic shrivels even before the label flares up.

"Great," Cassidy says. "Pollute the rocks we're going to be breathing."

"Like I can fail the Breathalyzer any harder?" Gabe says back.

"So what's with the antique?" Cassidy says about the rifle across Gabe's lap.

"Old man finally parted with it," Gabe says, holding it across to Cassidy, around the heat of the fire.

Cassidy racks the bolt back, clears it, studies the long goofy stock.

"Think it's for NBA players," Gabe says. "Forestock's long like that so they don't have to bend their arms too much."

"It shoot straight?" Cassidy asks, shouldering it, training it out into the darkness, one eye shut.

"Like anybody still has shells for something that old?" Gabe says. "He only shot bird shot and rock salt through it, yeah?"

"The Great Mouse War," Cassidy says, fake-pulling the trigger. "I bet I got something that'd work. You know when Ricky—I went out to Williston to get his stuff."

"Oh yeah. What'd he have?"

"Nothing. His dad said he was supposed to have all their rifles, but his shit'd been cleaned out a crew or two ago."

"Tighty-whities."

"All that was left of the rifles was a bag of random-ass shells. Think they're still in the glove compartment, probably, with whatever kid book Lewis was reading back then."

Gabe leans forward to see the old Chevy up on blocks.

"Good you put that pony out to pasture," he says. "She got stuck everywhere, man."

Cassidy sets the gun back against the trash barrel, away from the fire.

"I'm going to fix it up," he says. "Body's still good, mostly. Just need to find a hood, and a bed. Maybe some fenders, too. An engine, some tires."

"Still hide your shit in it for safekeeping?"

Cassidy breathes in, looks over to the eye shine of one of the horses, watching them, its big ears probably catching every word, saving them for later.

"Can't even keep the ground squirrels out of it," Cassidy says what he knows is a moment too late.

Gabe knows about the thermos? How can he?

"Got *just* the gun for taking care of rodents," Gabe says back, nodding across to the Mauser. "Take it instead of the cash, for this?"

"You really think it still shoots?" Cassidy says.

"No reason it wouldn't."

"Gimme a minute," Cassidy says. "I'm weighing you giving me something that's old and broke and stolen against you *being* too broke to ever pay me money you owe me."

"Ha, ha, ha, ha," Gabe says, his mouth open wide enough for a laugh this slow and fake. "You can sell it for a hundred fifty, I bet. Maybe more if it's historical."

"And when your dad comes looking for it?"

"Sell it to him, he wants it again. But he gave it to me free and clear, Scout's honor."

Gabe rabbit-ears his first two fingers up but then lowers the index, turns his hand around slow to flip Cassidy off at close range.

"Sure, leave it, whatever," Cassidy says.

"Only if it's cool with JoJo, man," Gabe says.

"She doesn't like it when you call her that," Cassidy says for the fiftieth time this month.

"It's like 'yo-yo,' but with *J*'s, man," Gabe says, and Cassidy isn't sure whether Gabe's calling Jo a toy or whether he's talking about joints. Either way, he flips him back off, *both* hands, which is when headlights wash across both of them like a snapshot.

SHIRTS AND SKINS

It's not the same car you rode to the reservation in yesterday, but it's the same dad, the same son.

The dad is standing from the open door of the car, his headlights still splashing white across Gabriel and Cassidy, their hands up to protect their eyes, their shadows blasting back across the big pile of moldy laundry behind them and then the horse pens and all the darkness past that, where you're standing, the tips of your long hair lifting from the hot air the car was pushing in front of it.

"We surrender, we surrender!" Gabriel calls out, trying to duck away from all that brightness.

The dad reaches down, turns the lights off, and while he's leaned down, his son shakes his head a bit in disgust, says, "So these clowns are tradish?"

"It's not about the sweat," his dad says, not really using his lips, just his voice.

It's not about the sweat, you repeat, trying to keep your face perfectly still like that. It almost works, except you're pretty sure your eyes are grinning.

The night's about to start.

"Then what *is* it about?" the boy asks.

The dad sits back down into the car, clicks the middle console open like he forgot something. "Look at these two jokers," he says, face tilted down. "They were you, twenty years ago."

Cassidy is shooting a spurt of water between his teeth at Gabriel, and Gabriel, trying to avoid it, is collapsing one side of his chair, and Cassidy is trying to save the chair from folding down on itself.

The boy has to chuckle.

"They're *alive*," he says.

"There used to be four of them," the dad says.

The boy pops his door open, hangs a leg out, swings his hair back over his left shoulder.

"All of us'll fit in that thing?" he says about the mound of sleeping bags the sweat lodge is.

"Just the three of you," his dad says. "I'm handling the rocks, that's my part of it."

"How long?"

"Long enough."

They stand together, their doors closing at the same time, an accident of sound that makes the boy straighten his back, like it's bad luck.

Gabriel is already pushing up from his broken chair to greet them. His face is shiny with water from Cassidy's mouth. "To Officer Victor goes the spoils . . ." he's saying, wiping at his cheek with his sleeve.

"What does that even mean?" the boy says to his dad.

"He read it in some bullshit book," Cassidy says from his chair. "Ignore his ass."

"Gentlemen," the dad says, shaking the hand Gabriel is offering.

"Victor-Vector sounds like a cop even when he's off duty, man," Gabriel says with a halfway smile.

"I'm never off duty," the dad says back, nodding down to the cop car he's driving.

The boy doesn't look to the car with Gabriel and Cassidy, but to the camper. All the windows are dark.

"How long since you've sweated it out yourself?" Gabriel is saying to the dad.

"This is for him, not me," the dad says, and all eyes settle on the boy. "Nathan," he announces, the big introduction.

The boy keeps looking at the camper, like considering how to take it apart. Or—he can't see your reflection in a window, can he? Just your shape, your silhouette, your shadow? Your true face?

If the boy were to tilt his chin out at you for his dad right now, this instant, and if his dad leaned forward, peered through the darkness at the wild-haired woman just past the light, then this could all be over in a rush, couldn't it?

But it's better nobody sees you. Yet.

The boy finally drags his eyes away from the camper.

"You play basketball, yeah?" Cassidy says to him, about the scrimmage jersey the boy's wearing black side out.

"I played ball, I'd be skins," the boy says.

"Got a little court right over there," Cassidy says, hooking his chin to the left of the camper, back toward the road. "Maybe we could shoot to cool down later."

"Got glow-in-the-dark balls?" the boy asks right back.

"Son," his dad says.

"They call you Nate, right?" Gabriel says.

The boy shrugs one shoulder, says, "Gabe, *right*? Seen you around."

Gabriel purses his lips about this for a fraction of an instant.

"You drug him back from Shelby or what?" Cassidy says to the dad.

"Farther than we ever got," Gabriel says, making a show of turning to finally see what the boy had been staring at so hard. "He ever done a sweat?" he asks the dad, no eye contact.

"You can talk to me," the boy says.

"*You* ever done this?" Gabriel says, making a production of talking *to* the boy.

The boy shrugs.

Gabriel says, "The idea is it's a purification, like. Consider it a dishwasher, yeah? We're the dishes. It steams us up spick-and-span, man."

"That what your friend Lewis and Clark was coming back for?" the boy says. "Clean the spots off his soul?"

Gabriel smiles a tolerant smile, looks back to Cassidy, who wows his eyes out like what did they expect?

"This is about you," the dad says. "Not all that. Got it?"

The boy stares across the dying fire at the paint horse.

"Y'all know Lewis was coming this way, though?" the dad says to Gabriel and Cassidy.

"Never off duty . . ." Gabriel singsongs, just generally. "Always trying to solve some crime, put another Indian behind bars."

"Lewis left, he was a ghost," Cassidy says.

"White woman," Gabe adds, all the explanation necessary.

"And one postal worker," the dad adds, looking around the place. "She was Crow, wasn't she? Saw her picture in the paper. Bet the wife caught him creeping across to her tipi."

"Lewis wouldn't," Cassidy says.

"Wouldn't what?" the boy says. "Cheat on his wife, or kill two people?"

Gabriel touches a place on the side of his face, by his eye.

The dad's still looking around.

"Where's your dogs, Cass?" he finally says.

Cassidy looks around like just missing them.

"Cass's dogs, they're the criminal sort, I guess," Gabriel says, unbuttoning his cowboy shirt. "They see tribal PD, *pew*, they're gone for the hills, man. Anybody with a badge, I mean. Even that way with game wardens, right? They can't tell Denny Pease from PD. Stupid dogs."

Cassidy stands, is unbuttoning his shirt now as well.

"You haven't eaten today?" he says to the boy, the cadence of his words old and Indian, and mostly fake.

"Just water," his dad says for his son.

"Same," Gabriel says.

Cassidy nods that him, too, yeah.

"ESPN's on at eleven, yeah?" the boy says to his dad.

"It's on again at two," his dad says back.

"Speaking of numbers . . ." Gabriel says, squinting like it's painful to have to be bringing this up.

The dad passes him five bills. Cassidy tracks this money into the pocket of Gabriel's jeans, off and folded on the arm of the chair.

"You ever wonder where the term buck-naked comes from?" Gabriel says, down to his saggy boxers.

"Listen close," Cassidy warns, stepping out of his boots, "you're about to hear some good lies."

"Settlers moving into Indian territory used to call us *bucks*, back when," Gabriel says with authority, looking around for what to lean on while he one-legs it out of his boxers. "Because we were always horny, I guess, right? They could tell we were because we were naked, since Levi's hadn't been invented yet. So, you know, them Indians coming in to the trading post, *They're all naked again, Jim, what are we going to do? Look, look, hide the women, those bucks are naked, man, they're* buck-naked . . ."

"Told you," Cassidy says, folding his pants over the back of his chair.

"Isn't there usually singing or a drum or something?" the dad says, studying the mound the lodge is.

"Doesn't have to be," Gabriel says, balling his boxers up in his hands, being sure they're touching every last one of his fingers, the boy notes with distaste.

"I've got some tapes," Cassidy says, making like to go over to his camper.

"Don't worry about it," the dad says.

"It's just—" Cassidy says, but this dad does his right hand flat, palm down, and moves it from left to right, cutting this idea off. It's a hand signal the boy—you can smell it on him, can see it on his face—remembers from a picture book in elementary: how the old-time Blackfeet used to talk with sign language when they needed to.

He hates being from here. He loves it, but he also hates it so much.

"Just send him in when he's ready," Gabriel, naked, standing there like a dare, says to the dad, and holds the flap of the sweat lodge open for Cassidy to duck in. "Cool?"

The dad nods a curt nod and an ass flash later Gabriel is in the lodge as well, the Army coat flapping shut behind him.

"You're serious about this, really?" the boy says to his dad.

"He always has a bunch of dogs out here . . ." the dad says back like a question, shining his flashlight all around, holding it at his shoulder exactly like the cop he can't stop being even for one night.

The boy leans back against the car and peels out of the scrimmage jersey all at once, turning it inside out in the process, so it's shiny white now. He folds it neatly over his arm, all the same, like turning it inside out had been just what he wantd to do. The air prickles his skin. He rubs his arms with his hands, hisses air out through his clenched teeth.

"That horse is watching me," he says.

"Sounds like it's you watching the horse," his dad says back, still studying the night for the chance of dogs.

"So what am I supposed to do in there?"

"Figure it out."

"It's bullshit, you know."

"When I was fourteen I knew everything, too."

The boy shakes his head, kicks his shoes off, is already counting the seconds of this night.

THREE LITTLE INDIANS

"This lodge is *dank*, Nate," Gabe says when the shape of Nate finally darkens the flap. He's been saving that line special for the kid, just so he can hate on it. It's good to give them focus.

"It's Nathan," the kid says, settling in on the missing point of the triangle, the chipped-out little pit between them already disappearing in the darkness again now that the flap's shutting. Evidently Victor was holding it up for his son to enter. Probably making sure Gabe wasn't making it *actually* dank in here. It's a sweat lodge, not a human-sized bong.

"Welcome," Cass says, still playing the ancient Indian.

Gabe hits him in the chest with the back of his hand.

"First time I did this, I wore a swimsuit," Gabe says, trying to dial them all up to today instead of a hundred years ago.

"Thought it was supposed to be all hot in here or something," Nate says.

"You ready?" Cass asks.

"We can't see you nodding, man," Gabe says. "I mean, if you're nodding."

"Ready, yeah," Nate says.

"And this isn't some toughest-Indian-in-the-world thing," Cass says. "You're supposed to get hot, but not hot enough to pass out."

"Well, that's where the visions are," Gabe says. "But whatever."

"Think I'll be all right."

"You'll think this is stupid, me saying it now," Gabe says. "But the cool air, it'll be down near the ground. If you need a good breath."

"And it's about praying, too," Cass says. "Talking to whoever you need to talk to, all that."

"With my dad listening right outside," Nate says.

"Too many sleeping bags," Cass says. "This is just us in here."

"We'll be talking to a couple of our friends," Gabe says. "Just so you know."

"Which one?" Nate says. "The killer one, or the one who got killed?"

Gabe licks his lips, looks down into the darkness of his lap. It's just the same as the darkness everywhere else.

"When we were your age, doing these," he says. "Our . . . our counselor, this old dude, Neesh—"

"That's his granddad," Cass cuts in.

"You're nodding at Nate, I take it?" Gabe says.

"Nathan," Nate says.

"Neesh Yellow Tail was his granddad, yeah," Cass says.

"No shit?"

"No shit," Nate says.

"Anyway," Gabe says. "Neesh, Granddad, whatever, he told us that none of the old stories are ever about a war party attacking a sweat that's happening. That it wouldn't just be bad manners to do that, it would be the worst manners. You don't even jump somebody when they're done, are all staggering out, weak and pure and shit. It's a holy place, like. It means right here where we are, it's about the safest place in the Indian world."

Nate snickers, says, "Safest place in the *Indian* world? That means we're only eighty percent probably going to die here, not ninety percent?"

"Nobody ever dies in a sweat," Cass says. "Not even the elders. I've never heard of it, anyway."

"This where we eat the mushrooms?"

Gabe drops his head back to smile up into the idea of the domed roof muffling their voices, says, "Different tribe, man."

"Unless you ordered pizza," Cass chimes in, finally joining this century.

"I can do that?"

"After, sure," Gabe says. "I like meat lover's. That's real Indian pizza."

"Nobody says 'Indian' anymore," Nate says, voice somewhere between insult and disappointment.

Gabe closes his eyes, lilts out, "*One little, two little, three little Natives,*" lets it fall dead between them all, then says: "Doesn't really sound right, does it?"

"We grew up being Indian," Cass says, something about his delivery making it sound like his arms are crossed. "*Native*'s for you young bucks."

"And *indigenous* and *aboriginal* and—" Gabe says.

"This part of it?" Nate cuts in. "I supposed to be getting all sweaty from this history lesson?"

"You didn't wear deodorant, did you?" Cass says, not missing a beat.

Silence.

"Does that matter?" Gabe finally asks, kind of quieter.

Cass calls out a deep *ho* to Victor.

"We have to be sure to thank him each time he brings a rock in," Gabe says, back to normal volume. "Otherwise—this is what your granddad told us—otherwise, feeling all unappreciated, he might deliver a warmed-up buffalo patty in for us to pour water on, breathe into our lungs."

"Bullshit," Nate says.

"Exactly," Gabe says right back.

"Here," Cass says, reaching behind Gabe for . . . ah: the ceremonial golf club. Of course. He uses it to guide the flap open enough for Victor to step one leg in. A cool sigh of night air breezes in as well.

"Careful," Victor says, making sure his path is clear. When it is, he angles the shovel in. Balanced in it is a rock so hot there's lava worms crawling all over it.

"Thank you, firekeeper," Gabe over-enunciates.

In the splash of light coming in, Nate, pushed back from the pit, nods a quick thanks as well.

Victor rotates the shovel handle, spilling the rock into the pit, along with the embers and ashes he'd scooped up. A vortex of sparks trails up into the domed ceiling.

"Did you wet the sleeping bags and stuff?" Gabe leans over to ask Cass.

"It'd smell like dog if I did," Cass whispers back.

Gabe nods, checks the fabric all around them again.

"Does dog hair burn?" he says, just out loud.

"Thank you," Cass says up to Victor.

"Another coming," Victor says.

When the hot rocks are in the pit—there's room for maybe three more, total—and the flap's closed, their faces all underlit dull red, Gabe looks across to Nate, says, "Last chance, man."

Nate shakes his head no.

Cass reaches back, slides the cooler alongside. The dipper is an aluminum scoop, like for feed. Cass does a humming up and up then down again drumbeat in his chest, and Gabe gets the lope of it, falls in. When they were the kid's age, they always called drum circles circle jerks. And now here they are, carrying the beat.

Gabe shakes his head, amazed at it all, and ramps up his humming drumbeat, smiles a smile he can't help. There's five twenties in the right front pocket of his pants on the chair out there, and at least three of them are his—would be eighty dollars, but Denorah can shoot the hell out of free throws, can't she?

"Here we go," Cass says, breaking his own drumbeat for a moment, and scoops a dollop of water onto the two hot rocks.

The steam hisses up, boiling the air.

Gabe chances a look across at Nate, and for the first time there's a hint of uncertainty in the kid's eyes, and for an accidental flash Gabe is seeing himself in the side mirror of his truck, when D asked if he was hunting again, and he thought he saw black hair behind his reflection, lifting up from the bed of his truck.

Except that couldn't have been. And the dogs weren't smelling anything back there, either. They're just stupid dogs.

Gabe breathes the heat in deep and holds it, holds it, eyes shut.

DEATH, TOO, FOR THE YELLOW TAIL

Victor plants the shovel into the ground by the fire after the next rock delivery—it takes two stabs to make sure it'll stand—then crosses to his car. Not to lean back against the fender until called again, but to settle down into the front seat, key the dashboard alive. He leans down to it, into it, comes up with a cassette tape. He holds it to the dome light to squint at, then flips it over to the side he wants, pushes it in.

Drumbeats well up from inside the car. Drumbeats and singing. It's been hot enough in the lodge for the last half hour that there hasn't been any singing, any talking, any anything. The last time he leaned in through that flap, he looked from face to sweaty face, gauging each of them in turn, then nodded, turned the shovel over, let the green jacket flop down.

Maybe it's working? Maybe this will have been a good thing?

Now he's looking at the green lights of the dashboard, is unhooking a handset from under the dash and clicking the connection open.

A crackling silence erupts from the top of the car, from a speaker up there. It's a loud nothing, full of emptiness and distance. Victor thumbs the sound away, pushes enough buttons or switches that the drumming and singing finally pour out of the top of that car all at once, making him flinch back from the suddenness. The sound swells, fills the night.

Inside the lodge one of them yips twice in celebration of this sound.

Victor nods with this, likes it.

He goes back to the fire, stirs it with the shovel, and notes the sparks drifting over to his son's scrimmage jersey. He saves it from the hundred airborne embers, folds it onto the broken chair set up by the lodge like an end table, so Nathan can find it first thing when he's done. Then he stirs the fire, watches the sparks spiral and climb even higher, like an invisible chimney, and then he leans the shovel against the trash barrel so he can inspect the rifle.

After making sure it's not loaded, he runs the bolt back and forth twice, swings it out like tracking something, and, of all the places in the night he could have pointed that barrel, he points it right at you, your head still turned to the side, your eye on the right side rolling back down that rifle at him.

Without even thinking about it—this is what you *do* when in a hunter's sights—you pull away.

Still, he sees . . . not you, but the motion of you. The idea of *some*thing.

He lowers the gun, stares out into the night.

"Jolene?" he calls out. "That you, girl?"

When you don't answer he flattens his lips and cuts a sharp whistle, slapping the leg of his jeans twice.

You're no dog, either.

Also: There are no dogs. Not anymore.

He settles the rifle back down into its place, watching the darkness the whole while. Moving mostly by feel, he pulls up three splits of wood from the pile, works them into the embers. Moments later one of them spurts a lick of flame up, and then all three are burning bright and orange and hot.

Victor stands in front of the fire, the dark silhouette of a hunter, still watching the darkness, the rifle in his hands again like a reflex, held crosswise down low.

From the lodge there's another *ho*, this one from Nathan—the first time he's been the one calling for more heat.

Victor considers the darkness, then finally turns away, trades the rifle for the shovel, and guides its blade under the burning logs, lifting a rock up and out. He shakes the shovel, ash and embers trailing off, and runs his gloved left hand up the handle, walks sideways to the lodge.

He taps at the door with his hip and it lifts up on a shiny silver strut, stays lifted.

Inside are three wet faces, each of them already spent. He deposits this next load of glowing rocks and just has his shovel clear of the lodge when one of the horses whinnies straight out of the heart of nowhere. Victor jerks hard enough to have dropped a burning rock if he'd still had any, but it's just a stupid horse.

Still Victor studies the night all around him, his eyes scanning and panning, trying to pick a shape out.

If he was smart, if he was listening to the horses, he'd already be gone.

You wouldn't leave, though, would you? You couldn't.

You stand over your calf until you can't stand, and then you try to fall such that your body can shield it. And then you come back ten years later and stand just outside the firelight, your soft hands opening and closing beside your legs, your eyes hardly blinking.

He can no more leave his calf than you could.

And now he's standing from his car a second time. With a beam of light to stab around.

You flatten against the ground, let that heat raze across your back.

But still, he knows. The way you can tell is the smell of the pistol at his hip. Its oily sick taste is in his hand now.

"Come on out!" he calls, his words rolling into the darkness, turning back to nothing.

The horses tell him about you some more, their warnings so clear, so urgent, so simple and articulate.

He had his chance, right? This is on him. He shouldn't have come out here.

Now his beam of light is disappearing behind the camper in hitches: walk two steps, shine the light all around, then jerk forward again, repeat.

When he's around the corner you can finally step out into the flickering light from the fire. The white and brown horse, the most articulate of the three, stamps her feet, shakes her head back and forth.

You shake your head just the same back at her.

The two you want are just right there, in the lodge three steps away, naked and helpless. Gabriel Cross Guns, Cassidy Sees Elk. The only two left from that day in the snow.

But you don't want to get shot in the back again, either. You can still feel the pain from last time, don't need this dad to blow that hole open all over again before you're finished.

When he walks around the side of the camper, you follow, right in the scent-path still swirling in the air so clear you could close your eyes and not lose him. You know to stay far from the camper, though, so he can't pin you there in a sudden pool of yellow. A camper isn't a train screaming past, trapping you, but it might as well be.

When he edges up to the outhouse he's so sure you're behind, your leg muscles bunch so you can—

He brings the light around, freezes you in its glare, your mind losing itself in that brightness.

"What—*who*?" he says, running his pistol back into its holster at his waist. "You trying to give me a heart attack, Jolene?"

It's her shirt and pants you've stolen off the line.

"Jolene," you say, your voice creaky because your throat is new. You start to clear it but there's a sound intruding on this moment. You both look over to the road.

A truck grinding up the road?

"Wait, you're not—" Victor says, then leans in to see better. "You're that Crow from the newspaper, aren't you?" he says. "The one who . . . who—?" Then he's raising the fingertips of his left hand to his right forehead, to show what he's saying: "But what happened to your eye?"

I got shot there, you don't tell him. *Twice.*

He takes a step back all the same, says, "I thought you—that Lewis ki—didn't he . . . What are you doing up here?"

In answer, you bring your face back around to him, eyes wild, hair lifting all around, and say, "*This*," then rush forward, show him.

METAL AS HELL

Cassidy should have done this years ago. Sweats should be a regular thing. Just like Neesh told them back when, he guesses.

Back then, though, this would have been just one more thing to sit through, one more thing between the four of them and the weekend. A sweat was never a ritual, was always just an ordeal.

Cassidy nods to himself that, yes, he's going to keep this sweat lodge going, maybe even dial it back from sleeping bags to layers of actual hide. And maybe he'll petition Denny for hunting privileges again, right? Why not? Denny's settled down and married these days, is at all the basketball games, even. And, ten years has *got* to be enough punishment for nine elk. It's been a clean ten years, too. Well, come tomorrow it'll have been a clean ten years. Cassidy has hardly even shot any animals, just a mulie or three out on the flats, that one moose that was asking for it, and the odd whitetail. But that's more like herd management, he figures. Herd management and subsistence—that's his right as a tribal member, isn't it? How can slipping back into an elder section one time take that all away?

And if Denny says no, then, well. Once Cassidy and Jo are legal, she'll have hunting privileges, he's pretty sure. Or, if not from marrying in, then he's pretty sure she can transfer her Crow hunting stuff up here, if she gives it up back home. Then, as long as she's in the field with her tag whenever Cassidy pops an elk or whatever, Denny won't be able to say a thing. Or maybe she'll line up on a big bull herself.

Beside him, Gabe scooches back from the heat the rocks are throwing, shields his face for a moment with his forearm.

All you ever want this deep into a sweat, it's a bit of reprieve. But you've got to push *through* that.

"Good?" Cassidy says across to Nathan.

Nathan's sitting with his knees up, his head hanging down.

He sort of nods. Either that or a sluggish death rattle. A last spasm.

Cassidy angles the cooler up onto a corner and lays the scoop down flat, its nose in that corner, then tilts the cooler back the other way to get at the last bit of water.

"For Ricky," he says, tipping a sip out onto the ground before taking a drink himself. It's as hot as ten-minute-old coffee by now.

He offers it to Gabe, who takes it like each time, says, "For Lewis," spilling a bit out, but passes it on around without drinking. Because, he said early on, isn't that the dog food scoop?

Horses, Cassidy hadn't corrected. And just oats at that, because Jo's paint was raised to expect more than hay or cake. But Gabe doesn't really know horses, doesn't really know how inert oats are, that this scoop is probably as clean as any spoon at the diner in town.

Nathan takes the scoop, his hand trembling, his hair plastered to his face.

"For Tre," he says, a little water shaking out.

It's the first words he's volunteered in nearly an hour, by Cassidy's reckoning.

The kid's coming around. Breaking down. Playing along.

Good.

Tre is the high schooler the wake was for a couple of weeks ago—which, now that Cassidy thinks about it, is probably about when Nathan split town, ran away into the wilds of America. He only made it to some skunky trailer on the other side of Shelby, but that counts.

Tre, Tre, Tre. The wake was the first time Cassidy knew that was the way that name was spelled. He'd always assumed it had four letters, like what you carry food on in a cafeteria.

How had he died, even? Cassidy can't dredge it up, not with the heat turning his thoughts to syrup. Was he Grease's nephew, maybe? But that can't be right, Grease isn't old enough. Georgie, then? Somebody who was a senior when Cassidy was a freshman.

"Kill it," Gabe says to Nathan about the last of the water, and, after confirming with Cassidy—just eyes, no energy to spare—Nathan tips the scoop up, cashes it, holds it back across.

Cassidy takes it. Good thing about aluminum is it doesn't heat up in a sweat. What'd they use in the old days, wood? Horn? A bladder? The skullcap of a wolverine, because the old days were metal as hell?

Doesn't matter. This isn't the old days. Exhibit one establishing that: outside the lodge, Victor's tape goes silent, to the end of itself again, and then there's a few seconds of silence while the deck looks for the first song on the other side again.

"This one again?" Gabe musters the breath to say, because he thinks he's hilarious.

"Try going on a trip with him," Nathan says back, his chest shaking twice with what Cassidy thinks is a weak attempt at laughter. The weakest attempt at laughter.

Gabe is having to waver to stay sitting upright. But he can do it until sunup, too, Cassidy knows. Of the four of them, Gabe would always be the one still sitting on the toolbox in the bed of the truck after everybody else had slouched over, passed out. It was like he was waiting for something. Like he knew that if he gave in, shut his eyes, he was going to miss it, was going to get left behind.

Of the four of them—and Cassidy hates to say it—of the four of them, Gabe's the least likely to still be aboveground, too. He's always been the first to jump, whether it's off a cliff into some big water or into the face of some cowboy outside a bar.

"Like this," he's telling Nathan now, lowering his own mouth right almost to the ground and sucking air in, making a show of swelling his chest out because the air down there is so much cooler, so refreshing.

"Where a hundred asses have sat," Nathan's saying back.

"Don't forget the dog piss," Gabe says, just giving in and lying on down.

Cassidy smiles, greys out for a second, maybe two.

This is for Lewis, he's telling himself. Lewis, who was trying to come home.

It's funny, almost: Lewis runs for home, dies on the way. Ricky runs *away* from home, dies on the way. Gabe and himself stay right here, are perfectly fine.

"Hey," Cassidy says down to Gabe.

"Just resting my eyes," Gabe mumbles back.

Nathan lowers his face again, his long hair a wet curtain, the rest of him mostly a silhouette in the ashy, humid darkness.

"About Lewis," Cassidy says.

Gabe gets an arm under himself, cranks up to a sitting position, dirt sticking all to one side of him because he's so sweaty, and because the ground is thawing under them.

"We really out of water?" he asks.

"They said he had an elk calf with him, right?" Cassidy says.

Gabe fixes his unsteady eyes on Nathan, but Nathan's just still. Either not listening or listening and not caring.

"Serious," Gabe says, about Victor's tape. "I like drums as much as the next red-blooded, red-skinned, beer-drinking—"

"He was carrying an *elk* calf home," Cassidy insists.

"Wrong season," Gabe says, waving this off. "Must have been *slow* elk."

"Wrong for them, too," Cassidy says.

"Horse."

"You don't run with a foal. It's too heavy."

Gabe repositions himself, but even the air is hot.

"I never told you," Cassidy says.

Gabe stills, looks to Nathan again, then back to Cassidy.

"That last hunt," Cassidy says. "Thanksgiving Classic or whatever Ricky called it."

"Thought that was *me*," Gabe says.

"That little heifer elk Lewis shot," Cassidy goes on. "She had one in the oven."

"I thought I shot her . . ." Gabe says.

"Your brain's melted," Nathan tells him.

Gabe shrugs like the kid's right, says to Cassidy, "It was—it was Thanksgiving, man. Maybe that little elk just had a turkey in the oven, yeah?" He pats his own belly to show what oven he's trying to mean.

"It was the Saturday before Thanksgiving," Cassidy corrects.

"Tomorrow," Gabe says with a goofy grin, looking down to the watch he's not wearing and also doesn't wear, and wouldn't be wearing in a sweat anyway.

"Lewis *buried* it," Cassidy says. "That—that unborn calf, whatever."

This silences Gabe.

"This is that same scrawny pre-cow he made us drag all the way up the hill?" he finally says. "The one got us caught by Denny the man?"

"We were getting busted anyway."

"This is when y'all shot up that herd?" Nathan asks.

Cassidy and Gabe both look over to him.

"Denorah told me," he says, like challenged to answer.

"You told her?" Cassidy says to Gabe.

"Who *else* that was there might have told her?" Gabe says right back, then does his lips like he's going to spit onto the rocks but can't muster any spit, so ends up just leaning over like a drunk old man telling important secrets to the ground.

"Oh yeah," Cassidy says.

Denny. Denny Pease. Of course he would have told Denorah this story by now. Anything to make Gabe look worse than he already does.

"What are you saying?" Gabe says then to Cassidy, picking the idea of that elk calf back up. "That Lewis was all messed up? That all those elf books finally caught fire in his brain, made him kill two women and run around with an elk baby until the soldiers shot him down?"

"It wasn't the books," Cassidy says.

"Elves?" Nathan says, watching the two of them now.

"Breathe, breathe, you're hearing things," Gabe says.

"How much longer?" Nathan asks.

"You cured yet?" Gabe asks back.

"Of what?" Nathan says. "Being Indian?"

Gabe chuckles without really smiling, which is a sound Cassidy knows. He puts his fingertips to Gabe's chest to keep him there, says across to Nathan, "You can leave whenever you want, man."

"Once you've been *purified*," Gabe adds unhelpfully, and then leans over to cough a lung up. Maybe two.

After nearly a minute of it, Nathan says to Cassidy, "He going to be all right?"

Cassidy studies Gabe, on his hands and knees now, nearly puking.

"One way or the other," he says.

Nathan shakes his head in amusement.

"My dad says he's busted him he doesn't know how many times," he says.

"White man's laws," Cassidy says. "Getting picked up, that just proves he's Indian."

"He says he busted you, too."

"Your dad's a good cop, mostly," Cassidy says. "Just messes up sometimes."

After a second or two, a grin crosses Nathan's face.

"He's standing out there like a cigar store Indian or something," he says.

"He called in sick on a Friday night for this," Cassidy says. "Because of being here, he's going to have to work shit detail for the next month, probably. He's doing this for you, man."

"He doesn't have to."

"Tell him."

"He doesn't understand anything."

"He was the first one into the Dickey house after that—Tina, with the gun?" Cassidy says, wincing from having to remember that. "He's scraped so many kids up off the asphalt he could probably write the manual for how to do it best so they stay in one piece. He's had to carry stoned babies to grandmothers and he's had to walk out into the grass to find other grandmothers. Some of the drunks he shakes awake in the morning, they're stiff, and he remembers them from second-grade homeroom. His first week, he was the rookie cop they made drag Junior Big Plume in from the shallows, when his face was all . . . he sent my brother Arthur to prison, how about that? He doesn't want you to end up there, too."

"I'm not like him and Granddad," Nathan is already saying, his lower lip trembling hard enough he has to bite it in.

"He'll stand out there and keep that fire going for you for as long as you need. That's all I'm saying. Not every Indian dad's like that. You got one of the good ones, man."

"It'll turn into an old-time Indian story," Gabe chimes in, his voice weak and spent from the coughing. He plants a hand on Cassidy's shoulder to pull himself upright again. "It'll—it'll be the story of the dad who stands outside the lodge for seven days, having to go farther and farther out for wood to keep the fire going, and then he asks the beavers to bring him some, meaning he'll owe them a favor, and then when the fire almost dies out once, he needs some kindling, so he has to—has to call a *hawk* down to deliver him some dried moss, so he's going to owe him something, too, then, then it's something with a muskrat, then, then . . ." but he loses it to coughing again.

Cassidy shrugs to Nathan like, *Yeah, that.*

"Aren't we supposed to be singing and praying and all that?" Nathan says, looking from Cassidy to Gabe.

"We are," Cassidy says.

After that they all stare into the glowing rocks.

"We need more water," Gabe finally says. "Maybe if we had, like, water guns in here, right? Old-time Indians never thought of that, I bet."

He finger-shoots imaginary streams of cool, cool water at Cassidy, at Nathan, then into his own mouth, just drinking it up.

"You could have drank some from the cooler," Cassidy tells him.

"Got . . . standards," Gabe says.

"I'll ask my dad," Nathan says—any chance for escape—which is right when the flap pushes in the way it does when Victor is nudging it. Except, no Victor. Are the dogs back, then?

"Here," Gabe says to Cassidy, and hauls the cooler into his lap.

Gabe lies back for the sacred golf club, aims it for the flap, and pushes.

Outside, instead of Victor's thick legs, it's a woman's long, very nice ones.

Nathan, naked and fourteen, pushes back into the darkness with his heels.

"Holy shit," Gabe says to Nate, impressed. "You really order pizza?" Then, to Cassidy, "Town Pump delivers out this far? Also, Town Pump *delivers*?"

"I got this," Cassidy says, and sets the cooler to the side, stands up through the flap.

"How's it going in there?" Jo asks.

"Hot," Cassidy says, riffling his hair with his hand and looking down his front side. "Pretty naked, too, I guess."

Jo cringes back from the droplets of sweat Cassidy's hand is spraying from his head.

He stops, looks at his hand. It's still wet, like the whole rest of him. Then he looks past his hand. Usually if he's sweaty, the dogs are using him like a Popsicle. In this chill, though, the sweat won't be sweat for long. Couple minutes and it'll be pneumonia.

"See Victor when you pulled up?" he asks, looking around.

Jo turns to the darkness all around with him, says, "Thanks for bringing my clothes in."

Cassidy considers this, can't get it to track. Maybe he's that great a boyfriend, and he just forgot?

"Everything good at the store?" he asks, meaning: *Why are you here when you're supposed to be there?*

Jo gulps a swallow down, gathers her words in her mouth, is about to say whatever it is when Gabe calls a weak *Ho!* out from inside the lodge.

Cassidy keeps watching her face.

"This isn't your fault," she says at last. "I want to be clear on that. But—I called home on break, yeah?"

Cassidy nods, knows that that's when she talks to her sister, because no one watches the break room phone.

"You know your friend who . . . who got shot?"

"Which one?"

"Out by Shelby. Yesterday."

"Lewis."

"He killed his wife and that woman he worked with?"

Cassidy nods, not much liking this lead-up.

Jo hooks her right elbow into her left palm so she can hold her hand over her mouth, look away again. "That was—that one he worked with at the post office, I guess, she was my cousin Shaney. Shaney Holds. My sister just found out."

"Oh shit," Cassidy says. "Oh, shit."

Jo tries to shrug it off, can't. Cassidy goes to hug her but remembers at the last inch how gross he is right now.

"So . . . so what does this mean?" he asks.

"It means she's dead," Jo says, maybe about to cry. "My aunt, her mom, she's—Shaney was her last, yeah?"

"Of how many?"

"Last one to still be *alive*, I mean," Jo says, threading her hair out of her face, peering around it to see Cassidy's eyes for a moment.

"Shit," Cassidy says again. It's all he's got.

"I talked to Ross," Jo says. "He said I can have three days, starting an hour ago. One day to get there, one to be there, one to drive home."

"Don't worry about Ross," Cassidy says. "Gabe's been in the hole with him. Take all week if you need. Take two."

"I know you can't go—"

"I can—"

"Third week of a new job and you need some personal time?" Jo says, and lets that settle.

She's right.

"I wanted to just go straight there," she says. "When I didn't show up in the morning, though, I thought you might—"

"Thank you," Cassidy says. "I would have freaked out, kicked everybody in town's ass."

"Because that's how you are," Jo says with a smile.

"Gotta do what you gotta do," Cassidy says, happy to have made her forget her cousin for a moment.

Jo steps away from the lodge, bringing Cassidy with her.

"How's he doing in there?" she says.

"Nathan?"

"He's the freshman?"

"Eighth grade, maybe?" Cassidy says. "It's good, it's good. I wish—back when, I wish I would have paid attention when his granddad was doing all this for me, though. So I could, like, pass it on better."

"His granddad?"

"He was—don't worry about it. You need to go. You need some money, though."

"I can—"

"Take it," Cassidy says, turning to the truck on blocks, the thermos of cash in the crumbly glasspack. "That's why we've been saving it, right?"

He walks over, hooks his hands on the old grille guard to slide under but then stops at the last instant, remembering again how sweaty he is. And how naked. And how sharp all the hanging rust is down there.

Jo's right there beside him already, holding his arm. Pulling him to her.

They hug in spite of his sweat, her loose hair matting on his chest.

"You're going to need a shower now," he tells her.

"I like it," she says back.

"Let me get my coveralls," Cassidy says.

"I'm not completely useless, you know," Jo says. "I can get the money myself."

"It was my friend who killed her."

"Feed Cali?" Jo says, about the paint.

"I'm not going to call her that," Cassidy says.

"In your head you will," Jo says, and takes his face in her hands, pulls his mouth to hers, kisses him bye, and holds him there, her eyes shut.

"Careful," Cassidy says. "I am naked here."

She reaches down, doesn't help matters any.

"Two days," she says, backing away.

"Monday," Cassidy says back.

"I'll leave some towels by the fire," she says. "Boys always forget there's going to be an after."

Cassidy turns to the lodge, has to shrug. She's right. They were just going to drip-dry, maybe. In the freezing cold. Standing in the snow.

"You're good to drive?" he calls across to Jo. She's on the steps to the camper.

"It's not even that far," she calls back, then, about the drumming coming from Victor's car: "One of your tapes?"

Cassidy shakes his head no and then she's gone, inside, packing, the camper creaking and groaning, all the windows yellow now, which pretty much means their one light is on. But still, it looks alive in a way that pretty much makes all of everything worth it.

Out in the darkness the horses are stomping and blowing.

"Don't worry," Cassidy says to them. Then, more to himself: "I'll bring your scoop back, sheesh."

But where *is* Victor?

Cassidy studies the darkness for ten, twenty seconds, each colder than the one before, then whistles loud and hard to pull the dogs in.

Stupid dogs. Stupid horses. Stupid Victor.

On the way back to the lodge, walking faster the closer he gets, his breath chugging white before his face, he scoops up two dripping handfuls of snow then lifts the flap with his leg, slow-spins in, already holding those two cool handfuls of slush out.

"Coconut?" Gabe says, drunk on heat, taking his handful of cold and looking over to Nathan for the rest of the joke: "He knows I like coconut flavor for my Icee."

Nathan takes his, crushes it into his face, holds his hands there to try to get this coolness to last.

"Coco*nuts*," Cassidy says, shaking his own before sitting back down, and Gabe considers his handful of slush, considers it some more, then dollops it down onto the rocks. Steam billows up, dialing the heat in the lodge up an impossible degree or two more.

"Ho!" he calls out to Victor, but there's no Victor to say it to, just drums and darkness, horses and cars, and, standing right there, so close now, you.

Cassidy lets the flap shut them in again.

THIS IS HOW YOU
LEARN TO BREAK-DANCE

The three things shuffling around for foot room in Gabe's head are:

1. a drink
2. a pee
3. Jo being out there now

What her being out there means is that staggering up and out into the cool air for the pee he desperately, desperately needs, even though he's drunk exactly nothing for this whole sweat, has to be deep in the negatives as far as fluids, really, what Jo being out there means is that . . . he needs a towel? A fig leaf? A Bible to cover himself with? Not one of the little green ones, but a big holy roller of a leatherbound book.

But—like there were never any naked dudes on the Crow rez?

Gabe chuckles to himself, slow-motions his fingertips up to feel his lips smiling, because his face isn't telling him anything at the moment.

"What?" Cass says.

Gabe just wobbles side to side, his wet head tracing secret figure eights.

The kid has his mouth down right by the melting dirt, is sucking its vapory coolness.

Cass passes him the cooler. The kid tips it up like a giant cup, sluices the last-last memory of water down his gullet.

"Feel like I've heard this one somewhere before . . ." Gabe leans over to say to Cass about Victor's stupid drums.

"Shh," Cass says, his eyes closed like he's trying to be inside himself, is trying to really get into this sweat.

Sure, great.

Gabe closes his eyes too, swims through that powdery hot blackness and feels his shoulders melt down, his ribs sighing in when he breathes everything in him out, his fingertips bulbous and heavy now, his legs and feet somewhere else altogether.

Maybe this is how it works, he tells himself, at the same time trying to be quiet in his head, because talking to yourself is exactly how it *doesn't* work. The body slipping away is what allows the rest of you to float up, over, out. Maybe see some shit for once, yeah?

Except what Gabe settles on, it's not real, he knows. It can't be.

It's his father sitting in his chair in his living room on Death Row.

He's watching that same channel as always: that camera angled down onto the parking lot of the IGA.

On his rounded little screen there's nothing and nothing and then some more nothing on top of that, and then—and then a tall dog trots through on some dog mission or another.

Gabe's father grunts approval and Gabe looks over to him like, *What?* Like, *This is what passes for action?*

His father chins Gabe back to the television.

The same nothing, like bank robbers have looped the footage, are cracking into the IGA, stealing all the heads of lettuce they want, for their big salad enterprise.

Gabe snickers.

"Listen—" he says, making to go, to be anywhere else than this, there's got to be better visions, but now there's a flurry of motion on-screen.

Not dogs this time. Boys. Four of them.

The skin around Gabe's eyes draws in. Either in the sweat lodge or his father's living room, he doesn't know, and it doesn't matter.

They were twelve then. Him and Lewis, Cass and Ricky.

What they have between them is a single Walkman with that one tape Cass had stolen from his big brother Arthur.

Lewis is first.

He puts the headphones on, Cass holds the Walkman out, keeping the cable free, and Lewis nods with the synthesizer the way it starts out, and then he looks around at Gabe and Ricky and Cass, his face deadly serious, and the way his head is bobbing, he lets that infect the rest of his body.

When the beat finds his hand, his fingertips lift out to the side in some Egyptian pose that's already crinkling back up along his arm, hitting his neck, throwing his head to the side like he can't help it, and around him Cass and Ricky and Gabe are bouncing with it.

This is how you learn to break-dance.

Gabe smiles, watching the four of them all those years ago, Lewis already passing the headphones to the next popper-and-locker, holding the Walkman himself now, the music still in his head.

It always will be, Gabe remembers thinking. Knowing. Promising.

It always will be.

And beside him now, his father is looking past the television screen, to the walls of his living room, to his baseboards, which are . . . are crawling with—

Cass.

It's Cass sitting beside Gabe, not his father. They're in the sweat lodge.

Gabe breathes in deep, the hot air roiling in his chest, cooking him from the inside, and he tries to muster a smile because *they're* the turkeys in the oven now, aren't they? But his lips are traitors, are slugs, are so far from his face. When he looks across to check on the kid, make sure he hasn't passed out onto the rocks, he sees two more shapes sitting there, eyes boring down into the heat.

Ricky.

Lewis.

Except . . . except, Ricky, his face is leaking down, is beaten in, stomped in, and Lewis, he's starting to look up, and there's finger holes of light poking through his chest, and . . . and—

Gabe stumbles up into the ceiling of the lodge and dog hair rains down.

Some of it finds the rocks, hisses a bitter taste into the air.

"I've got—I've got to," he says, ducking now, his hand on Cass's shoulder, and Cass doesn't stop him from feeling his way around to the flap, birthing himself naked out into the night air.

A moment later, gasping the coolness in, Victor's drum loop filling all the empty spaces in the darkness, the cooler comes through the flap as well, for Gabe to fill. Because somehow this ordeal isn't over yet.

Gabe leans back, stares up into the wash of stars.

Let Jo walk up, look him up and down, shake her head. So he's not the toughest Indian in the world. He *is* the thirstiest, though, he's pretty sure. And not for stale water from Cass's tank.

He's got his own cooler just over there in the truck, right?

He finds the Mauser by the trash barrels, uses it like a cane for a few steps, leaves it against Victor's cruiser, pats the car's hood like thanking it for holding this for him. He leans on one of the chairs to steady himself and looks all around, taking everything in.

Except for the camper and the trucks, it could be two hundred years ago, he's pretty sure. Not a single electric light for miles in any direction. But he's glad it's not two hundred years ago, too. Two hundred years ago there wouldn't have been bottles of chilled beer in the cab of his truck.

When he shakes free of the chair to get some of that cold-cold beer, Cass's shirt tangles in his wet fingers. He holds it over his crotch in case Jo's about to jump up from behind Victor's car.

Speaking of: "Um, firekeeper?" Gabe says all around.

Nothing.

"Hunh," he says, and finally settles his eyes on the outhouse just back from the camper, nods about the hanging lantern in there, glowing yellow.

Victor's in the can.

Gabe grins a who-cares? grin, pushes off the side of the cruiser he's staggered into again somehow.

It's so cool out here. So perfect. The snow crunching under the soles of his feet is the best thing ever.

At his truck he stabs an arm in through the open passenger window, flips the cooler open, shoves his hand down into the water that used to be ice. There's still chunks in there, even.

He draws a beer out to himself, rubs the cold bottle all over his face, his chest, his arms. The hiss of it cracking open is amazing, the mist swirling up the best promise ever.

"I've been thinking about you," Gabe whispers into the mouth of the bottle, and tips it up, tries to go slow so he won't throw up.

While he's drinking, he left-hands a pee. Cass is always saying not to piss too close to the camper, either go on out to the trees or use the outhouse, that the whole place is going to start smelling yellow if everybody just splashes pee all over, but screw it. Victor's in there anyway, and Gabe can't wait.

Liquid in, liquid out.

With a gasp he finally breaks his long kiss with the beer, wipes his lips with Cass's shirt, oops, and manages a look down to what he's peeing on.

It's one of the dogs.

He angles his stream away, lets it sputter out, shakes off, and doesn't zip up since this isn't exactly a zipper situation.

He looks over to the camper, all its lights on. To the outhouse, hunkered down over its deep hole. To Victor's car, drumming its loud beat out into the night.

And the dog.

It's one of the two pups, not Miss Lefty, but . . . Dancer, yeah. Dancer the dead, dead, very dead dog.

Gabe squats down gingerly, unsurely, and touches the dog's matted coat.

"What stepped on you, girl?" he says, petting the dog's haunch.

Her guts are ballooned down into the interior skin of one of her back legs. Gabe's seen it happen before, to dogs that have been run over.

But this dog, it's been . . . *stomped*?

Her chest has been crushed, too, and because there was no-where for the lungs and heart and liver to go, most of it's splashed out the mouth in what looks like a single chunky gout. The tongue is hanging, not swollen up yet.

"What the hell?" Gabe says, standing, looking out into the dark-ness instead of behind him, where you are, on the other side of the truck. If he just turned around, chanced a look into the passen-ger window, through the cab, there you'd be out the driver's side, watching him. Glaring hard at him, your five-fingered hands balled into fists.

He doesn't, though. And he won't. His whole life he's been looking in the wrong places. Why should tonight be any different?

"Cass," he says then, like trying it out, "one of your horses, man, it got out, I think. And it doesn't like your dogs."

He steps carefully around this dog, deeper out into the night.

Two slow steps later are the other two dogs.

Ladybear is dead, but Miss Lefty is still trying.

"Shit," Gabe says, dropping to a knee.

Miss Lefty whimpers.

"Shit shit shit," Gabe says, and sets his beer down in the snow, holds it there a moment to be sure he can let it go without it tipping over.

He feels around with his right hand for a rock, finds a good heavy one, then, with his left hand, makes sure where the dog's head is.

She's dead now.

He sets the rock back down, slumps on his thighs.

When he stands it's without his beer, without the shirt. When he looks back to his truck there's nobody there through the tunnel the windows make. Walking back, he runs the hair out of his eyes and smears blood all across his face.

That rock he used, or meant to use, it was the same one you used.

It's almost funny.

Back at the truck he grubs a rag up from under the seat, cleans his hands and face, then, with his other hand, liberates another beer, drinks it down all at once, and turns, does a running throw to sling the bottle out as far into the darkness as he can.

It doesn't land for seconds and seconds, and doesn't shatter when it does, just *thunks*.

Cass is *not* going to like this, he knows. Nobody likes all their dogs being dead at once. But it's not Gabe's fault, either. And if—if he leaves pretty soon after the sweat, then he won't even have to get involved in this, will he?

"You were never even here," he says to himself, looking around to make sure Jo's not suddenly standing there behind him, listening in.

Why would he even be thinking that?

"Getting jumpy in your old age," he mumbles, and hauls the cooler of still-cold water up through the window.

It'll be better than the water from Gabe's tank. And they'll need something better to dip it out with.

Gabe sloshes the cooler onto the hood, opens the passenger door and digs behind the seat, eyes staring straight up so his fingers can feel farther. Finally he comes up with some random metal thermos. He twists the cap off, dumps it into the floorboard then blows into the thermos once, hard, already turning his face to the side.

No mice skeletons or bug husks come back at him.

He holds it upside down, taps it against the front tire to break loose anything stubborn, and when nothing cakes out—it would just be coffee anyway, right?—he fixes its thin lip into his mouth, carries it like that, the cooler in both hands like the biggest, squarest, most refreshing fig leaf.

He's going to be a hero, bringing water back with actual chunks of ice still floating in it. And the dogs dead in the snow? They haven't even happened yet, aren't even real.

On the way back to the lodge he raises his voice, singing with the singers, walking with the drumbeat, Indian-style.

BLACKFEET INDIAN STORIES

Nathan remembers some stupid summer program years ago, where all the ten-year-olds were supposed to be learning traditional stuff. This was back when he had three braids, was still being groomed to be an All-Star Indian. Before he started being who he really was.

Tre had been there, too, his hair in traditional braids as well.

What they were learning for that week wasn't riding or archery or any of the cool stuff, but how to dry meat on a rack.

Sitting in the heat of this lodge, that's exactly what he feels like: one of those thin strips of meat on that rack of twigs, a slow fire burning under him, the sun baking him from above.

Except there's words cycling through his head, shaken loose by the steam. From when his granddad was taking him through the language. From when talking like that made sense.

Kuto'yiss.

Kuto'yisss"ko'maapii.

Po'noka.

Kuto'yiss is where his dad drove him back from yesterday, pretty much. The Sweetgrass Hills, but use it in a sentence: *I went out to Kuto'yiss maybe to die, Granddad. To be with Tre. But your stupid son dragged me back. I went there because you were always talking about the Sweetgrass money, do you remember? What America kept not paying us for the hills it stole?*

Use it in another sentence: *I'd rather die out in Kuto'yiss than under a car upside down in Cutbank Creek, like Tre.*

And what about Kuto'yisss"ko'maapii? It's not Sweetgrass Hills plus "ko'maapii," which was hard to wrap his head around back then. And also now.

What it means is Blood-Clot Boy, the hero kid born from a clot of blood, back when shit like that was always going down, at least according to his granddad, waving one more kid into the lodge for story time.

Nathan had never told anybody, but used to, second grade maybe, his dad braiding his hair before homeroom every day, he'd secretly known he was Kuto'yisss"ko'maapii. That he was here to save the people, then become a star in the sky. Then in seventh grade Mr. Massey had explained how every young Indian thinks he's Crazy Horse reborn.

Denorah Cross Guns had stabbed her hand in the air about this one, and Nathan sneaked a look back at her, like always.

"Not the girls," she said.

"You all think you're . . . *Sacajawea*," Mr. Massey told her with a shrug, his mouth tumbling down through all those syllables like the best joke.

Because Denorah Cross Guns didn't know enough of the old-time Indians to pick someone better, someone not a traitor, she'd saved it all up for the game that night, and fouled out, had to be dragged off the court for fighting, and her new dad had had to keep her real dad from crashing down onto the court as well.

Nathan had been there in the stands as well, yelling for her with the rest of the crowd, yelling that it wasn't her foul. But even if it had been, right?

Denorah Cross Guns isn't anybody's Sacajawea. And Nathan, he isn't any Crazy Horse *or* Blood-Clot Boy. He knows that now. Those three-braid days are over and done with. Never mind all this sweat lodge bullshit. Never mind his dad playing the drums out there.

When Gabriel offers the new cooler, Nathan takes it into his lap, uses the black metal thermos to scoop up some of that water that's so cold it almost hurts.

Cass nods at him to go on, that he's doing good.

Nathan dollops some of the water out onto the rocks and steam spits up between the three of them, stranding them in their own individual sweat lodges, almost.

Are the rocks even really supposed to be this hot?

Nathan doesn't think so.

No way could anybody stand this for more than an hour or two. Not without coming out cooked. A round or two ago Gabriel said he'd been *baked* before, sure, but this was another level.

There's still half the thermos of water left.

Nathan swishes it, swishes it again, and is about to drink when he remembers the rule: honor your ancestors. Which is what Cass told him. What Gabriel said was just to say somebody's name, somebody who might not be getting a drink otherwise, yeah?

"Granddad," Nathan says, loud enough for the two clowns through the steam to hear, and pours out half of what he was going to drink.

Across from him, he's pretty sure Cass nods that this is good, this is good. Now keep it going.

Back in his place in their triangley circle, Gabriel is next to get the cooler. The one he just delivered.

"Neesh," he says, like agreeing with Nathan, and tumps a splash down, doesn't take a drink himself. Meaning he probably drank his fill while he was out there.

"Think he's had enough?" Gabriel says just generally, passing the cooler to Cass.

Cass looks up, not following, so Gabriel explains: "His grand-dad, man. That's two drinks already. He's gonna have to go pee soon, think?"

He smiles after this, his mouth loose like his face is melting.

"What do you think ghost pee smells like anyway?" Gabriel's going on now. "You think it's like all around all the time?" He tries to haul his foot up to his nose to smell for ghost pee.

"Not hot enough for you?" Cass says back to him, then angles his face over to the flap, calls out a deep *ho* for another hot rock, even though the last one hasn't come yet.

Gabriel slumps in response, looks up into the ceiling like for something to save him, and big bad Officer Yellow Tail was right, Nathan kind of knows: Gabriel and Cass *are* him and Tre, twenty years down the road. Or, they would have been, if Tre were still around. Or, if he were over with Tre now.

This is all you really need, isn't it? Just one good friend. Some-body you can be stupid with. Somebody who'll peel you up off the ground, prop you against the wall.

Example fifty-eight, about: Gabriel has sharpened his hand into a blade, is touching Cass's shoulder with it, just enough to get a jolt of electricity from Cass, a jolt that can travel up his arm, cock his head over to the side in the stupidest, least ro-botic way.

"Shh, this is serious, man," Cass hisses to Gabriel, and Nathan shakes his head about the two of them, one grooving while sitting on his bare ass, one ceremonially dipping the new scoop into the water, holding it up like you have to look hard at it before tipping a little out for the dead to drink.

But then he doesn't tip any out.

He's still studying this black, onetime-pricey thermos.

"What?" Gabriel says, stopping his slow-motion serpentine groove. "I mean, I know it's not a dog food scoop, man, but some of us have higher—"

"Where'd you get this?" Cass asks, zero joking.

Gabriel shrugs, doesn't answer, goes back to his stoned swaying, and only looks around slow when Cass is up and gone through the flap, taking the black thermos with him.

"This mean it's over?" Nathan says to Gabe, and Gabe tunes back in, looks all around the lodge, finally settles on the cooler Cass let spill on his way out.

"Quick, kid," he says to Nathan about the spilling water, "say the names of all the dead Indians you know, be right back," and then he's gone just the same, and Nathan knows this was the plan all along: To strand him here alone with his thoughts, with his demons. With his granddad.

He shakes his head at the stupidity of it all.

What would Crazy Horse do? he asks himself. Probably stay in here all night, then stare everybody down when he walked out naked, all the rocks cool, outlasted.

Either that or he'd count to one hundred, be done with this Indian bullshit.

Highlights are on at eleven, he reminds his dad, out there somewhere.

How about we make them?

AND THEN THERE WAS ONE

Ten years and now you're here at last.

From the herd, you have the scent and the taste and the sound of Richard Boss Ribs getting beat to death in that parking lot in North Dakota, and you felt Lewis Clarke catching bullets with his chest, his body dancing against your own, his arms holding you like you were all that mattered, but this time you're going to *see* it happen.

It's going to be different. It's going to better. It's going to have been worth the wait.

Before, you were standing by the horse pens, close to the dogs. Now you're on the other side of the driveway, from walking back from the outhouse, your chin and mouth black with blood.

Neither of these last two know you're in the world at all. That day in the snow they shot you, to them it's just another day, another hunt.

That's why it has to be like this.

You could have taken them at any point over the last day, day and a half, but that's not even close to what they deserve. They need to feel what you felt. Their whole world has to be torn from their belly, shoved into a shallow hole.

The first one out of the lodge is the Sees Elk one, Cassidy. The name already leaves a bad taste in your mouth. He's standing in front of the lawn chair he left his clothes on. At first he'd grabbed the boy's bright white shirt when it was right there by the lodge, but he put it back, even trying to get it folded again, patting it into place. His own shirt isn't on the lawn chair anymore, but his pants are still there. He's trying to put them on but he's sweaty and they're tight and it's not working.

He grunts with frustration, sits in the chair and then straightens out in it, flattening his body to try to find less resistance. It's not the angle, though, it's the stickiness. The chair folds over, the left pair of hollow aluminum legs bending in.

He stands from the tangle, his pants halfway up, and slings the chair around and around, launches it as high and as far as he can, out past the horse pens.

It's because he watches it fall that he sees his shirt, a smear in the darkness over to the left of the trucks.

"Gonna shoot those dogs," he says, and takes up the black thermos, stalks out there.

A moment later the other one, Cross Guns—*Gabriel*, the first one to shoot his rifle into the herd that day in the snow—is standing naked in front of the lodge, watching his friend stalk off into the darkness.

For once he doesn't say anything.

Slowly, he becomes aware again of the lights in the camper still on, and of his own nakedness. He covers himself with his hands, darts to his own fallen-down bent-over chair, does the pants dance just the same as the other one.

"Victor?" he says all around, his voice deep like that can balance out his nakedness.

He rolls his shirt on sleeve by sleeve and you remember what the boy said before, about one team being shirts, the other skins.

"Guess the ceremony's over," Gabriel says, still watching Cassidy.

He's wrong. The ceremony's just starting.

Look over to the other one now.

Cassidy yanks his shirt up from the ground, tries to shove his right arm through the sleeve, but . . . it's wet, it's soaked something up, something more than just snow.

He peels back out of it, studies the spreading stain.

Blood.

It's then that he registers what he's standing in the middle of.

The dogs. *His* dogs.

All he came out here to do was shimmy under his truck, check the muffler, see if his black thermos is still there, if it was just bad luck that his friend had hauled an exactly matching thermos in from who-knew-where. Cassidy isn't trying to solve the big mystery of what happened to his dogs. Five seconds ago, there wasn't any big mystery. The dogs were just dogs, off doing dog things.

Like dying, evidently.

Like having their heads smashed in with . . . did the horses get free, stomp them? The dogs are forever harassing them. But still.

Cassidy looks over, the horses' eyes shining in the dull glow from the dying fire, nostrils wide from this death in the air. They're still in the pen, couldn't have done this.

So.

He comes back to the closest dog, sees the guilty rock. He edges over, lowers himself to his knees, the crust of snow sharp against the top of his feet. Right beside the blood-crusted rock is one of Gabriel's beers.

Cassidy is breathing hard now.

He looks over to the fire, to the lodge. To Gabriel, struggling to button his pants, having to hop on one leg so his other can be straight enough.

There's nothing funny about him right now.

You can read Cassidy's thoughts on his face, in the way his top lip is drawing up on one side: *Good-time Gabe. Dog-killer Gabe. Gabe the bank robber.*

Cassidy places his hand to the rock and, instead of hauling it up immediately, senses a presence the same way Victor Yellow Tail did. Not you this time, but—a pair of sudden and out-of-place eyes looking right at him from just a few yards away.

The Crow, the one who lives here, the one who leaves her scent everywhere, especially in her clothes. She's under the old truck just like she said she would be, one of her arms up in the chassis for that glasspack, but now she's motionless, doesn't know what this night is trying to turn into. "Is it there?" Cassidy says across to her, not loud enough for Gabriel to hear, and the Crow doesn't answer. "Never mind," he says, standing with the black thermos. "I already know."

With that he steps out, is standing by Gabriel's truck.

He pulls the passenger door open for the dome light.

Gabriel cocks his head over, says, "Cass?"

"Did you think I wouldn't notice?" Cassidy says.

Gabriel steps closer, eyes squinted.

He's heard his friend dial his tone down like this, but never for him, and not for years, probably not since . . . narrow your eyes so you can inhale it . . . not since Cassidy's big brother went to prison and Cassidy drank that whole bottle and broke into the high school at night, to wrench his brother's old locker door off, save it for him.

"Notice what?" Gabriel says, still edging in. "That I brought a lot of cold-ass water into that sorry excuse for a lodge, and then you spilled it all?"

Cassidy's body shudders with a sick laugh.

He punctuates it by slamming the thermos into the passenger side mirror of Gabriel's truck. The glass shatters, the frame swinging down on the lower part of the bracket still bolted to the door, the top arm scratching a raw arc into the paint.

"*What the hell!*" Gabriel says, in close now, leading with his chest.

Cassidy stands right into him for once, says, "Let me see your hand."

Gabriel backs up.

Cassidy reaches across, takes Gabriel's left hand in his own, turns it over for inspection. "She hardly even bit you," he says about the two punctures ringed with bruise.

"What are you—?"

"Is that how you justified it to yourself?" Cassidy goes on.

"The—" Gabe says, then sees it in Cassidy's eyes: "The dogs, no, yeah, I mean—that wasn't, I was going to—"

"Not the dogs," Cassidy says. "The money, Gabe. There was nine hundred *dollars* in there, man."

"In where?"

Cassidy spins the black thermos into Gabe's chest, says, "You *know* where."

Gabe fumble-catches the thermos, sets it purposefully onto the hood of his truck.

"You think I have nine hundred dollars on me?" he says, incredulous. "You think I've ever had nine hundred dollars to my name all at once?" To prove his innocence he shoves both hands into his pockets, rabbit-ears them back out all at once, five twenties fluttering out and down.

"I just got that from Victor," he says. "You saw, you were there, man."

"And that?" Cassidy says about his other hand, still wrapped in a fist, around whatever was in *that* pocket.

Gabriel looks down at that hand like he wants to know, too.

But he can feel it against his palm, too, can't he?

He steps back from Cassidy.

"I don't—this isn't mine," he says. "It wasn't here when I took those pants off."

"*What?*" Cassidy says, reaching in.

Gabriel steps back again. "Are these even mine?" he says, looking down to his pants.

"Show me," Cassidy says, his voice low and no bullshit.

Gabriel locks eyes with him, says, "Listen, I don't understand what's—" and holds his hand out between them, palm up, and opens his fingers, peek-looking at whatever he's holding.

It's the ring. The one Cassidy was keeping at the bottom of the thermos, for the Crow.

"*This* is how bad you don't want me with her?" Cassidy says, huffing a sort-of laugh out.

"No, wait, I don't—" Gabriel says, depositing the ring carefully on the hood of his truck to show how little he wants it. How little he stole it.

"And then you kill my dogs on *top* of that?" Cassidy says. "Did you catch whatever crazy Lewis had? I don't understand what's happening with you, Gabriel fucking Cross Guns. Tell me why you're doing this—no, no, don't even try. Just tell me where the money is."

"Listen, somebody's . . . I don't know what you're—" Gabriel starts, but then Cassidy cuts him off by one-handing the black thermos off the hood, spinning it in his hand to get the hold he wants, and slamming it into the windshield of Gabriel's truck, leaving a deep crater, the thermos in the white center like it's something that blazed down out of the sky for this truck and this truck only. Gabriel looks from the windshield to Cassidy then back to the windshield, his eyes flaring up at last.

"Right?" he says, matching Cassidy's rising tone, and steps in, wrenches his mirror the rest of the way off, holds it by the bracket and swings it into the rain gutter of the cab until the roof wedges in, making a deep, unfixable notch. "*C'mon*, man!" he urges. "Let's beat it to hell, yeah? Stupid truck, stupid truck, always getting stuck right when, right when . . ."

When Cassidy doesn't fall in, Gabriel slings the mirror out into the darkness, is facing Cassidy now, his chest heaving.

"But it's not the only truck that was always getting stuck, right?" Gabriel says, and brushes hard past Cassidy, is picking up speed by the time he pushes off from his own taillight, is already running before Cassidy can catch him.

"No!" Cassidy screams, diving, his fingers just hooking into Gabriel's right rear pocket.

For a moment Gabriel slows, but then the pocket rips away, shows ass.

"Gabe, Gabriel, *no!*" Cassidy screams from the ground, but it's too late.

If either of them looked just six feet into the darkness to the right, they'd see the white slash of your smile.

This is it. They're doing it.

Gabriel curls around to come at the old truck from the side and drives his shoulder into it with everything he's got.

He doesn't weigh much, but he weighs enough.

Cassidy is up and running already, but his pants aren't buttoned and are too long without boots and he doesn't get there in time, could never have gotten there in time.

The truck sways to the side, sways back, and Gabriel catches it in rhythm, pushes back hard enough that one of the cinder blocks under the front axle housing explodes, the driver's-side front lurching down like a horse taking a knee. No: like an elk that just got shot, doesn't understand, is crumbling down.

"*No!*" Cassidy screams, and hooks his fingers into the wheel well on the passenger side right as that cinder block comes down in stages as well, taking the two blocks under the rear axle with it.

For an impossible moment Cassidy holds the truck up, screaming, his mouth open as wide as he's ever had to open it, wide enough Gabriel even panics, wedges into Cassidy's foot space, hooks his hands in the wheel well like keeping this truck up is suddenly the most important thing in the whole world.

The truck doesn't know that, though. It hitches down farther through the cinder block, crushes down all at once.

Cassidy falls with it and goes lower, his face sideways to the snow in an instant, to look under, but there are no tires anymore, no wheels, even the brake drums are gone. The truck's sitting down on its frame. There's no seeing under it.

He hits the side of his fist into the ground over and over, and Gabriel's just standing there watching him.

"Hey, man, I got a good enough jack in the truck, we can—" Gabriel says, but Cassidy stands right into him, shoves him away.

Gabriel falls down, watches Cassidy from there.

Now Cassidy is . . . trying to force the hood open?

"Here," Gabriel says, pulling himself up and stepping in, but Cassidy elbows him away hard again.

"What's got into you?" Gabriel says.

Cassidy is crying now, sputtering, can't catch his breath.

Gabriel goes back, drives his elbow down into the mismatched hood once, twice, trying to remind the springs how they work.

The ancient catch releases and the hood pops up a few inches.

Cassidy pushes his hand in, forces the rust-frozen hook over to the right, and, with his other hand, lifts the hood in a screech of metal. He collapses back, covering his face from whatever's in there.

Gabriel looks from the ball of pain Cassidy is to the truck.

There's no engine, so he can see straight through to the ground.

It's the Crow. Part of her, anyway—her hair, matted deep in blood and brains, all of it soaking into a nice Hudson's Bay blanket. The crossmember at the back of the engine bay, right about where the front of the transmission would be, looks to have come down on her face, crushed her forehead in. And back out.

She was trying to ball up in the safety of the engine compartment, Gabriel can tell. She knew the truck was falling, she was scrambling ahead, pulling with anything she could grab on to.

It would have worked, too. It should have worked.

But they couldn't hold the truck up long enough. The truck that didn't even need to be falling in the first place, except to make a dumb-ass point. Except to get Cassidy back for bashing a windshield in, for some money and dogs Gabriel hadn't even had anything to do with it.

Still.

Gabriel covers his mouth with his hands, can't get his lungs to suck air in the right way anymore.

Now Cassidy's stalking back from the patrol car. With the Mauser.

Gabriel steps out into Cassidy's path, drops to his knees, offering himself, but Cassidy goes right around him, for the truck now sitting on the Crow.

He hauls the passenger door open and leans in, a great cloud of dust billowing up into the cab.

"Cass, man, I didn't—what was she—" Gabriel says.

And then he sees what his friend is doing. It's what Cassidy said earlier—that he probably had a stray shell that would fit the old gun. One of the ones from Ricky's foggy bag of stolen ammo.

Cassidy tries the first shell, and when it won't load he drops it, moves on to the next.

"You knew this is where I keep my money," he says to Gabriel like an explanation.

"Dude, *dude*," Gabriel says, standing, holding his hands out like they can fend off accusations, like they can stop bullets, like they can make all of this make sense.

Cassidy rams another shell in, works it back out, tosses it.

"Shut up," he says. "You're always talking. You never shut up. If you'd just listen for once in your life—"

"*I would never have hurt her!*" Gabriel screams.

They both hear it when the next cartridge slides in perfect, like made for this moment. Cassidy slams the bolt into place and steps out of the truck, the gun at port arms, his head loose like he's really getting ready to do this thing.

"We grew up together," he says, sort of crying, lips firm as he can get them. "I loved you, man. You saved my life so many times, and I saved yours back. But—but it was *her* now, don't you understand? I loved *her* now. *She* was saving my life. I was saving hers! Everything was *working* for once, don't you get it? And now . . . now . . ."

With that he shoulders the rifle, backs up enough to level the barrel dead-center on Gabriel's face.

Gabriel is breathing in spurts, shaking his head no, no.

When there's nowhere to go that Cassidy can't reach him with the rifle, he drops to his knees a second time. The rifle follows him, is tethered to the bridge of his nose.

"Do it, man," he says. "Fucking do it already. I don't deserve to— *Just do it!* Nobody will even know, nobody will even miss me, man! You're the only one who would, even. If—if you're . . . *Just do it!*"

To make it easy, he lifts his chin, stares straight up. A moment later he starts singing, kind of with the drums still bleeding out from the top of Victor's patrol car but kind of more, too. Something else.

"Shut up!" Cassidy yells down at him, stepping back from this, stepping back from *having* to do this.

But he keeps seeing the Crow, too, you know, the Crow through that engine compartment, under the truck *Gabriel* knocked over.

"What are you even doing!" he yells to Gabriel.

"My death song," Gabriel sputters. "Shh, this next verse is tricky."

"You're just making that up!" Cassidy tells him. "Everything that's Indian, you just make it up!"

"Shit, somebody's got to," Gabriel says, and goes back to the song.

It's not even words, is just that old-time sound, always rising higher and higher and then resetting, starting the climb again.

"I don't . . . I don't—" Cassidy says, lowering the gun, looking at his friend on his knees, tears coming down his traitor face, running down by his ears into his neck, into his shirt.

Cassidy is crying as well.

He wipes his tears away, raises the rifle back, can't hold it steady enough, but he's only ten feet away. It's how far Lewis was from you when he shot you the second time, in the head. And the third time.

It's the perfect distance. It's the distance they've earned.

Except this one is losing his resolve, is losing his anger, is falling into a grief hole inside himself. But he's on edge, too, the barrel of the rifle coming up like he means it, then dipping down again. His every nerve is frayed. What that means is that, when Cassidy sees a white flurry of motion directly behind Gabriel, he flinches back in response, startled, and tries to pull the rifle with him, ends up putting that jerking pull into a trigger he doesn't really know.

The sound is thunder, deep and bass and ragged. It splits the night in two, both halves falling neatly away, leaving Gabriel standing in the silence between them.

He looks down to his chest for the hole that should be there. And then he feels his face gingerly. Finally he pats the side of his head, comes away with blood.

His ear. His ear has a new notch in it.

He smiles with wonder, says, "Coup," and looks across to Cassidy, but Cassidy is dropping the rifle, is shaking his head no, his breath hitching in deep again. But this time it's with fear.

"What?" Gabriel says, unable yet to even hear his own voice, and looks behind him, to whatever's got Cassidy shaking his head no.

It's—Gabriel is trying to process it, trying to resist it—what he sees is what he's most terrified of ever having to see: the girl with the basketball, the Finals Girl. His daughter in her scrimmage-white jersey. Her name shapes itself on his lips a bit at a time, like trying to add up to her: *D, Den, Denorah.*

She's still standing, her hair spilled forward, her face angled down at the blood spreading over her bright white jersey like checking to see if this is really real, if this is really happening.

Gabriel falls back, unaware of his fingertips on the ground, unaware of anything except what's just happened, what can't be taken back, what can never get undone.

His little girl, she—earlier in the day, at the little pad of concrete behind her house, she'd toed up to that charity stripe, she'd used textbook form, and she swished forty dollars' worth of free throws through that net.

It was impossible, no kid could shoot like that. But she could. For forty dollars.

"I'll bring it to the scrimmage tomorrow," Gabriel'd said to her out the window of his truck, the engine already turning over to bring him here.

"It'll be gone by then," she'd said back, with her mother's mouth. "And, you can come to the gym again?"

"It's a scrimmage, not a game."

"If I'm playing, it's a game."

"I don't even have it yet," Gabriel told her, shrugging like this was the truth, the whole truth, and nothing but.

"Who's giving it to you?" she'd asked.

"Victor Yellow Tail," Gabriel said. "Tonight. Police money. That's the best kind, yeah?"

"For Nathan's sweat?"

Yes.

Denorah had logged that, he knows now and doesn't want to know, she'd logged it and weighed it and considered it, and now she'd caught a ride out here to collect before her loser-dad could spend what he owed. Before he could let it blow away across the snow.

Only, Cassidy shot her with a 7.62mm round before she could even announce herself, had shot her so clean that it hadn't even thrown her back into the lodge, had just blown a ragged plug of meat out behind her.

But she's not meat, she's my daughter, Gabriel says inside, screams inside, can't stop screaming about inside.

Exactly, you say back to him.

Gabriel slashes forward to catch her, but she tips forward onto her face before he's even two steps closer. He falls to his knees by his own truck, pushes his whole face into the ground, his lips right to the dirt all the tires have cleared of snow.

His girl, his baby girl. She was going to take the team to state, she was going to take the whole tribe into the pros, into legend. Everybody was going to quit painting buffalo and bear footprints on the side of their lodges, were going to have to learn to draw all the lines in a basketball. She was the one who could plant her feet, get the rim in her sights, and drain ten free throws in a row. Twenty. Fifty. A hundred.

She was going to make it out of here, like Gabriel never had. Like nobody ever did. Exhibition one: Ricky. Exhibition two: Lewis.

Had he really seen her earlier today at lunch, walking away from school in the cold in that same white jersey? Was seeing her like that supposed to have been a warning? Was it a vision? Is Trina parked down at the cattle guard? Did she hear the shot? Is she standing from the opened door of her car, listening with mom ears for the next shot? For footsteps running in the dark? For her ex, trying to come up with one more excuse?

Shit. Shit shit shit.

And: *no*.

There is no excuse. Not for this.

When Cassidy drops to his knees beside Gabriel like *What have we done here*, Gabriel pushes him hard enough that Cassidy falls and slides, hard enough that the recoil drives Gabriel over into the side of his truck.

"You *shot* her!" he screams, standing, his hands balled into fists. He's crying harder than he was, now. But at the same time he's mad, mad enough to reach around to his own cratered-in windshield, come back with the black thermos.

"And you—you pushed a truck onto Jo . . ." Cassidy says.

"Not on purpose!" Gabriel says, and then, just like he's supposed to, he steps out into the darkness after his best friend since forever, and when Cassidy crawls back, away from this thing trying to happen, Gabriel steps faster, finally comes down with his knees to either side of Cassidy's hips.

The thermos is alive in his right hand, is both completely weightless and the heaviest thing in the world. He rolls it for a better grip, for a final grip, for the best way to hold it when doing a thing like this.

"You shot her, man," he says, like he's pleading. Like he's trying to explain. "You shot *Denorah*. You shot my little girl . . ."

Cassidy is holding his hands over his face.

He nods that yes, yes, he did.

His body is hitching and jerking under Gabriel, and it's like a current is passing between them. Like they're kids again, learning to break-dance.

"I'm sorry," Gabriel says, and brings the butt of the thermos down with the weight of all their years of friendship.

Because he's holding it wrong, his pinkie finger is between it and Cassidy's eyebrow.

The thermos glances off and dives into the ground, its open mouth standing it up in the crusty snow.

Cassidy lowers his hands, blood sheeting down over his face.

He looks up through it to Gabriel, and they're both crying, neither can breathe right, neither wants to breathe ever again.

With an unsteady hand, Cassidy claps the snow for the thermos, finds it, passes it back up to Gabriel, and you have to cover your bloody mouth with your palm, because even in your most secret dreams you never would have guessed this part, would you have?

It's perfect, it's amazing.

Gabriel takes the thermos, their fingers touching over that black metal, and Gabriel remembers it all over again: D, yesterday, turning back to him with that sharp smile, no-looking free throw number ten just like Jordan, and it hurts so bad that he closes his eyes, brings the thermos down again, with a crunch. The next crunch is wetter, the one after that deeper, punching through into a darker space.

The muscles closest to Cassidy's shin bone are the last to die.

Gabriel leans back, wavers, an insubstantial shape of a person.

Past Cassidy's head is a dead dog, and a beer, still standing.

Gabriel crawls over, trades the bloody thermos for the beer, and drains the bottle.

He still can't breathe. His right hand is slick with blood, and his face and shirt are spattered with it, and he doesn't know whether to laugh or die, really. Both seem reasonable.

He struggles out of the shirt and it'll hardly come, so he tears it, balls it up, stands to throw it as far as he can. It flutters, doesn't go anywhere. He kicks back through the snow for his truck and stumbles into the Mauser, is a skin now along with Cassidy, meaning they're on the same team, like always.

He looks at the rifle and then looks at it some more. His breath finally comes, washing through his head, leaving him dizzy.

The Mauser, yes, he decides. The Mauser, for the pest that he is. He can—he can be another statistic, he can make it so the pamphlets are right about Indian suicide rates, can't he? He can keep the numbers good, keep everyone from having to print up new pamphlets. He can go—he can go with Cassidy. Maybe even still catch up to him.

He picks up the Mauser, falls to the old truck, the one the Crow's dead under, and grubs cartridge after cartridge from Richard's foggy bag, only stops when he cues into an eye watching him.

"Jo," he says, like of course.

The hole he shot through Cassidy's floorboard all those years ago, it's pushed down now over the Crow's face, her eyeball bulging up through it. Gabriel turns away shaking his head no. His fingers are shaking too much to get a shell in right, though. He fumbles the one 7.62mm he finally finds into the snow. His chest shudders with laughter. He can't even do this right. He lets the rifle fall away, is looking back to the fire, squinting like to see it better. Or to see something over there better.

Denorah. Den. D.

He pushes away from the truck, makes himself take the walk to her. Just to hold her again. He wants to repeat her season average to her, and project what would have been her junior year on varsity, her senior year in the state tournament. He wants to tell her about all the games she would have won, all the posters they would have made with her on them. The line of shoes that would have been named after her.

Did you get the new Cross Guns yet?

They're so dope.

Do I look like her when I come up like this, on the toes?

And then he's there, stepping around the sparking fire.

"D?" he says.

Not because it's her. Because it's not. It never was.

Gabriel looks back to the mound in the snow his best friend is, then to not-Denorah again.

It's the—it's the *kid*? In the scrimmage jersey he has no reason to be wearing, that's black on the outside, bright white on the secret inside. His hair is down and everywhere, could be Denorah's hair, *was* D's hair.

"N-Nate?" Gabriel says. "*Nathan?*"

Where the Mauser caught him is low down in the left side. Not the kill zone, but close enough. The kind of shot where you just have to follow whatever you shot back into the trees, wait for it to collapse at the end of its blood trail.

But he's not dead yet. Not quite.

"Hard to kill, aren't you?" Gabriel says with an almost smile.

It shakes the boy awake, and, maybe because Gabriel's standing over him bloody-handed, bloody-faced, the boy jerks away, pushes with his heels, shaking his head no, no, and something else, the syllable and sounds coming fast, in a tumble, over and over.

Po'noka?

Gabe narrows his eyes, has to hunt deep in his head for this old word, then stand real still in his thoughts, wait for it to stand up from the snow, a brown form against all that white.

"*Elk?*" he says, and, following the boy's eyes, looks behind him, looks all around, but you're not there anymore.

When Gabriel comes back to the boy, the boy's still trying to get away, leaving more and more blood in the dirty snow.

"Wait, wait, let me get your dad," Gabriel says, going to his knees and holding his red hands up and out to show he's no threat.

It doesn't help.

The boy pushes back and back, past the lodge, under the lowest rail of the horse pen, leaving dark smears on the pipe.

"No, listen—" Gabe says, trying both to follow and not be scary, but he stops when the horses whinny in their panicked way about this intruder underfoot. "Shh, shh, guys," he says to them, stepping in, but the way he smells—they shy back, rear up, rise and fall in the darkness, and there can't be room in that pen for all four of them, can there? Their weight coming down shakes the ground and Gabriel looks away, kind of numb, finds himself just staring down at a clot of the blood the boy left behind in the slush. A clot of blood he probably needs, or would have needed, if the horses hadn't done their thing to him.

"Another fine job," Gabriel says, walking away from this, kicking snow with his bare feet, his hands running through his hair. He sits on Victor Yellow Tail's hood and stares into the fire, the drums beating, voices rising, his mind working, mouth muttering: Why did he think the kid was D, even? Why *would* he? It was . . . it was because the kid had been wearing a *black* jersey, right? And the last time Gabriel had seen the daughter, she'd been wearing white?

Still, was an inside-out jersey, plus long black hair, really enough for him to think Nate was Denorah? Was he not thinking right because Cass had just clipped his ear? Because Jo had just—Why was she even *under* that truck? Why was she home at all? Didn't she work most nights?

"What the hell is happening here tonight?" Gabriel says, pushing away from the car and looking all around.

"Po'noka?" he says at last, trying it out like it might be the key that opens everything up.

What would an elk have to do with this, though? How could an elk make them all kill each other? Why would an elk even care about two-leggeds, unless the two-leggeds were shooting at them?

And why is he even thinking like that? *Two-leggeds?* Has he fallen so far back into himself that he's sitting in Neesh's lodge again, listening to the old bullshit stories? If he's there again, though, then he's there with Cass and Lewis and Ricky, he figures. Back when there were four of them.

He rubs that spot beside his eye.

"One little, two little, three little Indians," he singsongs, and kind of laughs, kind of cries. It turns to coughing again, and when it won't stop he stumbles to the camper, tries the locked door, then feels his way around to the outhouse. All he needs is tissue, some toilet paper, something for his nose or he's going to suffocate.

When he swings the outhouse door open, Victor Yellow Tail is there, a bib of blood on his uniform shirt, his head lolling, his pistol in his hand like he had plans.

An elk mother will use her hooves when she can, but she'll bite if she needs to.

Gabriel closes his eyes, opens them again, and Victor Yellow Tail is still there, still dead.

"Then there was me," Gabriel mumbles, smiling a sloppy smile, and closes the door. It swings back open, so he shuts it again, and again and again and again, slamming it shut enough that none of this can even have happened.

But it did.

And he's the only one still standing knee-deep in it all, he knows. He's the one they're going to say did it, who cares why. Because he's an Indian with a Bad Track Record. Because a Tribal Police Officer Came Out. Because He Didn't Like His Other Friend's Fiancée. Because His Mind Boiled Out in a Sweat. Because His Murderer Friend Just Got *Shot*. Because the Great White Stepfather Stole All Their Land and Fed Them Bad Meat. Because the Game Warden Wouldn't Let Him Get His *Own* Meat. Because His Father Reported Him for Stealing a Rifle. Because the Rifle Was Haunted by War. Because because because. He did it for all those reasons and whatever else the newspapers can dream up.

Unless he runs.

Unless he runs to the mountains and lives there the old way, never comes back down, even for beer. But, maybe just to go to one of his daughter's games? Maybe just to stand by the Boss Ribs's grave fence? And wherever Cass gets buried? And Lewis?

He shuffles up to the fire, opens his palms to that wonderful heat. He's shivering, his teeth clanking against each other. He looks to the lodge, sprayed now with Nate's blood, hates himself for being thrilled it's not his *daughter's* blood, and then he studies the old truck, its frame on the ground. Finally his eyes settle on the mounds out in the snow.

He goes there, past the dogs, and drops to his knees beside his best friend.

"It's just you and me, man," he says down to him.

He sits down, the snow not even cold anymore, even though one ass-cheek of his pants is flapping. He works his legs under Cassidy's head, cradles his face, lowers his forehead to what's left of his friend's, and then he looks up fast, as far into the sky as he can.

"It wasn't her, man," he says, knocking his forehead into Cassidy's twice, kind of hard. Love taps. "It wasn't D, C."

Cassidy just stares. His eyes don't look the same direction anymore. In death, he's an iguana. Gabriel braces himself for Cassidy's mouth to open, for a great tongue to roll out, slap at something.

It wouldn't be the worst thing this night's had to offer.

"This is—this is goodbye, man," Gabriel says. "I'm going to—they're going to think it was me. And I guess it was, for Jo. And the kid, too. And you. Definitely you, man. You should have just—you should have pulled your shot an inch to the left, man."

He drills the pad of his middle finger into the dot of scar tissue by his right eye, the same place he's been touching since he was a kid.

"You always were a terrible shot, though," he says, then closes his eyes hard. "*But it wasn't D*," he whispers, thrilled to be delivering this news. "It wasn't D. That's the main thing. She's all right. Now I'm . . . I'm going up to live with the—"

When he looks up to the snow crunching then not crunching, you're standing there, holding the Mauser across your hips, left hand ran all the way up the forestock, to the uneven checkering. It hurts to touch it, to even think about touching a *rifle*, but this is the only way now.

You can feel your eyes are the hazel and yellow that feels right, and that they're maybe a smidge or two bigger than makes sense for this face.

Gabe nods, says, "It was you who did all this, wasn't it? Lewis too, right?"

You don't owe him an answer. You don't owe him anything.

"Anybody ever tell you you've got eyes just like an elk?" he says. "Not the—the color. But . . . something, I don't know."

Down the slope the herd is already waiting for you, drifted in like ghosts, not even one of them bleating or calling. The ground under them is churned and dark and raw. The smell is so wonderful. You can't breathe it in deep enough.

"The kid saw you, didn't he?" Gabriel says, laughing it true. "P-Po'noka, right?"

"Ponokaotokaan*aakii*," you say down to him. Elk Head *Woman*.

Gabriel works through this, gets it enough, looks up to you and nods that he can see that, sure.

You hold the rifle out to him. An offering.

"Why?" he says, shying away from it, but finally having to catch it when you throw it sideways down at him.

He plants the Mauser's butt in the snow to prop himself up, says it again. "Why are you doing all this?"

If you tell him, he would get to die knowing it was all for a reason, that this has been a circle, closing. Which would be more than you ever got, that day in the snow.

You nod to the rifle he's holding, say in his bitter English, "Do it or I go after your calf for real."

He watches you for maybe five seconds here, and then he looks to this rifle.

When he racks the bolt back, the wet brass flashes in there for a bright instant.

"I dropped that shell in the snow," he says.

"It stinks," you tell him back, crinkling your nose.

"You'll really leave her alone?" he says, ramming the bolt home in a way that straightens your back. "You won't touch her? She's— you know she's going to get away from here, don't you? You can see that?"

It would be so easy for him to angle that barrel at you, wouldn't it?

But he's not thinking like a hunter right now. He's thinking like a father.

"Okay, okay," he says at last, and angles the awkward rifle around, the barrel chocking up under his chin, his head having to tilt up because the rifle's long. "Like this?"

His breath is fast and shallow like getting ready, and then he closes his eyes, pulls the trigger all at once.

Click.

"Oh shit," he says, flipping it back around with a halfway laugh, the barrel pointed right into you now, his finger still on the trigger, his thumb figuring the big obvious safety out.

"You promise you won't come after her?" he says one last time.

You shake your head no, so he'll get the rifle back under his chin. But then he stops, says, "Wait, does that mean you will or you won't go after her?"

He finally smiles when you're just drilling your eyes into him. He leans back a bit, says, "I always—I wanted it to be like those two Cheyenne I read about, yeah? I wanted to run my horse back and forth in front of all the soldiers, so it would be like . . . it would be heroic. Like the old days. Not like—not like this."

"Now," you tell him.

"Okay, okay, geez," he says, "at least let me—" and instead of using his own hand, he shoves his friend's dead index finger through the trigger guard.

"I killed his almost-wife," he explains, getting the finger positioned just right. "This is—he's avenging her, like. It's an Indian thing. You'd understand if you were, you know, a *person*."

He opens his mouth, swallows the barrel in deep enough that his eyes fill with tears. The metal rattles against his teeth. His breath is fast and shallow, like it matters anymore how much air he has.

"D, D, D," he says around the barrel, and nods once to himself for rhythm, then again to be sure, and on the third time he raises his fingers over his friend's hand and gallops them down one after the other, until the last one, the one that makes the trigger pull, and right as the sound blasts a fist-sized hole through the top of his head you realize that he's made his fingertips into horse hooves, that it's still the cavalry taking a shot at him, and finally getting lucky.

The rifle is angled away from you but the red mist of him rises, plumes over, coats your face.

You wipe it off, don't lick it away, then look back down the idea of the road, to the cattle guard out there in the deep dark.

Now there's only one left, one you just promised you wouldn't go after.

Killing a calf is the worst of the worst, you know.

Beside it, breaking a promise is nothing, really.

Nothing at all.

MOCASSIN TELEGRAPH

Say we're all in a John Wayne movie. Say your trusty reporter here has his ear pressed right down to the railroad tracks, so he can listen up the future.

What am I hearing? you ask.

The bus tires of Havre leaving their parking lot for tonight's big scrimmage with the girls, sure. But you don't need to be a real Indian to know the Blue Ponies are coming to town for a grudge match, to prove that last year's tournament win was due to skill, not injury.

No, you come to this column for the real dirt, don't you? Let me dish. And, as always, you didn't hear it from me.

Word has it that a certain big-time college scout has been seen in blaze orange down at the diner. Further word has it that, once his lunch schedule was established, it's completely possible that a certain coach may or may not have sidled up to his table, mentioned where the elk have been the last week or two, and kind of, shall we say, bundled that tidbit in with a certain scrimmage going down tonight.

Supposedly, the trade was that if a certain scout bagged his trophy early enough in the day, well, that would leave his evening free, wouldn't it?

And, if he was free enough, why not come for the junior high game as well, right? You thought I was talking about a certain high school coach, not the coach who wears her hair in two pigtails?

For shame.

Junior high coaches know as well as high school coaches that all the elk are bunched together up towards Duck Lake all this week. The game wardens have been trying to scare them back over to the park, or onto the old folks' happy hunting grounds, but elk are elk, right?

This isn't the Fish & Game column, though. This is what you won't hear anywhere else, unless you have your ear to the rail like me. Trust me, a certain junior high coach either has or hasn't got a big-time college scout out to watch her star player. You know the one. You've seen her after practice, smoking the varsity girls and boys both? We've never had a player like her, niiksookowaks. This is history in the making. I'll be there, trying to read over the scout's shoulder.

And, remember, you didn't hear this from me.

IT CAME FROM THE REZ

SATURDAY

Denorah can tell the order the sweat lodgers got there last night.

Cassidy was first, of course. It's his place. He didn't so much get there as just never leave. Her dad was next, front tires cocked at what he tells her is a rakish angle, like his truck just stopped there in the middle of some crazy slide and he had to wait for all the dust to settle before kicking the door open, stepping down, peeling out of his sunglasses one side at a time. After that dramatic or *not* dramatic entrance had been Victor and Nathan Yellow Tail, the cop car nosed right up to the fire like claiming it for its own, its tracks in the snow showing where it had to step off the sort-of road to get around all the trucks that thought they were so important.

Last, this morning probably, when her shift was over, was Jolene, pulled up right behind Cassidy's old truck that used to be up on blocks but is flat to the ground now, like embarrassed about something it's done.

None of the sweat lodgers are up and about yet. Denorah would think it was for the usual reason—beer-after-ceremony, which her dad would have claimed was "rehydration"—but then Victor's car wouldn't still be there. And no way would *Officer* Yellow Tail let *minor* Nathan drink with her dad and Cassidy, even if Cassidy's finally settling down a little, according to Denorah's mom.

"Hello?" Denorah says, still a good walk away from it all. She could have screamed it if she wanted, she supposes. Near as she can tell, the place is dead times two. Even the sweat lodge is collapsed, smoke and the lines of heat blurring the air above it, the blankets and whatever smoldering, meaning it's a trash pit now. Next time, the sweat will be somewhere else.

It's good Denorah's mom didn't see that smoke.

"I'm only letting you do this because that Crow from the grocery is there," she'd just told Denorah at the cattle guard, after confirming the presence of Jolene's truck. "I'll be back in one hour, got it? You're lucky I had to return this to Mona."

"This" was Mona's casserole dish that had wended its way from Tre's house to Denorah's, because Trina is always coming up this way to smoke cigarettes with Mona in her new trailer. There's an old bear that gets after the berry bushes just down from the trailer in the spring, and Denorah's mom is forever talking about that—as she calls it—silly old bear. Silly or not, that bear is her mom's excuse for one more cigarette, one more pack, one more carton. It's like she's the most willing prisoner in Mona's little window nook thing, that Denorah thinks looks like the cockpit of a spaceship, like the two of them are plotting some big escape, once Denorah's out of the house.

"One hour, right here," Denorah said back to her mom.

It feels military, repeating commands back so there's no confusion, but it seems to result in less grief, so Denorah plays along.

Still standing at the cattle guard, Cassidy's place either a ghost town or a junkyard, no dogs even—no dogs?—Denorah looks back to the road for her mom's car. Past where the road ducks down to the right there's just snow and snow and more snow, though, and then the shimmer of the lake where her dad told her one of his running buddies died, way back.

But her dad's got a story for every place on the reservation, doesn't he? If not someone he used to run with in high school, then a coulee where he popped a blacktail once, a ridge where he found a little pyramid of brass shells for a buffalo gun, a place he once saw a badger humping it across the grass, an eagle dive-bombing it like it thought this was the biggest prairie dog ever.

When she was a girl Denorah had soaked every one of those stories up, and then, later, her mom told her to be careful what she took for gospel. The dead friend stories, though, Denorah still kind of believes those. Because it would be bad luck to lie about that, she thinks, and her dad's the kind of superstitious he thinks nobody notices. Case in point: That day him and Ricky and Cassidy and Lewis popped all those elk back in that section they weren't supposed to be in, the one down by the lake? He's never mentioned that to her even once, even in defense, even to give her the rest of the story, how it wasn't like it sounds, the story her stepdad told her isn't the real story, isn't the one with feet on the ground and smoke in the air, bang bang bang. And the reason he hasn't said anything to her about it, she's pretty sure, it's because to talk about it out loud would throw his sights off next time he was lining up on an illegal elk, those being the only kind he can shoot anymore.

The same as he's never told her his version of that elk massacre, he's also never told her *how* his friend died at the lake. Just that that's where his body was. To talk about what actually happened might get him in Death's crosshairs, the way he thinks. So, because he won't speak directly about that story, she kind of believes it, in spite of her mother's warning. But still, her dad's got to *think* of that dead friend still, doesn't he, even if he won't talk about him out loud? How could he not? Every time he's out here to see Cassidy he probably stops halfway across the cattle guard and looks back to Duck Lake. He says that when his *other* dead friend Ricky found his *lake*-dead friend, Ricky got hauled into jail himself. Not because he did it—everybody knew who did it—but because he'd had to break into one of the summer people's lake houses over there to call in about that body, and the cops couldn't look past a breaking-and-entering, not when there was property damage.

It was all part of a lesson her dad was trying to impart, Denorah's pretty sure, which was why he was even talking about the whole thing at all, but she isn't sure if it was a warning against calling the cops or against finding a dead body. Maybe both at once? Probably the idea was that when you see somebody dead and floating like that, you just keep walking, let somebody else find it, or nobody.

She knows the joke about how Indians are crabs in a bucket, always pulling down the one that's about to crawl out, but she thinks it's more like they're old-time plow horses, all just walking straight down their own row, trying not to see what's going on right next to them.

Speaking of horses: Cassidy's?

Last time she was out, her dad had let her sit up on that paint horse, the one Jolene calls Calico, like a cat, but that was . . . was it last summer? Was Jolene living here by then? Yeah, she was. That was when her dad was still calling her Dolly, like the best joke ever, and Cassidy had even played along at first, faking like he had a beard—like, if his girlfriend was Dolly, that meant he was Kenny, ha ha ha. It had been so stupid that it had been hard for Denorah not to smile about it. The way they were fooling around so natural made her kind of see her dad and Cassidy twenty years ago. It had been a good day. But now the pens are empty, the gate flapping. Cassidy wouldn't have sold his Indian ponies, though. They're probably grazing in some meadow, won't trail back to the barn until dark.

Also: Who cares?

Denorah's here for forty dollars, not to conduct the Big Horse Poll and Headcount.

She nods to herself about this and leans up the road, follows its loop around and down, keeping to the ruts because the snow's crusted hard and she doesn't need to hyperextend a knee before tonight's game.

She's almost to Jolene's truck when the driver's door opens and Jolene cocks her right foot up on the duct-taped armrest, to tie a high-top tighter.

Her long hair blows out over her knee.

"Hey," Denorah calls ahead, to keep from getting shot.

Jolene flinches around, clears her hair from her face, from her blown-red right eye, and she *isn't* Jolene.

"Whoah," Denorah says, stopping hard, looking around at everything all at once, to be sure this is still Cassidy's place.

Not-Jo snickers, keeps tying her laces.

"Who are you?" Denorah asks.

"Don't worry," Not-Jo says, "this isn't a raiding party, little girl."

"*Little girl?*"

"Young lady?" Not-Jo stands from the truck, sways her back in, extending her arms to either side, wrists up, stretching. It's a full-body yawn. She's wearing black gym shorts and a faded yellow T-shirt with the arms scissored off, the neck cut out, maroon sports bra.

"Where's Jolene?" Denorah says, not even trying to reel the accusation in.

"You're Gabriel's girl," this woman says, angling her head over to study Denorah. "You *do* look like him. That's not an insult."

"You're Crow, aren't you?" Denorah says.

"Your dad would have been pretty—I mean, if he was a girl," the woman says. "I'm Shaney, Shaney Holds. Jolene's best cousin. Maybe the best cousin of all time, jury's still out on that one."

"What are you doing here?"

"Getting interrogated by a kid?" this "Shaney" says with a smile, then reaches importantly back into Jo's truck and hauls out a basketball, claps it in front of her like something's starting.

"You play, right?" she says, passing the ball across to Denorah. "Your dad says you're pretty good."

"Where is he, do you know?" Denorah says, casting around Cassidy's place a third time.

"Good luck with that," Shaney says with a smile.

"What do you mean?"

"That kid . . . Nate?"

"Nathan Yellow Tail."

"He heard the dogs bawling after something down that way," Shaney says, hooking her chin downhill to where the trees start. "His dad, that big cop guy, he thought it would be all super-Indian if they rode horses down to check it out."

"My dad can *ride*?" Denorah says.

"Just glad they're gone," Shaney says. "I can't shoot the ball when the horses are in their pen. I think one of them's gun shy or something, I don't know. Gets them all riled up. But, now that they're gone . . ."

She opens her hand for the ball and Denorah underhands it back to her.

"Why's the sweat lodge burning?" Denorah asks.

"They used plastic for the frame," Shaney says with an amused shake of the head. "It kind of melts in the heat, I guess? Whole thing collapsed in on the rocks. They told me to watch it, make sure it doesn't catch the grass."

Denorah nods. That sounds about right for her dad.

"Even Nathan rode a horse?" she says, incredulous. "He's always being all gangster."

"Two hundred years ago, the gangsters rode war ponies,"

Shaney says, and shuts the truck door with her hip. "Twenty-one till they get back? I want to see if your dad was lying about what you can do out there."

Denorah looks to the goal poking up from the grass maybe fifteen yards to the left of them, over from the outhouse. It's a square, rotting-away backboard nailed flush to a tribal utility pole—the kind of court where if you don't slash in from the base-line for a layup, then where you come down, it's into a rake of creosote splinters.

"Got a game this afternoon," Denorah says.

Shaney nods, looks out to the grey trees, like for the men.

"You can hang in the camper if you're cold," she says. "Or sit in the truck. I think they broke all the lawn chairs around the fire last night."

She's right: the chair by the dead fire is folded over, the one by the lodge is bent in on itself, and the other is sideways, thrown out in the grass and snow.

"Did you play?" Denorah asks. "In high school, I mean."

"I used to *eat* basketballs, little girl," Shaney says, clapping the ball hard in her hands, and Denorah knows right then she's not sitting in any camper, she's not sitting behind the steering wheel of any truck.

"Maybe just twenty-one," she says to Shaney. "Until they get back."

"Sure your coach won't mind?"

"Not if I play like I play, she won't."

"How old are you?" Shaney asks, the crow's feet around her eyes crinkling with amusement.

"How old are *you*?" Denorah says right back.

Shaney hooks her head for Denorah to fall in. Denorah does, and, turning away from the drive, she sees that her dad's wind-shield is caved in on the passenger side. It stops her for a moment, but that could be anything. Knowing him, he's got six different stories cooking already for what happened, each more epic and unbelievable than the last, none of them involving him being at fault.

The seventh story will probably be about how he needs this forty dollars toward a new windshield. Does his Finals Girl want him to freeze, come January?

Denorah follows the path Shaney's picking through the hard snow. It's rocks and dry patches, but it gets them there without wet feet or bleeding shins.

Shaney bounces the ball high off the concrete and tracks it while working a hair tie off her wrist, gathering her hair behind her neck. On the ball's third bounce she rabbits forward, snatches it on the way to the bucket, then stops on a dime, fakes once, and goes up, executing a neat little fadeaway that banks in like money.

"Your coach let you Reggie Miller your left foot out like that?" Denorah says, down on one knee to retie her right shoe.

"Crow ball," Shaney says. "What do y'all play up here? Big on the fundamentals, all that boring-ass stuff?"

Denorah switches to her other shoe, battens it down tight, making sure the bows are even. Not because she's superstitious but because it makes sense to have them both the same.

"Done stalling yet?" Shaney says from the pole, and snaps a bounce pass across.

Denorah has to stand fast to catch it at her stomach, keep it from slamming into her face.

Shaney has her by six inches, she guesses. But tall girls are never the ball handlers, at least not in small schools—not in reservation schools. Tall girls get trained on boxing out, on rebounding, on posting up and setting screens, using their hips and elbows. All of which a team needs to win, for sure. None of which are much use one-on-one, which is a game of slashing, of stopping and popping.

Denorah dribbles once to get the right feel for this ball, this court.

"Warm up?" Shaney says, bouncing in place.

Denorah snaps the ball back to her, says, "So you can clock my dominant hand, my favorite place at the top of the key?"

Shaney chuckles, says, "There's no key out here, little girl. Just you and me."

"The Blackfeet and the Crow . . ." Denorah says.

"If that's how you want to look at it," Shaney says, stepping out to what would be the free-throw line and waiting for Denorah to step into position in front of her.

Denorah takes her time, won't be rushed.

"Don't want to wear you out for your big game or anything," Shaney says with a little bit of bite, dropping the ball in front of her for Denorah to check.

Denorah takes the ball in both hands, spins it back toward herself, and makes a show of looking around, says, "What, there another baller out here I'm not seeing?"

"Cocky, I like that," Shaney says, taking the ball back. "Just like your dad."

"Done stalling yet?" Denorah says, getting down in the stance, palms up, tapping her forearms on the outside of her knees twice like activating Defense Mode.

Shaney dribbles once, high by her right hip, and then turns around, giving Denorah her ass, backing her down already, which is what you do when you have a size advantage.

When you're on the wrong end of that size game, though, then you can time it out, stab an arm in, slap the ball away.

Denorah gives ground like she's falling for this, then, the next time Shaney goes for a bounce-against, the round of her back to Denorah's chest, Denorah steps back—pulling the chair out, Coach calls it—comes around with her right hand, reaching in for that blur of orange leather.

Except Shaney wasn't backing her down. She was baiting the trap.

What she does now is peel around the other way, her long legs giving her what feels like an illegal first step, and by the time she's done with that step, throwing the ball ahead of her in a dribble she'll have to chase down, Denorah's already out of position, can just watch.

She's never been spun on like this.

To make it worse, Shaney doesn't just lay it in, either. She catches her dribble in both hands, rocks her elbow out hard to the right, and plants one high-top on the pole about chest-level and uses that to push higher, twisting in the air to come around the right side, having to guide the ball *around* the net on the way, like having to fight through the trees to get to the bucket.

She lays it in gentle with both hands, lands already jogging backward.

Fucking-A, Denorah knows her face has to be saying.

This might be a game.

THANKSGIVING CLASSIC

15–15, and Denorah isn't having to run her flyaway hair out of her face anymore. Now it's pasting to her skull with sweat.

She dribbles in hard to the left, Shaney bodying right up to her but not tangling their feet somehow, and stops, makes to rise up, getting Shaney's long body into the air. It's one of the only two strategies she's found that are worth anything against this tall, slashy defender. Trick is, long bodies stretched out, they take longer to recoil back down, go a different direction.

Instead of letting her feet leave the ground, Denorah reels the ball back, both hands because Shaney will slap it out into the snow again, and leans over to the right, ducking ahead under Shaney's already-coming-down arm.

Position, yes. When you're outgunned, all you can do is whatever you have to for position. Not that there's a ref to blow a whistle, but even a Crow knows that bringing an elbow down into the neck and shoulder of a player in the motion of shooting, that's a do-over.

Now Denorah lets her feet leave the ground, still exploding forward under Shaney's wingspan, and she teardrops the ball up and over, *in*, just enough soft touch, because this bullshit plywood backboard isn't trustworthy, not for someone who hasn't killed a thousand sundowns out here, the clock always ticking its last three seconds down.

"Cheap . . ." Shaney calls out, just generally.

"Sixteen," Denorah says back, collecting the rebound before the ball can get slick in the snow.

She dribbles it slow back to the top edge of the court, bounces it across to Shaney, who, Denorah's satisfied to see, is finally breathing hard as well, her mouth moving like she's the kind of player who's used to having a piece of gum in her mouth. Or used to chewing cud, ha.

"How long you been playing?" Shaney asks. "Your dad never said."

"Was born on a court," Denorah says, Shaney lowering the ball right to the concrete, rolling it slow between them, giving her time to crowd in.

"So this is what's most important to you, right?" Shaney says. "Basketball? Matters more than anything to you?"

Denorah fixes Shaney in her eyes for a moment, like taking stock. "And you think you can take it away from me?" she finally says. "That you can break my pride before the game tonight? You a Blue Pony in disguise?"

"Home court advantage, little girl."

"You're *far* from home," Denorah says, lowering into triple-threat, leading with her face. In practice, Coach will put a big hand on Denorah's forehead while she slashes the ball back and forth and all around to pass, to shoot, to dribble. Now Shaney does the same thing, her rough palm right between Denorah's eyebrows. It's a violation, would be a foul in any game with a whistle, but, too, it slows the whole world down, lets Denorah sort of see this not from her triple-threat position, but from the

side, in ledger art, like this battle between the two of them is so
epic that it's been painted on the side of a lodge, and inside that
lodge, an old man with stubby-thin braids is recounting the story
of that one time the Girl played a game for the whole tribe. How
each dribble shook the ground so hard that over in the Park great
mountainsides of snow were calving off, rumbling down, shaving
the foothills of trees. How each time the ball arced up into the
sky it was merging with the sun, so that when it came down it
was a comet almost, cutting through that orange circle of a rim.
How each juke was so convincing that the wind would come in
to take that player's place but then would get all scrunched up
because the player was already back in that space, cutting the
other way, her path as jagged and fast as a bolt of lightning.

This win isn't just for pride, Denorah tells herself, in order to
push harder, be faster, jump higher. It's for her tribe, her people, it's
for every Blackfeet from before, and after. "You don't win today,"
she says, speaking right into Shaney's wrist.

"And you do?" Shaney says back, getting light on her feet for
what she must think Denorah's move is about to be.

"I am," Denorah says, and pushes hard with her forehead,
nudging Shaney back just enough to clear some space.

She uses it to launch up and back, up and back. It's improper
form, is even poor practice, as it's nearly impossible to replicate all
the variables of a fallaway like this, but you can't always go by the
textbook, either. Some games, you are Reggie Miller. And, if you're
really good, you're maybe even Cheryl.

Denorah rises and rises, falling back at the same time, Shaney
lowering her arms to swing them up together, extend enough to
block this shot, but that smidge of time it takes to lower and jump,
gather and push up, it gives Denorah just enough window to release the ball through.

Still, because of Shaney's length, Denorah has to adjust at the last instant, arc the shot even higher than she'd wanted, make it even more of a prayer.

It *just* clears Shaney's fingertips.

Denorah lands on her ass in the snow a full second before the ball catches the front of the rim, shudders the whole thing, and then—bounce, bounce, jiggle-jaggle—it drops through. Denorah rolls over three times in celebration, snow and dry grass all over her. She's spent more hours on the court than off, she'd bet, and played against girls her age and older, guys, too, on Sunday nights when the gym's open, she's even had the ball at the end of the game more than anybody on her team, but still, this shot, this one lucky roll, it's better than any of the rest of them.

"*Two*," she calls out, because that's how they've been playing, and Shaney's pissed enough she rips the hair tie from her ponytail, runs to the edge of the concrete to throw it as far as she can. It's a scrunchy, though. Too much air resistance. It flutters, dies, doesn't go anywhere.

"You can't beat me," she says—*growls*, really.

"Eighteen," Denorah says, standing, keeping a close eye on Shaney.

Riled up like she is, there's something almost animal about her. In a game it's the kind of thing Denorah could use to get to the free-throw line. Out here miles from anybody, it's more likely to earn her an elbow in her ribs.

It'll just mean she's winning the real game, though.

Shaney gives her the ball, bodies up close enough that Denorah gets a bug's-eye view of her knitted-together, scarred-up forehead, and Denorah fakes back like to repeat that Hail Mary fallaway but Shaney doesn't take the bait, is all over her when she puts the ball down to drive.

Still, Denorah gets the step—you can always get the step, if you want it bad enough—runs the ball as far out in front of her as she can to flip it up at the last possible moment before her next foot touches the ground.

It's pretty, and it's on target, but Shaney's been *on* this ball since the moment she checked it. She doesn't just slap it down, either, she smothers it, she collects it, she wraps around it like a fullback, falls hard enough back into the pole that rotted wood from the backboard rains down over her.

She waves it away from her face, shakes the pain off, her hair almost completely hiding her face now, her teeth flashing in that black shroud.

"You all right?" Denorah says.

"Check," Shaney says, leaving the ball behind her as if disgusted by it.

Denorah uses the toe of her right shoe to flip it up to her hands, a move Coach would be all over—hands, hands, basketball players use *hands*—and, on the way to the top of the key she chances a look back to the dead fire, the smoldering lodge, the horse pens, all the empty trucks. The camper, the outhouse. The whole reservation as backdrop.

"Where are they?" she says, kind of just out loud.

"They're not going to save you, little girl," Shaney says, already in her place.

Not even a *dog* has made it back, though? And what happened to the windshield of her dad's truck?

"I'm not a little girl," Denorah says.

Shaney starts to say something about this but swallows it.

"My mom's coming back by in about fifteen minutes," Denorah adds.

"She can play winner, then," Shaney says, clapping twice for the ball.

Denorah rolls the ball to her slow enough that the lines don't even blur.

Shaney snatches it up the moment it's close enough, follows through on that forward dip of her body, twitches ahead like enough with the bullshit finesse, this time she's going *through* Denorah.

Because she can't get too banged up for the *other* game she's playing today, Denorah flinches back, ready to give ground, sacrifice a point to save her body, but then at the last moment Shaney breaks right, the exact same move Denorah just used on her: get the first step, then stretch out, flip it in.

The reason it didn't work for Denorah was Shaney's length, which Denorah doesn't have.

One blurry dribble and then Shaney's flipping the ball up.

It catches the backboard high and comes down slow, flushes down and through, the net popping up behind it exactly like an old man's lips after he's leaned over to spit.

"Good one," Denorah says, chocking the ball under her arm.

Her legs are trembling, spent, her lungs raw, her heart beating in her temples. This is no way to prepare for tonight's game. Still, if her mom's car crests over the cattle guard, she's going to hold her hand out, tell her to wait, she's got to finish this.

Forty dollars or not, right here's where the real money is.

"Sixteen–eighteen," Shaney says.

"Give up now, you want," Denorah says back. "There's no shame. I'm younger, faster, play every day. You've taken this farther than anyone else would have."

Shaney laughs at this.

"You should probably be asleep now anyway," Denorah says, "right? Or you and Jo on different schedules or something?"

"I slept for ten years," Shaney says back.

After a breath to make sense of this, to *not* make sense of this—she didn't step on a court for a whole decade, and can still play like this?—Denorah bounces the ball across.

Because she's winded, Shaney takes the ball up into the Crow version of triple-threat, which more and more Denorah's thinking might actually be some sort of quadruple-threat, and turns around to back her defender down, probably muscle her back at the end of that, fall back on one leg, bank it in. Not showy, but, if there's no three-second violations, generally effective in one-on-one like this.

But now Denorah knows not to try to reach around, slap the ball. That's what Shaney's waiting for. Probably she's just *acting* spent, is really ready to spin off Denorah, go up and under, lay it in.

Denorah thins her lips, shows her teeth where Shaney can't see, and shakes her head no to the chance of that happening. Not on *this* defender. Not in *this* game.

Still, when Shaney bounces back into her, she can't help but give six inches, a foot.

Again, again.

Denorah steps in to regain ground, leading with her hips now because Coach says that's where women are most solid, and when Shaney's hair is in her mouth she spits it out but doesn't raise a hand to guide the strands out, because being grossed out doesn't matter, not when a point's at stake.

Except—

There's something *wet* on Denorah's chin?

Now she does raise the back of her hand, to wipe at it.

Blood?

Did she bite her tongue? Bust a lip?

No.

She backs off a full foot, to study Shaney's back.

"Hey," she says, stopping the game. "You're bleeding."

The whole back of Shaney's pale yellow shirt is red and dripping, her hair all matted in it.

"When you hit the pole that last time," Denorah adds.

Shaney keeps dribbling, the ball a metronome. Her face shrouded under her everywhere hair.

"We're playing," she says.

"But—"

Shaney spins against nothing, is playing mad now, is up against an imaginary defender.

She slashes past Denorah, is already pulling the ball up under her arm and behind her like protecting it for a bust-through, and, because she can, because she hasn't been in this backed-off of a position yet, Denorah reaches an easy hand out, slaps the ball from around Shaney's back, doesn't even have to shift her feet.

It's not a defensive move, it's a time-out.

The ball rolls off Shaney's knee, out into the crunchy grass and snow. Shaney, her momentum already gathered, has no choice but to keep surging forward. For the second time in as many plays she slams into the utility pole, shaking the janky backboard, more splinters and bird-nest trash sifting down. Denorah steps out of that bad rain, clocks Shaney coming down hard and awkward right *on* her back, like somebody cut her legs out from under while she was up there walking on air.

She flips over fast, onto her palms and toes, and then she rolls her shoulders slow, her hair all around her face, and screams straight down into the concrete, screams for longer than her lungs should have air for.

Denorah turns her head, like studying this from a slightly different angle can make it make sense.

"Hey, hey, are you all—" she tries, leaning ahead with her hand open like to help, but now Shaney is standing in her easy, athletic way, her body loose and dangerous again.

She guides the hair out of her face and . . . her eyes. They're different. They're yellowy now, with hazel striations radiating out from the deep black hole of a pupil. Worse, her eyes are too big for her face now.

Denorah falls back, sits on the concrete with maybe half her weight, the rest on her fingertips.

She's not making the game tonight, she knows.

"What—what are you?" she says, breathing hard from fear now, not exertion.

"I'm the end of the game, little girl," Shaney says, then twitches her head around, stares hard at Cassidy's camper.

Dad? Denorah says deep inside, her heart fluttering with hope.

She looks to the right, trying to will three or four horsemen up from the grey trees, dogs weaving ahead of them.

There's nothing.

"The end of *your* game, anyway," Shaney goes on.

"Why are you doing this?" Denorah says, her voice getting more shaky at the end than she planned.

"Ask your father," Shaney says right back, still watching whatever she's watching over at the camper, or the sweat, or the cop car.

"My dad? Why? What did he do? He doesn't even know you."

"We met ten years ago. He had a gun. I didn't."

To prove it she whips her hair away from her melty forehead, leans forward so Denorah can take a long look.

"He . . . he wouldn't—"

"Shouldn't, wouldn't," Shaney says. "*Did.*"

"Just—just let me go," Denorah says. "You win, okay? We can . . . this is between you and him, then, right? Why do you even need me?"

Shaney settles her weird eyes back on Denorah.

"You're his calf," she says, like that explains anything.

"You're not really Crow, are you?" Denorah says.

"Elk," Shaney says back with a grin.

"My mom's on the way," Denorah says.

"Good," Shaney says back.

Denorah stares at her about this.

"What if I win?" she finally says.

"You won't," Shaney says. "You can't."

"I was," Denorah says. "I am. Eighteen-sixteen."

Denorah stands, staring into Shaney's nightmare face the whole time.

"I don't care what you are," she says. "When you're on this court, you're mine."

"And that's precisely what I'm here to take away from you," Shaney says back. "Before I take everything else."

Denorah gives Shaney her back, steps out into the snow to collect the ball, comes back to the pad of concrete, and cleans the soles of her shoes on the opposite legs of her shorts.

"My ball, right?" she says.

Shaney doesn't say yes and doesn't say no, just takes the check pass.

Denorah walks to her place facing the goal, says, "It's my ball, and"—pointing with her lips—"I'm putting it right there, and there's not one single thing you can do about it."

This is word for word what her dad used to tell her when she was a kid and they were playing in her granddad's driveway, when she could hardly even hold the ball, when he would have to scoop her up under the arms at the last moment of the layup, hold her up to the basket.

But sometimes he'd set her up in defensive position, get loose in the shoulders, his head rocking back and forth, and look up to the goal, tell her he was going to put it right there, and there's nothing Denorah can do about it.

Which is where it all started, she knows.

"What's wrong with your back?" Denorah says, catching Shaney's rolled ball under the sole of her right shoe.

"I'm dying," Shaney says, easy and obvious as anything.

"Serious?"

"But not yet, don't worry."

Denorah isn't sure what to make of this so she just looks to the opposite two corners of the court like confirming with her teammates, and then she feels her mouth curl into her dad's reckless smile. Whatever this is, it's about to happen.

Shaney, whatever *she* is—some Indian demon from way back, some monster her dad found buried on some hill out here, a ghost woman he left in a rolled-over car—she steps in, gets down into defensive stance, her long fingers ready, her teeth showing.

Denorah turns to the side, dribbling with her left and taking stock, and in her head she says a silent apology to Coach, for the move she's about to try.

One thing about Coach, she *does* believe in the fundamentals. Nothing fancy, nothing showy. Three times already this season Denorah's been benched for showing off. Once it was for circling the ball around her waist before a layup on a breakaway, never mind that the crowd all came to their feet for that. Another time it was for passing between a defender's legs, which made that girl mad enough that she ended up getting kicked out a quarter later.

The third time Coach benched Denorah, it was for dribbling behind her back when there was no advantage to do it. Coach had been right, too—it *had* been completely for show, for joy, had been one hundred percent because Denorah *could*.

Never mind that she almost lost the ball, had to step long to keep up with it.

Alone on the little court at her house, though, she's been practicing a new move.

About a third of the time, with no defender, when she's holding her mouth just right and the wind's in her favor, she can stick it.

Okay, one time so far she's sort of nailed it. Everything but the actual shot at the end.

Still, "Bet they didn't teach this at elk school," she says, and then, before Shaney can react—*using* that moment of confusion—she flips the ball around her left hip with her right hand, more a bullet pass than a real dribble, one she has to hula her hips forward a smidge to allow.

The ball bounces once with her serious English on it and then it's beelining for the right corner of the concrete pad and Denorah is already in motion, diving for it, her body blocking Shaney out behind her. Two out of every three times she's done this at home— okay, nineteen out of twenty—she can't catch the ball, has to run her effort off in the grass and snow. It's nearly impossible to catch it, much less turn it back toward the bucket. It's a move Coach would have outlawed for sure if she'd ever seen it. It's a move the crowd would shake the roof off the gym for, if they ever saw it. More important, it's a move that'll break the heart of any defender, Denorah knows. More important than *that*, it's the very last arrow in her quiver, and it's already slashing across the court, is going to bounce out of bounds if Denorah doesn't—

She *just* gets her fingertips to that spinning-away leather, Shaney so close that her hair is coming around Denorah's own face. Committing all of her weight and muscle and hope, cashing in every hour she's spent sweating it out in practice, Denorah pulls that ball tight to her ribs, hands clamped hard to each side so it can't be poked away, and turns on the ball of her left foot, her right shoe already coming up, and up.

She's too close already, though. This court is so small. The burst of speed she needed to catch up with the ball, it's left her already under the basket, where the only thing she can do is the first thing Shaney did to *her*: plant that right shoe as high up the utility pole as she can, wait for her weight to collect behind it. It gives her enough grip for the sole of her shoe to stick when she pushes off, when she forces her already-twisting body up into the air, the net scratchy against her face, her mouth open not in a scream but a war cry, her face full of Shaney's hair because she's right there, is coming up with Denorah, is going to slap this one down no matter how high Denorah climbs.

The only thing Denorah can do, her only hope, it's to extend the ball as far from her body as possible now, *around* Shaney's side where any defender would least expect it, meaning Denorah's one-handing it now, has just enough grip to spin it up, kiss it soft off the other side of the board, and then she's falling away, is falling for miles, back into legend.

The concrete jars her from tailbone to neck, leaves her spitting tongue blood and cheek gristle, but still she sees the ball slip through neat as anything, a pretty little reverse by a player who shouldn't even have that kind of reach, that kind of vertical, that kind of English.

It's about heart, though, Coach is always saying.

When Denorah smiles, she's sure her teeth are red.

"Nineteen," she says, chocking her face up like does Shaney have anything to say about *that*, and then she cringes away all at once, from . . . from—

From splinters in the air?

And sound. Her head is full of it.

A *gun*shot.

She looks up to where Shaney is glaring.

Cassidy's camper.

No, the outhouse.

Victor Yellow Tail is wavering a few feet from it, the door open behind him, his whole front soaked in blood, a pistol flashing in his right hand.

What he just shot was the utility pole.

The backboard is raining more of its rotted wood down.

Shaney bares her teeth, her whole body quivering.

"I killed you," she says across to Victor.

"*Where's my son!*" Victor loud-whispers back—no throat to speak with—and loosely aims the pistol again, shoots.

This time the concrete in front of Shaney chips up. Her leg snaps back and away and Denorah can tell she wants to explode away from this spot, run and run, be miles away.

Now Victor's falling to his knees with the effort of shooting, of screaming, of bleeding so much. But he's still pointing that drooping pistol ahead of him.

Shaney turns her head to the side like he better not, but he pulls the trigger.

This shot catches her in the right shoulder, flings her off the court, into the frozen grass and snow.

Denorah stands, doesn't know what to do.

Instead of just lying there and hurting, like would make sense, Shaney is flopping and writhing in the snow, screaming from the pain, the fingers of her left hand digging into her shoulder, and . . . and: no.

Her face.

Her head.

She arches back, her fingers deep in the meat and muscle of her shoulder, and her face is *elongating* from the strain.

Her cheeks and chin tear with a wet sound and the bones crunch, resettling.

At the end of it her long hair is blowing away from her, isn't connected to her scalp anymore, and her face, it's, she's, her face is—

Not a horse, which is what Denorah thinks at first.

Not a horse, an *elk*.

Elk Head Woman.

Denorah falls away, stands again, knows only to run, to leave, to not be here for whatever's next.

Where she runs is straight to Victor, the cop, the one with the gun.

She slides to her knees in front of him, grabs on to him, and his right hand falls across her back, the pistol hot at the base of her spine.

"Na-Na-Nate," he manages to say.

"*What is she?*" Denorah says, crying, holding so tight on to his bloody shirt, but then with his left hand he guides her away from him, pushes her behind.

Elk Head Woman is standing, is walking this way, her ungainly head turned to the side to better see them with her right eye.

"Go," Victor whispers to Denorah, "*run*," and she does, on all fours mostly, and when Victor's pistol fires again she falls ahead from just the massive cracking *sound* of it, and where she falls, it's into the smoldering lodge.

It's a pit of bodies.

The first she sees is a dog, mouth open, eyes staring at nothing.

She pushes away, trying to climb out, and then it's Cassidy, his face caved in and half burned away.

Denorah screams, can't breathe, can't do anything.

The hair in her hand is, it's—this is her dad.

She opens her mouth, doesn't have any sound left.

Behind her and all around her then, Victor screams through his bloody throat from whatever Elk Head Woman is doing to him.

Denorah rolls around, sees just grey sky above her, and then her right palm finds an ember. She snaps her hand back, holds it to her chest, and, just working on automatic, on instinct, fights her way up from the lodge, her knees and clothes and all of her sticky with ash and gore.

On the other side of the lodge, through the scrim of smoke but staring right through it, is Elk Head Woman.

"*You killed them all!*" Denorah screams through the smoke, holding her right hand with her left. "You killed my . . . my—"

Instead of answering—her mouth is no longer shaped for human words—Elk Head Woman steps forward, over what's left of Victor's broken body, his head just hanging by tendons now, and the way she looks down to get her feet in the right place, it's because her eyes are on either side of her head now.

Denorah steps back, falls down, comes up already running.

In practice, there's a drill Coach makes the team do maybe once a week. More than that would leave them too beat-up to play. But, once a week, she'll line all the girls up on the baseline and step in among them, the ball rocked back to let loose.

The whole time before she blows that whistle, too, she's yelling to them like a drill sergeant, asking, *How bad do you want it? How bad do you want it?*

At the end of a game or the beginning, it doesn't matter, it's never the fastest or the strongest player who gets that rolling-away ball. It's whatever girl dives the hardest. Whoever fights for it. Whoever doesn't let anybody take it away. Whoever doesn't care about their precious hair or skin or teeth. It's all about who-ever wants it the worst.

This is the drill Denorah's running right now.

Only, this time it's no drill.

ONE LITTLE INDIAN

The first place Denorah's going is Mona's. If she can cut across, find the road, it'll take her right to Mona's trailer, and, and, and maybe that old bear will be there, maybe he never went to sleep this winter, maybe he'll smell an elk and stand up, forget about waiting those berries out.

It's a good plan—it's a stupid, stupid plan—until, maybe a mile out, her lungs raw, her shins bloody from how hard the snow's crusted, her feet soaking wet and numb forever, Denorah runs right up to the lip of a drop that's probably a hundred rocky feet down.

The wind coming up it pushes her back, saves her life.

Down at the way-bottom there's an old broken-down corral and a stone something, but nobody's lived down there for eighty, a hundred years. This is one of those far-out allotments that some-body tried to make work, but Blackfeet aren't farmers, Blackfeet aren't ranchers.

"*Nooo!*" Denorah screams down into that big empty space she can't cross.

She looks back like she's been telling herself not to, and maybe a quarter mile back, not even that, it looks at first like a horse is cresting the rise. Her heart swells, thinking it's her dad on one of Cassidy's horses, but that was a lie, the men never went down to see what the dogs had tied into, the dogs were already dead by then, they all were.

And this still isn't a horse head.

It's Shaney, whatever she is. Elk Head Woman.

She walks forward, has human shoulders, a woman's arms, one arm red from all the blood coming down from her shoulder. Long gym shorts and tall socks. Wide eyes fixed right on Denorah.

"*Why won't you even run!*" Denorah yells back.

Elk Head Woman just keeps coming.

Denorah bounces on her feet, her back to that long drop, and looks left and right, her only two choices.

Right is more of the same: what looks like snow forever, all the way over to the Park, but with coulees gouging through deep and sudden. Left is that same snow for maybe a mile, but then there's the lake out that way. The one her dad's friend drowned in, or whatever. And—and that's where his other friend got arrested—

"Oh yeah," Denorah says.

There's *lake houses* over on the shore. Cabins with steep roofs and canoes lashed to the porch across the door, like that would really keep anybody out. Her dad's friend Ricky had broken into one to report that body floating facedown in the water—to *call* and report a body in the water.

Meaning: a phone.

Denorah can call Mona's from there, she can call the Game Office, her dad, her new dad, she can report the massacre, report an officer very, very down.

Denorah looks back to Elk Head Woman, gone again, slogging through the deep snow that's between the rises—she only walks in a straight line, like following a ridge would be undignified, would be the land making her do something.

Picking her foot placements as carefully as she can, so she's walking where the wind's scoured the snow away, Denorah goes left and keeps low, always picking the side of the brush that threatens to drop her down the cliff instead of the other side, where she can be seen.

She remembers some grade school teacher talking about how Indians having long hair—it was Miss Grace, a French-accented blond woman from Canada—how long hair, it helped with hunting. When hanging down, it wavered back and forth like grass, and it hid the recognizable human features.

It had been bullshit, of course—hair isn't grass, faces are faces—but Denorah has never forgotten it, either.

Running now, half certain that Elk Head Woman anticipated which direction her prey would take, is cutting across on the diagonal, is about to step over this rise *right here*, Denorah hooks a finger into the tail of her braid and runs the band off, combs the rest free with her fingers.

In her head she's practicing what she's going to say into the phone.

My dad, Cassidy, she killed them all, you've got to—

No. Start with Victor.

Your . . . your cop, your officer, Nathan Yellow Tail's dad, he tried shooting her but she . . . she—

Also: *Her back is already hurt. That's where you need to shoot her. If you shoot her from the front she'll just pull the bullet back out.*

Like she's even going to get to call. Like she can even make it the two more miles to the lake. Like she's not going to fall one too many times, roll over, find Elk Head Woman standing over her.

Why would a phone even still be hooked up out there over winter?

But where else is there to go?

Denorah shakes her head, her hair down now.

She imagines Coach behind her, blowing the whistle.

The next time she looks back, there's no elk head cresting. It doesn't mean anything, she tells herself.

Run, run.

She does, harder, and it's good that she does. This time when she looks back, Elk Head Woman is right there, maybe forty yards back.

She stops, turns her head to the side to get Denorah in one of her big eyes.

"I beat you," Denorah mutters, not even close to loud enough, and forces herself up a steep rise, comes over it at a shamble, into . . . into—

Somebody's old place. A ramshackle house low to the ground, all the windows gone, the walls peeling away. Two old hatchbacks left where they died, it looks like. A barn or shop that's blown over except one corner. The only structures still standing, not caring about the wind and snow and loneliness, are three rusted-purple boxcars parked nose to tail, the kind people use for storage, the kind her stepdad recommends all around the reservation since they're about the only thing bears can't get into. Whoever set them up here was playing with a big train set, it looks like— no, of course: they were trying to get a snowbreak going. Giving the snow something to drift against, to keep it from building up against the house, but these boxcars are train-tall, too, are sitting on blocks or actual wheels or something.

"*Hello!*" Denorah yells down to the place, but it's obviously abandoned.

And, is she hearing footsteps behind her? *Hoof*steps?

She surges downhill, sliding on her butt and the heels of her hands over and over. When she looks back this time, Elk Head Woman is walking a straight line down the hill, not slipping even once, because elk always know where the foothold will be.

Denorah turns, frantic, considers trying to stay on the other side of one of the hatchbacks, always moving to the front when Elk Head

Woman comes around the back, but all it takes to lose that game is one good trip. And the house, going in there she'd just dead-end in a bedroom, die there when Elk Head Woman filled the doorway.

Denorah shakes her head no, there's nothing for her here. This is just a place to run through. She does, deciding at the last moment that burrowing down *under* the middle boxcar might slow Elk Head Woman down. If she only walks in straight lines, maybe she doesn't bend over to go under things, either, right?

It's as good a guess as anything.

Denorah slashes forward, Elk Head Woman only two car lengths behind now, and forces herself through the wind-scoured crust of snow packed between . . . probably not wheels, but it doesn't matter.

Immediately she regrets closing herself in like this, and panics hard, digging with her hands, kicking with her legs until she surges ahead into . . . a dry cave under this boxcar. A magic kind of place. So quiet but not quite dark: the sunlight's seeped in through the thousand-million crystals of snow packed all around her, making the walls glow blue like ice.

Not a cave, she tells herself, though. A tomb. A grave.

She gathers her will and pushes into the far blue wall, takes a deep breath to push through, but then each sidearm of snow she sweeps away, ready to break into open air, there's just more snow, and more snow. She gasps her lungs empty, tries to suck a breath in but there's only snow everywhere, in her mouth. She gags, bucks, gets her feet under her as best she can and just *pushes*. Into more snow.

But her hand, it's through, it's out there.

She's swimming now, swimming up through a slushee, not quite surfacing but pulling enough crusted snow down that a sort of sinkhole to the sky opens above her. Her mouth at the bottom of that funnel, she draws as much air in as she can. And again.

Like whoever put the box cars there planned, and like she didn't think to anticipate, the snow on this is drifted deep-deep, and sloped out for probably thirty feet.

Denorah trudges out through it, the crust cutting into her neck, then her chest, then her stomach, thighs, shins.

On level ground at last, she lowers herself to her fingertips, shakes her hair out of the way, and looks back through the chasm she just made, that'll probably hold for a few more minutes yet.

Elk Head Woman's high-tops and tall socks are there through the opening, blurry through the wall of icy snow on the other side. But they're not moving. For the first time, they're not moving.

What? Denorah says to herself.

She stands, ready to run, but then doesn't. She looks through again.

Elk Head Woman's high-tops and socks again. Still.

"What the hell?" Denorah says, looking left and right to be sure this isn't a trick, that Elk Head Woman isn't coming around either side.

Has . . . did Shaney get stupid when her head went all elk? Is she *acting* like an elk now more than a person?

Denorah stares at the backside of the drift she just clawed up from.

Jutting up from it, to the roof of the boxcar, is the built-on ladder.

This is what smart girls do, she tells herself. When the killer's right on their tail, they run up to someplace they can't get down from.

But she has to see. She has to know.

Denorah nods to herself, nods again, then backs up and rushes ahead, to run up the side of the icy drift, clamp a hand onto that lowest rung.

She makes it three steps before the drift swallows her whole for a second time.

Ten sputtery seconds later she bursts up through the drift partway up the ladder, stabs a hand up one rung higher, pulls herself free.

She clambers to the top, hooks a leg over, and just tries to breathe.

She's wet head to toe now, which isn't wonderful.

It's windier up here, too. Of course.

Denorah hugs herself and inches forward, being sure of each footstep before giving it the rest of her weight. She does *not* need to fall through, into whatever got left behind in this boxcar.

The last four feet are on her stomach, her hair coiled in her hand so it doesn't blow over the edge ahead of her, give her away.

Elk Head Woman is just standing there, her ungainly head cocked a bit to the side, the boxcar locked in her glare.

Denorah smiles.

You're afraid of trains, she doesn't say out loud.

But it's true.

Elk, which is what Elk Head Woman must be in there somewhere, maybe more and more with each step, they're train-shy. Her dad told her this. It was a story from one of his great-uncles, about how once all the men in town had backed a herd of elk up to the tracks, blown them away when the train came. They hadn't meant to use the train as a fence, were just using it for sound cover since they weren't supposed to be shooting in town, but it had turned into a fence all the same. The one or two elk that got away, her dad said, had told the rest the Truth About Trains, and that was that, no more using train tracks to hunt.

Evidently trains themselves are even scarier, never mind that there's no wheels on this train. Never mind that the cars aren't even actually connected. Never mind that there aren't any *tracks*.

Elk might be tough and fast, Denorah figures, but they don't seem to be the best problem-solvers. Still, it's not going to take

Elk Head Woman forever to figure out that this train is only three cars long, and not making any sparks, not filling the world with sound.

Elk Head Woman opens her mouth and a low bleat eeks out, like testing this situation, like announcing her uncertainty, like asking the herd for help here. When none comes she steps back, like the train trance she's in is losing a bit of its grip.

Denorah turns, crawls back to the ladder, hand-over-hands it down into the drift, kicks out the other side, walking her previous churned-up path.

Still no Elk Head Woman.

"Choo-choo, crazy lady," Denorah says, tossing a middle-finger salute off her forehead—another thing she learned from her dad, every time they'd just passed a cop.

The lake, she's saying inside.

She can make Duck Lake now.

The one time she looks back, there's no Elk Head Woman rounding either side of the boxcars. But there will be, she knows. There will be.

Denorah quickens her pace.

BLOOD-CLOT BOY

She should have crossed the dirt road she needs ten minutes ago, Denorah knows. Twenty.

It's like—it's like all the roads are gone. Like the reservation's dialed back a hundred years, to before cars. Like that broken-down corral back there, like it's probably still standing, has a stone house beside it now, smoke curling up from the chimney.

Either that or Denorah's a town girl, knows every inch of the basketball court, but the ungreat outdoors? Not so much.

One tree is the same as the next. All this snow looks like all the rest of the snow.

The lake, though.

Every few hundred yards she'll work her way up a rise, see it shimmering in the distance.

What time does it get dark? Four?

Coach is going to flip when her star player doesn't show up an hour before the game. But that's good. Wait, no: That doesn't matter. By then Denorah's mom will have called in the National Guard, probably. She'll have walked up Cassidy's long driveway, found all the bodies burning, seen the blood splashed on the court, found Victor Yellow Tail over by the outhouse, killed twice.

And . . . and there are tracks in the snow, aren't there? Denorah looks behind her to be sure.

Hopefully Elk Head Woman is still stuck on the wrong side of that ghost train. But: Don't count on that, Denorah tells herself. Elk Head Woman's got to be close already. Don't look now. Okay, don't look again, and again.

Denorah sags to her knees, makes herself push up, push on.

Her first wind was spent before Cassidy's camper was even out of sight. Her second wind didn't even register. She's going on pure need to survive now. Need to survive and the conditioning Coach is always saying can decide a game.

All that plus a little hope: the lake houses.

Maybe some crazy hermit of an ice fisherman is down there, snowed in. Maybe some of the high schoolers have broken into one of the cabins like always, are partying this weekend. Denorah can . . . she can take one of their snowmobiles, tear out of there, run for Canada.

Are there any train tracks between here and there? She's not counting on bears to save her anymore, but train tracks.

Run, run, she tells herself.

Last three seconds of the game, *push*. And again.

Her lungs aren't burning anymore, they're cold, and there's blood in the back of her throat she's pretty sure, what Coach calls lung cheese. But Denorah should have blown all that out two months ago, when practice started. And she's lactose-intolerant anyway, she says about the lung cheese, trying to make a joke out of it. The saddest, most-alone joke.

She breathes a long hair down her throat and has to stop to cough it up, puke a little besides.

She's not going to make it.

Is the lake still the same distance away? It can't be.

Denorah closes her eyes tight to reset, to find herself in all this pain, all this cold. Distantly, like it's someone else, she's aware that she's on her knees, that her hands are over her face.

The road has to be up here somewhere. It *will* be up here.

What's happening is that she's thinking like she's in a car, where distance goes by fast. But she's on frozen wet feet, and not taking anything even close to a straight line, and the road *does* swerve the other way anyway. She's probably just coming in above that bend, meaning the road will be farther.

Don't panic, girl. Gather the ball, collect your wits, and check the time clock.

Denorah lowers her hands, looks up to the hazy sun.

At least three hours left, she decides. Three hours before Elk Head Woman is stepping out of every darkness, which will be all there is.

But you'll be dead long before then, she reminds herself, and brings her face down. To a long brown face watching her from maybe twenty feet ahead, just behind the next rise.

Denorah knows not to flinch back, knows better than to scream, but still, inside, all her big plans are falling off their flimsy metal shelves, clattering down into the pit of her stomach.

This is it, then.

Denorah stands, her hair lifting all around her, her hands opening and closing by her thigh because she's about to be gouging eyes and tearing ears, whatever she can get to—you come at a reservation girl, bring a box of Band-Aids—but then . . . then—

It's a buck. A mule deer. She knows because back when she still had to stand up on the seat of her dad's truck to see over the dash, he taught her how to tell mulies and whitetails apart. It's size, sure, and how their racks are shaped if they're male, but before all that, it's color. Mule deer are dusky brown for life out here on the flats, and they don't have white rings around their mouth and nose so much, and, according to her dad, they taste better, but color's an easier tell than running one down, taking a bite.

This one's just staring at Denorah with his big black-marble eyes. Waiting to see what she is, his tail twitching out the seconds.

And then he's looking past her. Behind her.

"No . . ." Denorah says, turning around all the same.

Elk Head Woman, plowing ahead, leading with her wide forehead.

Denorah turns back to tell the mulie to go but he's already gone, running down some frozen creek bed, probably—yep: on cue he bounds up like off a hidden trampoline, floats for a span of ground Denorah is completely jealous of. The instant he hits the ground his hooves are already digging in, churning him forward.

"Hit it, brother," she says, and urges her own self forward as well.

She's got maybe a quarter mile of space between her and Elk Head Woman, if that.

What was that little kid story her dad told her about whitetails? He said he'd heard it from his granddad, but Denorah learned later that he never knew her great-granddad—their years hadn't overlapped, quite. He's heard it from *some* granddad, then. Either way, when he told it, it was so real. The way whitetails got that white ring around their mouth and nose, according to him, it was because they were always sneaking into Browning to drink from the bowls of milk everybody used to leave out, from back when there weren't any reservation dogs, only reservation cats. That was why the whitetail could come into town like that: no barking. But the cats were too good, they got the mice all so scared that the mice got smart, started living so deep in the walls of the houses that the cats couldn't get to them, so one day all the cats just left. It was two, maybe three days after that the first dog trotted into town with a stupid grin on its face, looked around for what it could pee on.

Denorah hates that she'd believed that, once upon a time. And she wants to cry for not getting to believe it anymore.

Yes, the deer drank milk, and that left their mouths ringed white. Fuck it.

Run, run.

She tells herself not to, but she looks back all the same.

No Elk Head Woman. Meaning—meaning Denorah can wait for her to slog up from whatever dip she's in, or she can cover some more ground.

She moves, moves.

What she's counting on now, since the lake isn't getting any closer, is finding the road before her mom's driven down it, finding it and then flagging her mom down, not even letting her stop the car all the way, just climbing in, locking all four doors, and waving her ahead, Go, go, faster, I'll explain later, *go*.

Denorah falls, gets up, falls again, gets up again, and now the horizon is wavery. Not from heat, but from exhaustion. From cold. From no more adrenaline. From too many last three seconds.

But then . . . then: Elk Head Woman *is* Crow, right?

Denorah stands, pushes on, making herself run again.

No way does a Crow win. Not today, not here.

Even *if* the world's blurry. Even *if* Denorah's lungs aren't working. Even *if* she can't feel her legs at all. Even if she's seeing ledger art come to life now in front of her.

She slows, shakes her head, tries to clear her eyes.

The ledger art remains. It's there not fifteen feet in front of her.

A dying Indian slumped forward on a horse, what she sees at every booth at every powwow: The End of the Trail. The only difference is that the tired war pony, it's usually either in silhouette or just white, to better see the dying Indian's bare leg on that side.

This horse is a paint.

It raises its head, gives an obligatory whinny about Denorah.

"Calico?" Denorah says weakly, sure this must be a death vision.

Calico whickers, blowing her lips at the end, and Denorah tracks up the horse's neck.

Tangled in its long mane, tangled tight, are fingers. Behind them, on Calico's back, his blood coating down her side, is the dying rider—

"*Nathan!*" Denorah screams, running to him, hardly registering that they're up on the hard hump of exactly the road she's been trying for.

She gets to his left leg with her hand, and that nudges him awake. He looks around, then down to her.

"D," he says back with half a messed-up smile.

"Are you—what—let me," Denorah says, no clue where to start or how to start it.

At which point Calico dances to the side, away from Denorah.

"Po'noka," Nathan says, sitting all the way up now.

Denorah tracks from his eyes to where he's looking: behind her.

She turns around already shaking her head no.

Elk Head Woman.

So close.

Two free throws away and walking in a straight, pissed-off line. Probably because Nathan's supposed to be dead, not still dying.

"*Go, go, go!*" Denorah says up to him.

He reaches an arm down for her, to haul her up onto Calico with him, but the effort nearly tilts him off, and grabbing onto her looks like it would rip him in half anyway. *More* in half. Denorah pushes him onto Calico's back with both hands, holds him there.

"*No,*" she says, "I'll—I'll lead her to the lake. Tell my—go to town, can you do that? Ride right the fuck into town and tell them, tell them all . . . You know where the Game Office is? Just . . . find my dad, tell him I'm headed to the lake, the one that Junior guy died in, Duck Lake, tell him—"

"Your . . . your dad," Nathan manages to say. "He's—isn't he dead?"

"My *other* dad!" Denorah yells, then grabs on to Calico's head, hauls her around, and slaps her hard on the ass, screaming at the same time.

Calico explodes ahead hard, even wheelie-ing up at first, which Denorah knows is called something else when it's a horse, but there's no time, there's no time.

Elk Head Woman steps up onto the packed dirt of the road.

She's looking at Nathan and Calico, is considering them.

"*Hey, you!*" Denorah says, bringing that long elk face around to her. "Nineteen-sixteen," she says, touching her own chest, then pointing across to Elk Head Woman. "Thought we had a game to finish here."

Denorah gets the full attention of one of those big yellow eyes, and she doesn't wait, she's already running.

This isn't a second or even a fourteenth wind, she knows. This is running on hardpack with feet she can't even feel. This is running downhill, toward water.

This is the real last three seconds.

WHERE THE OLD ONES GO

It doesn't make sense that Denorah is just now getting down to where the lake sort of is. She's been running for *years*, she knows. For her whole life, maybe. And not running the whole time, either. At least three times now she's crashed and burned, just flattened out there, ready to give up. Her chin is raw from scraping, the palms of her hands are bleeding, and she's not thankful that she can feel her feet again. Her feet are full of needles.

In her head she mumbles apology to Coach. Players are supposed to save their legs for game day. Denorah's not going to be able to walk for a week, she knows. If then.

But first she's got to live.

The last time she fell and decided to just rest her eyes for a moment, for a breath, for two, okay, the hard dirt so right and perfect against the side of her face, she came to all at once, instant panic, and rolled over to see Elk Head Woman just two fence posts behind her.

She's walking on the road now too, even though the road curves and twists, banks and falls away in places. If this were fair, if Elk Head Woman were sticking to her own rules, she'd still be taking a straight line, wouldn't she? She'd be getting bogged down out there in the deep stuff. Even elk bog down, right?

But elk walk the road, too, Denorah knows. She's seen them doing it, all in a long line, heads drooping like it's the Elk Dust Bowl, the Great Elk Depression.

"*What do you want?*" Denorah screams back, standing her ground, leaning forward from screaming so hard. "What did I ever do to you?"

For the first time Elk Head Woman's pace steps up.

Denorah falls back, turns it into another push, another run.

What's it going to take? What else can she do? And, how has she missed her mom? There isn't some other road out here, is there? If only her dad were here. He knew all the old poacher cut-acrosses, all the shortcuts if you had four-wheel drive.

Denorah falls again, leaves even more hand-meat and knee-meat and mouth-blood on the road, and then she rises again, not running anymore, just stumbling.

She's not going to make the lake by dark. She's not ever making the lake.

And—and Nathan, he probably fell off Calico a hundred yards out. He doesn't know horses any better than Denorah, and he was already half dead anyway.

It's just Denorah and Elk Head Woman, then. One-on-one.

Denorah walks backward a few steps, sees that distinctive head crest over the road, ears pasted back.

She shakes her head no, no, please, and nearly falls down again, has to catch herself on one of her raw hands, push up hard before it turns into a dirt nap.

Ten, twenty steps later, there's a break in the grey trees beside her. A—a *gate*.

Denorah looks back and Elk Head Woman is gone for a moment, so, no time to think about it, she steps out onto one side of the big corrugated silver tube that runs under this offshoot road, and she jumps from it to the top wire of the gate and flops immediately and unintentionally over the top strand, praying she's not leaving tracks. Without looking back, she staggers ahead, her right hand patting numbly at the point of pain in her belly, probably from a barb. But that hardly even matters at this point. The road's a two-track, but one that hasn't been used for however many snows there's been so far this year.

She tries to keep to the hard hump in the middle but loses the road almost immediately, is in some trees now, is using them to stand, to pull ahead.

Don't look back, don't look back.

Just forward, go, keep moving.

Maybe there'll be a phone booth right up here, she tells herself, her thoughts getting loopy now, the trees smearing into a wall of upright logs. Denorah hand-over-hands down along that wall, feeling for the opening. When she finds it, she was so sure the wall was going to go forever that she falls straight through, is sliding downhill, scraping and rolling through rocks and bushes and dead wood.

She lands in a ball of pain maybe ten seconds later, looks back up.

Oh. She was on a ridge. The road must have hooked back to the right to keep this from happening to all the trucks. But, unlike a truck, she'd gone straight.

Denorah pulls herself up with a bush that scratches every part of her face, even her lips—is this what her dad calls *buckbrush*? Or, used to call, she reminds herself.

"But I'm a doe," she says, drunk with the pain of it all, and puts one foot in front of the other, and then repeats that complicated process, and a court length or two into that she realizes that this is what it's like to die, isn't it?

You hurt and you hurt, and then you don't.

It's soft at the end. Not just the pain, but the world.

And at least she'll die with that, she knows: The *world* killing her. Not the Crow. Not Elk Head Woman. Not the thing that got her dad.

"I'm sorry," she says to the idea of him.

Not because he died however he died, but because she never told anybody to let him stay when they were dragging him from the gym. Because she pretended she didn't know him. Because she was embarrassed. Because—because she's still that girl standing on the bench seat of his truck beside him while he's driving, her hand on his shoulder, the cab full of his stories that were all true, she knows.

Because because because.

Her breath hitches deep and she stops, her hand on an aspen, a birch, she doesn't know stupid trees, trees are only good to make basketball courts from. This tree holds her up just the same. She pats it in thanks and looks past it, to where she's going to die.

It's a field of . . . not spikes of snow, no, there's no such thing. *Bones.*

"What?" she says.

She—she can't be *that* far out, can she? Marias, that massacre or whatever? The bones from that wouldn't still just be lying out there, would they?

Bones don't last that long.

Unless. Unless she already died a few steps back, and is walking forward through her people's past now, maybe. Is that how dying works?

She looks behind her—nothing calling her back—and steps forward gingerly, to crack this last Big Indian Mystery.

It is another world, the kind she wants to hold her breath in. Not to keep it from getting into her lungs, but because it's sacred. There's skeletons all around her. Not Indians, she can tell that now, not people at all, but . . . cattle? Her new dad's told her about grizzly stashes, but those are always back in the trees, not out in the open like this.

No, this is something different, something worse.

Elk.

Denorah nods to herself, puzzling the bones together in her head.

Elk, definitely.

There's one side of a rack tilted up over there, even, unbleached and frozen, and—she looks around faster now, more desperate.

This can't be *that* place, can it? The place her dad would never tell her about, where him and his friends blasted all those elk ten years ago?

But it is that place.

Denorah swallows, settles down to her knees, her hand tracing the gentle curve of a weather-smoothed rib until it's shattered about halfway down. And the rib beside it as well, just the same. From a gunshot. Maybe even from a bullet shot from her dad's gun.

Denorah looks up the steep slope, can almost hear the rifles, can almost see her dad and Cassidy, Ricky and Lewis, so proud, so thrilled with their luck, with what great hunters they were.

Her heart beats once, seems to stop in her chest.

"Dad," she says.

This is where it happened.

Part of her new dad's story of this, too, the end of it, was her real dad and his buds throwing their caped-out trophy bull back down the slope, after trying to bargain to keep just it, please, not even any of the meat, not even the young little elk.

That's when she knew it was a true story. Because that's exactly the kind of thing her real dad would have asked for: the horns.

But, that story being true, it also means—it means her dad really and truly did this, doesn't it? Instead of being the one down in the encampment, bullets raining down all around, punching through the hide walls of the lodges like she knows happened to the Blackfeet, to Indians all over, her dad was the one *slinging* bullets, probably laughing from the craziness of it all, from how, this far out, they could do anything, it didn't even matter.

"I'm sorry," Denorah says to the elk rib she's touching, and closes her eyes.

This is a good place, she tells herself. A good enough place. She can lie down here with them, can't she? If they'll have her.

When she opens her eyes ten, twenty seconds later, it's from snow crunching behind her.

She sways her back in but she has to do it, has to look around.

Elk Head Woman.

This close, her head is even more wrong.

But she's not looking at Denorah, has forgotten all about Denorah.

Elk Head Woman falls to her knees too, her human hands to these elk bones, her nose dipping down to touch a skull, and staying there.

Denorah is breathing heavy, can't move.

All at once Elk Head Woman thrusts up, casts her long head around, looking for, looking for—

There.

Just an icy patch of grass like all the rest.

But not to her.

She makes her way over, falls to both human knees over it, lowers her head.

"You—you were here that day, weren't you?" Denorah says, and Elk Head Woman snaps her face over, her eyes hot and fierce.

Denorah starts to reach a hand across, like the daughter of Elk Head Woman's murderer can do anything good here at all, but then she remembers Victor Yellow Tail's broken body. And

Cassidy's, and Jolene's. Her dad's. She pulls her hand back to her chest, holds it there.

Now Elk Head Woman is leaning forward on her right arm, her palm to the bare dirt, like she can feel something down there.

Denorah can feel it writhing around down there, too.

"What is it?" she asks without thinking, but Elk Head Woman is already digging, frantic, her elk mouth making desperate little chirping sounds.

Denorah, shaking her head no, leans in just enough to see the birth: a fragile brown leg kicking up from the dirt, ten years after it should have rotted away, and then a thin little flank there under a swipe of earth, and now Elk Head Woman is digging faster, more desperate.

An elk calf, still wet, shivering.

She pulls it up to her human chest, its neck too weak to hold its head up, its chin on her shoulder.

Elk Head Woman's whole body hitches up, and then sighs with the perfectness of this skin-to-fur contact.

Which is when the rifle shot opens up the world.

Just past Elk Head Woman, a spurt of snow geysers up, the powder hanging there while the sound rolls away. Denorah looks back up the long slope, to . . . to—

"You made it," she says, in wonder.

It's her new dad, in his Fish & Game shirt.

Meaning—meaning *Nathan* made it. He Paul Revere into Browning with half his blood gone, must have ridden right up to the Game Office, stayed conscious long enough to tell Denny Pease that his new daughter, stepdaughter, she was out by the lake, Duck Lake, and there's a . . . there's a monster—

Her new dad knew just where to go, and just how to get there. There's only one spot Gabriel Cross Gun's daughter would end up. Where *his* daughter would be.

His next shot slaps into the ground just in *front* of Elk Head Woman, like showing her he can shoot past her, and he can shoot just short of her. Translation: she's next.

Elk Head Woman understands this, resists all her instincts to run, instead turning to curl around her calf, give her back to the slope, hoping her body can be thick enough to keep her calf safe. Because that's what an elk mother does, isn't it? That's the only thing you've ever really wanted to do this whole time, ever since you found yourself suddenly back in the world. Just—your anger, your hate, it was coursing through you so hot, and you got lost in it, and—

Denorah looks up that long hill, into the winking scope and dead eye of her new dad, and then she looks to Elk Head Woman, to the calf, and she sees now that both her fathers have stood at the top of this slope behind a rifle, and the elk have *always* been down here, and it can stop . . . it *has* to stop, the old man telling this in the star lodge says to the children sitting all around him. It *has* to stop, he says, brushing his stubby braids out of the way, and the Girl, she knows this, she can feel it. She can see her real dad dead in that burned-down sweat lodge, the back of his head gone, but she can also see him up the slope ten years ago, shooting into a herd of elk that weren't his to shoot at, and she hates that he's dead, she loved him, she *is* him in every way that counts, but her new dad shooting the elk beside her isn't going to bring him back, and as long as she keeps dribbling behind her back when she doesn't have to, then her real dad won't even really be gone, will he? He'll still be there in her reckless smile. Because nobody can kill that.

So—this is where the old man looks from face to face of the children in the lodge with him, a blanket of stars spread out around them, this is where he says to all the children gathered around the fire that what the Girl does here, for Po'noka but also for her whole tribe, what she does is slide forward on her bloody knees, placing her small body between that rifle and the elk that killed her dad.

She holds her right hand up the slope, palm out, fingers spread—the old man demonstrates—and she says it clear in that cold air: *No, Dad! No!*

Is it the first time she's called him that?

"It is," the old man says. It is.

By slow degrees, the rifle raises, its butt settling down onto Denny Pease's right hip. He's just a silhouette all the way up there. Just another hunter.

For a long moment Elk Head Woman doesn't move, is just hunched there around her calf, but then her long head wrenches around, ready to flinch from that next shot boring into her back, to take her legs away again, to start this whole cycle all over.

Instead, the man-shape up there, he's sliding his right hand sideways, palm down, left to right like this, the old man says.

It's the Indian way of saying a thing is over. It's what he used to end every meeting with, when he was trying to pull Gabe and Cass and Ricky and Lewis back, keep them alive. It's what he would have told his grandson, if he could have.

It's over, enough, it can stop here if you really want it to stop.

The Girl nods about this, knows what this hand signal means. She turns back to Elk Head Woman beside her, but Elk Head Woman is jerking now without even being shot, is falling over onto her side, still holding on to her calf, protecting it from whatever this next thing is.

It's her collapsing into the snow, her legs and arms kicking and reaching, twisting and creaking. Finally her right leg kicks through its human skin, is coarse brown hair underneath. Then an arm pushes through, has a clean black hoof at the end of it.

An elk cow stands up from the snow and lowers her face to her calf, licks its face until it wobbles up, finds it feet, and that's the last anyone ever sees of those two, walking off into the grass, mother and calf, the herd out there waiting to fold them back in, walk with them through the seasons.

Because it's the end of the story, the old man holds his right hand up again, like the Girl did that day, and all the children do as well, and then, just like the Girl does four years later, when her team loses State in double-overtime, he balls that hand into an upraised fist. What the Girl will be doing with that held-up fist at the end of that forever game, it's honoring the Crow team that finally figured out how to shut her down—the first defense to ever do that, and one of the last.

That show of sportsmanship, of respect, of honor, it's what gets silhouetted on thousands of posters all through high school sports, all across the land that used to be hers.

It's not the end of the trail, the headlines will all say, it never was the end of the trail.

It's the beginning.

ACKNOWLEDGMENTS

I don't write this novel without Ellen Datlow—not sure how I would write horror at all without her being her—so, thanks, Ellen, always. Not sure how I'd write *this* novel without how Louise Erdrich's *The Antelope Wife* lodged in me, either. But that's everything she writes. Her stories and characters and scenes are shattered all through my heart. Remove any one of them and I bleed out fast. Too, there's Elizabeth LaPensée's *Deer Woman: A Vignette*, which I picked up at the first Indigenous Comic Con. Or, I think Lee Francis IV maybe gave me a copy when I was there? I don't remember for sure, but somehow I ended up curled around that comic book, and couldn't stop thinking about it. And I'd be lying if I didn't also cite the seventh episode of season one of *Masters of Horror*, "Deer Woman" by John Landis. I really liked how that woman kicked whoever needed kicking in that story. I want that for all Indian women. I also want them all to live, too, please. Some of them are my sisters, my nieces, and all of them are my cousins, my aunts. And Joe Lansdale is always kind of my model for how to write, how to get heart and laughs and action and everything good on the page, in whatever genre. And . . . somehow James Dickey's poem "A Birth" is either really deep in the grass of this story or it's part of my writer DNA in a way I can't shake. The timid steps that new horse takes in that poem, into my world, that's the way the elk walk for me in this novel. They're looking at me while they graze, I mean, and if I don't do them right, then they're coming for me. I probably won't hear them either, since my music's always blasting. Example: when very first starting this novel, the song I had on repeat is D-A-D's song "Trucker." Rounding the corner to done, though, I needed people, not music. I think Matthew Pridham and Krista Davis were the first to read it, but Matthieu Lagrenade and Reed Underwood and Bree Pye and Jesse Lawrence and Dave Buchanan were close behind. Thank you all. Hope I'm remembering everybody there. If not, then write your name here: _____. Thank you, _____. Thanks as well to Alexandra Neumeister and David Tromblay and Theo Van Alst, and Billy J. Stratton, none of whom read this while I was writing it, but talking about different things with each of you nudged me this way in the story instead of that way. Thank you for those talks. And, talking about talking, I don't speak Blackfeet, but Robert Hall and Sterling HolyWhiteMountain were able to make that all right and proper for me, along with a lot of Browning and Blackfeet Reservation details, which I didn't know, <u>as I didn't grow up there</u>. Which isn't to say I didn't still manage to jack it all up. But, if so, it's on me, not them. Thanks, Robert and Sterling. And, okay, Sylvester Yellow Calf too, you're on every page. And Pat Calf Looking, my great-uncle, you're maybe on some as well. While finishing this, I taught a grad seminar on the haunted house, which was so helpful. Won't list all the students in there, as I'm probably already getting the staredown (I'm really stretching "one paragraph" here . . .), but our discussions in that classroom were so vital to me, getting this novel together, as were some old and not-so-old haunted house discussions with Nick Kimbro. Too, thanks to my brother-in-law

Oliver Smith, for doing some last-moment eyeshine research deep into a writing night. And thanks to Migizi Pensoneau for helping me get some Great Falls facts . . . I won't say "right," as I tend to change things in the writing of them, but "less wrong," anyway. I hope. Maybe. Thanks also to Jill Essbaum, who doesn't yet know I smuggled the opening line from her *Hausfrau* up onto the rez, with some slight liberties taken. Really, though, thanks for always being my lifeline on the mountain, Jill. I can't write if I don't come back down, right? And, talking about making it down the mountain mostly in one piece: thanks to my dad, Dennis Jones, for taking me out before dawn morning after morning, when it's so dark that everything's sort of glowing light blue, and you can hear the elk so close that you're pretty sure you can reach your hand out, touch them. Only, they're ghosts, aren't they? They're so much smarter than I'll ever be. Mostly what I come back with are stories. But stories last longer than meat, I say. One of those stories is from my great-uncle Gerry Calf Looking. It's about how one time a herd of elk came to Browning, and how the train came through right when it needed to. And I bet either some of John Calf Looking's actual stories are in here, or I stole the way he tells those stories. But I also stole the way Delwin Calf Looking said "Tasco" once when we were out after deer, so, you know: stealing's what I do, yeah? Or: I'm always listening, anyway. And, the next-to-final reader this time was Mackenzie Kiera, who didn't just give this novel a pass, she stepped inside it, looked out from it, and guided me back in, walked me through all the story's rooms, one of which is the living room of the house I'm currently renting. It has this high, slanted ceiling, I mean, and this crazy-eyed light that doesn't know what to do with electricity. So, thanks, ridiculous, probably-haunted light. I'd have never looked down through the blades of my ceiling fan without you. Thanks also—and this is maybe the first time I've done this, and I might still delete it, because who can believe me—to the dog that grew up with my kids, Rane and Kinsey. You were Harley here, Grace. You were the best girl. And? Thanks also to a dude I worked with at a warehouse a long time back. Butch. I hijacked you, man, renamed you Jerry. But it's just because I miss you. You're also in my "Discovering America" story from better than twenty years ago, I guess. I can't quit writing about you. And, after all of that to get the novel together, after all the hijackings, all the lifelines and late-night texts, all the people talking me down from the many ledges ringed around each and every novel, thanks to BJ Robbins, first for making it better, for asking the good questions that I was kind of hoping nobody would think to ask, and second for believing in it enough to get it on the right editor's desk. That editor was and is Joe Monti. Since it's my name on the cover, you maybe can't see the impression his hands have left in this story, this book, but, really, this novel didn't find its final form, the one you're holding in *your* hands, until he kind of shrugged and asked, "What if it was this way instead of that way, yeah?" It's this way now. The other way—what was I even thinking? But sometimes, some books, it takes the right editor to push it those last few steps, into what it *can* be. Thanks, Joe, thanks, BJ, thanks, Lauren Jackson, best publicist ever, thanks to Madison Penico for helping me get this one right line-by-important-line, thanks, first, second, last, and current readers, thanks to everybody, especially the people I'm forgetting, the animals I'm keeping secret, but mostly, as always, thanks to my beautiful wonderful smart and perfect wife, Nancy, for putting herself between me and the world time and again, leaving me little pockets out of the wind where I can sometimes write a book or three. I write nothing without you shielding me like that. But, really, thanks just for seeing me across a wash of sand when we were both nineteen, and holding my eyes that one little moment longer, a moment that's lasted and lasted for us, and still has a lifetime to go.